ANTIQUES ROUND-UP

Also by Barbara Allan

The Trash 'n' Treasures Mysteries

ANTIQUES ROADKILL
ANTIQUES MAUL
ANTIQUES FLEE MARKET
ANTIQUES BIZARRE
ANTIQUES KNOCK-OFF
ANTIQUES DISPOSAL
ANTIQUES CHOP
ANTIQUES CON
ANTIQUES SLAY RIDE (e-book)
ANTIQUES FRUITCAKE (e-book)
ANTIQUES SWAP
ANTIQUES ST. NICKED (e-book)
ANTIQUES FATE
ANTIQUES FRAME
ANTIQUES WANTED
ANTIQUES HO-HO-HOMICIDES
ANTIQUES RAVIN'
ANTIQUES FIRE SALE
ANTIQUES CARRY ON *
ANTIQUES LIQUIDATION *
ANTIQUES FOE *
ANTIQUES SLAY BELLES *

* *available from Severn House*

ANTIQUES ROUND-UP

Barbara Allan

SEVERN HOUSE

First world edition published in Great Britain and the USA in 2025
by Severn House, an imprint of Canongate Books Ltd,
14 High Street, Edinburgh EH1 1TE.

severnhouse.com

Copyright © Max Allan Collins and Barbara Collins, 2025

Cover and jacket design by Piers Tilbury

All rights reserved including the right
of reproduction in whole or in part in any form.
The right of Max Allan Collins and Barbara Collins to be
identified as the author of this work has been asserted
in accordance with the Copyright,
Designs & Patents Act 1988.

British Library Cataloguing-in-Publication Data
A CIP catalogue record for this title is available from the British Library.

ISBN-13: 978-1-4483-1492-8 (cased)
ISBN-13: 978-1-4483-1864-3 (paper)
ISBN-13: 978-1-4483-1493-5 (e-book)

This is a work of fiction. Names, characters, places and incidents are either the product of the author's imagination or are used fictitiously. Except where actual historical events and characters are being described for the storyline of this novel, all situations in this publication are fictitious and any resemblance to actual persons, living or dead, business establishments, events or locales is purely coincidental.

No part of this book may be used or reproduced in any manner for the purpose of training artificial intelligence technologies or systems. This work is reserved from text and data mining (Article 4(3) Directive (EU) 2019/790).

All Severn House titles are printed on acid-free paper.

Typeset by Palimpsest Book Production Ltd.,
Falkirk, Stirlingshire, Scotland.
Printed and bound in Great Britain by
TJ Books, Padstow, Cornwall.

The manufacturer's authorised representative in the EU for product safety is
Authorised Rep Compliance Ltd, 71 Lower Baggot Street, Dublin D02 P593
Ireland (arccompliance.com)

Praise for the Trash 'n' Treasures Mysteries

"Amusing"
Kirkus Reviews on *Antiques Slay Belles*

"This humorous, conversational cozy, lovingly set in the Mississippi River town of Serenity, is framed with details about antiques"
Booklist on *Antiques Slay Belles*

"A mystery that has it all: zany characters, antiquing tips, and recipes to brighten your day"
Kirkus Reviews on *Antiques Foe*

"Framed by small-town life in Iowa, with interesting details on antiques, this fun cozy includes recipes and tips"
Booklist on *Antiques Foe*

"Allan delivers the cozy goods"
Publishers Weekly on *Antiques Liquidation*

"For readers of cozy mysteries who enjoy small-town living, humor with a side of murder, and cute canine companions"
Library Journal on *Antiques Liquidation*

About the author

Barbara Allan is the joint pseudonym of husband-and-wife mystery writers, Barbara and Max Allan Collins. Barbara is an acclaimed short-story writer, and Max is a multi-award-winning *New York Times* bestselling novelist and Mystery Writers of America Grand Master. Their previous collaborations have included one son, several short story collections, twenty-one novels, and most recently a Trash 'n' Treasures film, *Death By Fruitcake*. They live in Muscatine, Iowa—their Serenity-esque hometown—in a house filled with trash and treasures.

www.barbaraallan.com

For
Paula Sands
and
Alisabeth Von Presley

Thank you for bringing the Bornes
to life in *Death by Fruitcake*.

Brandy's quote:

*Spring has sprung,
The grass has riz,
I wonder where the birdies is.*

– Anonymous

(Note to Brandy from Mother:
I don't think you're taking our dedication
responsibilities seriously)

Mother's quote:

*Nothing is sufficient for the person
who finds sufficiency too little.*

– Epicurus

(Note to Mother from Brandy:
Wise words, but maybe
you should take your own advice)

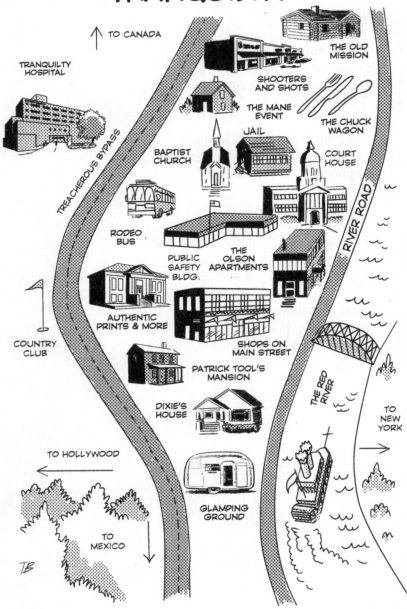

ONE
Westward Ho!

Spring.
 The season of rebirth, hope, possibilities, and a chance to lose the ten pounds I put on during a cold and stressful winter (*Antiques Slay Belles*). Actually, three of those ten were still around from the year before, and two from the year before that. You understand how they can start adding up—right, one bite at a time.

But on this sunny, unseasonably warm March afternoon—a Saturday in our picturesque town of twenty-five thousand souls nestling on the banks of the Mississippi River—I wasn't thinking about my weight. Instead, I was caught up in a conversation with Mother in (and about) our antiques shop, Trash 'n' Treasures, regarding the dwindling state of our coffers.

Customer traffic all day had been nonexistent, anyone with half a brain outdoors, working in yards, uncovering tarps from boats, or taking motorcycles out for a spin after winter storage.

I was, and am, Brandy Borne—thirty-three, blonde by choice, divorced by misadventure, medicated by anti-depressant; Mother was, and is, Vivian Borne, over seventy, under eighty, Danish by ancestry, widowed by thirty, medicated bipolar. The third entity present in our little family was Sushi, my diabetic brown-and-white shih tzu, spoiled by us.

Allow me to further set the stage: I was seated on a high stool behind the check-out counter; Mother stood in front of it; and Sushi slept nearby in her leopard-print bed.

She was saying (Mother, not Sushi), "We need a serious buying trip, dear. And not merely to purchase the same old, same old."

"What do you suggest?" I asked, for once in immediate agreement. Our merchandise had grown stale and predictable, and even moving it around fooled few customers. And few customers were what we were attracting lately.

"What we need are antiques and collectibles," Mother replied, as if sharing some special knowledge, "that will bring in new buyers."

I raised a hand as if wanting to be called upon in class, and pointed out, "But we can't wander too far from what's regionally popular."

Lighthouses didn't sell well in the landlocked Midwest, as attested to by the half-dozen ceramic collectibles Mother had bought several years ago when lighthouses became all the temporary rage.

"Agreed," she said, her eyes blinking behind the big-framed, magnifying glasses, which made her seem less attractive than she really was. "What category has been our fastest seller recently?"

I drew the portable computer screen closer, and opened the inventory file that tracked the dates each item had been tagged and sold.

Scrolling through the list, I noticed a recent trend.

"Actually," I said, a little surprised, "all those Western antiques we'd bought are gone."

A restaurant called the Wagon Wheel in a nearby town had closed when the owners decided to retire. Unable to entice a new buyer, the couple put the building and contents up for auction, including the authentic Western antiques they'd amassed for years as they'd systematically added new finds to the walls and various glass display cases.

Mother and I attended the auction, but bottom-feeders that we were/are, shrewdly waited till the end to buy what was left for minimal cash out-lay.

Still blinking behind the magnifying lenses, which made her seem even more eccentric than she was, she asked, "Surely you can't be including the armadillo lamp?"

"Yes. I *am* including the armadillo lamp."

Of course I was. I'd been against taking that taxidermied creature on, its unfathomable existence dishonored by its shell being used as a lamp shade (if you are not familiar with this practice, *don't* look it up), banishing the grotesquery to our basement display of man-tiques.

Mother said, "I'm glad it found a suitable home."

"As long as I don't have to visit it there."

"Well, then," she said, moving on, "clearly we need to purchase more Western-themed items. They can be arranged together in one of the upstairs bedrooms."

For readers not familiar with our shop (others can skip to the paragraph beginning "Why don't we go to Round Top?"), our business took up an entire house perched at the end of the downtown commercial area where residential homes began.

We had bought the 1920s-era two-story clapboard with its wide front porch and picket fence for half market value because long ago an axe murder had taken place in the parlor. Previous owners hadn't stayed long, claiming the house was haunted. And indeed, after we'd moved our merchandise in, rockers would rock by themselves, doors would slam suddenly shut, and small articles would move to other spots, as if the victim (an elderly lady) didn't approve of where they had been placed. But after Mother and I solved that long-ago case (*Antiques Chop*), the strange occurrences ceased. I like to think the woman finally found peace.

From the beginning, we decided to organize everything in the rooms where they belonged (estate-sale style, only not sad). We arranged kitchen articles in the kitchen, bedroom sets in the bedrooms, linens in the linen closet, bathroom fixtures and paraphernalia in the bathroom, steamer trunks and old doors in the attic. Downstairs, formal furniture was displayed in the parlor, dining sets in the dining room, books in the library, and (as I mentioned) man-tiques in the basement. Even the knickknacks were placed where one might expect to find them in a cozy, older home.

During business hours, the wafting aroma of freshly baked cookies (peanut-butter today) would lure patrons to the kitchen, where they were welcome to sit at the yellow-and-white boomerang-print laminated table and partake of the free goodies, along with a cup of coffee—no purchase required, but fresh gossip appreciated.

Customers often claimed that shopping at Trash 'n' Treasures gave them the impression of visiting an elderly relative—a grandmother, perhaps, or kindly old aunt. Only you didn't have to wait to inherit something that might catch your eye; for the listed price (or maybe a haggled-over lower one), you could walk out with a treasure right now.

"Why don't we go to Round Top?" I said.

I referred to an extraordinary antiques show in Texas that stretched along twenty-five miles of highway through five towns, and boasted over a thousand vendors. Texans did everything in a big way.

Mother seemed immediately intrigued. "When is it being held?"

I consulted Google. "March twenty-fourth through the thirty-first."

She mulled that for a moment, then said slowly, "While that *does* seem enticing, I foresee more than a few negative factors."

I thought, *Such as it was my idea*, which I edited down to, "Such as?"

Mother began counting the fingers on one hand with the forefinger of the other. "With so many vendors, prices will be high. The event has been going on for years, so merchandise is bound to be picked over. We would have to buy tickets to participate. Obviously accommodations and food always prove expensive." At this point, she ran out of fingers and recruited her thumb. "Plus, Houston is a long way to drive with gas prices as exorbitantly high as they are."

She did present a good case: large vendor participation often drives prices up, not down, due to their own expense attending; the first antiques show in Round Top happened over fifty years ago, so it was well-established; any event requiring patrons to buy tickets in order to spend more money limits the appeal; booking separate rooms—getting there and back, plus once we arrived—would be necessary because Mother snores, which sometimes turned me into an insomniac; and I'd be doing all the driving as she'd lost her license, due to her various infractions. (Don't ask. Let's just say her infractions had fractions.)

"Any other options?" I asked. "Or is Round Top the only game in town?"

"That, dear, may depend upon the town . . ."

She moved to the end of the counter where we kept a rack of antiques publications, and carefully selected one.

"This caught my eye the other day," Mother said, thumbing through the pages. "Here it is—a small notice in the back." She began to read. "First-ever city-wide yard sale to fund a new library. Saturday March sixteenth. Location: Tranquility, Texas.'"

Just one week from today.

"Surely that couldn't compare to Round Top," I said skeptically, avoiding up-talking so as not to annoy Mother.

"It's a hidden *gem*!" she exclaimed. "A diamond in the rough!"

I squinted at her, as if bringing her into focus was an actual possibility. "How can you tell by that one little item?"

Mother sighed. "Dear. Sometimes you do disappoint me."

"If I stopped disappointing you," I said, "you'd *really* be disappointed."

Ignoring that, she slapped the page with the back of her hand. "It's all here. First ever? City-wide? New library?"

I shook my head. "Books are slow sellers and we have plenty already."

She sighed. "It's for a new library. They want to be able to *buy* books, not sell them. Think big! First ever? City-wide?"

"Oh. It'll have all new stuff."

"And?"

"Citizens will be scouring attics and basements for treasures. And the kind of collectibles some people dismiss as trash."

"Which means . . .?" she asked, working at being patient, a teacher coaxing a slow student.

My eyes went to the top of my head for the answer and, what do you know, I found it there. "Prices will be reasonable, even *cheap* . . . because it's for a good cause!"

"Excellent, dear."

I basked in the praise Mother seldom doled out; not just to me, frankly, but anyone. Except herself.

She went on: "Now the next question is . . . how far into Texas is Tranquility? It's a rather big state, you know."

I did know. I consulted the computer. "Just over the border of Oklahoma."

"Satisfactory," she said, invoking Nero Wolfe, her favorite fictional detective. "If we left early enough in the morning, we could make it to the town in a single day."

Point of that possibility: there'd be no hotel expenses getting there and back.

"Sounds doable," I said, nodding. We seldom got on the same page so quickly. "If we leave Friday morning, and get back late Monday night, we'll only be gone four days."

And for two of those four—Sunday and Monday—our store was closed anyway. And when our doors opened, there would be fresh stock.

But now Mother was shaking her head. "I want to go Thursday morning."

"Why? That'll put us there a day before the sale." And add an extra night of hotel expense, doubled. If you ever heard Mother snore, you'd demand your own room, too.

The eyes behind the magnifying glasses slitted. A forefinger rose. "Dear, I will need to do recon before the Saturday sale."

I frowned. "What *kind* of recon? Nothing shady, I hope."

Mother splayed a hand on her chest. "Shady? Moi? Why, I'm honest as the day is long."

Well, the days weren't very long right now.

She continued, as if to assuage my fears, "We do need to get familiar with the lay-out of the town."

Usually, in city-wide sales, maps were handed out the day of—not beforehand, to discourage early buying—detailing which homes and businesses were participating. And being unfamiliar with the town did put us at a disadvantage.

Mother sighed and changed the subject. "I admit being concerned where this leaves Jake."

Jake was my fourteen-year-old son, who lived with his father, Roger, my ex, in Chicago. Jake's dad was an investment banker, his new wife, Laura, a pediatrician. In January, Jake came to stay with us to attend our high school, after he'd been thrown out of several private schools. So far, he's been getting good grades and staying out of trouble. You may find this hard to believe, but Mother and I were a good influence.

"We won't have to worry about Jake," I said, "because he'll still be on spring break, visiting his father and stepmother."

Mother nodded, remembering. "That's right! . . . Let us repair to the kitchen for sustenance and further colloquy."

Yes, she really did say that.

As soon as we made a move in the kitchen's direction, Sushi sprang from her bed (I swear she sleeps with one eye open), attuned to the possibility of a treat.

Settling in at the boomerang-print table with cups of coffee and a plate of peanut-butter cookies for a centerpiece, we discussed preparations for the journey. Or rather Mother did while I nibbled a cookie.

She began, "We can bring in Joe to run the shop for the days we're gone . . ."

A friend I'd made during my one year at our community college, Joe was a benignly eccentric soul we at times employed. He'd served in Afghanistan and came home with PTSD, and lived with his widowed mother.

". . . even though," Mother continued, "Joseph can be rather off-putting to certain customers."

As in, all of them.

But I had a warm spot in my heart for Joe, whose apparel ran to fatigues and combat boots, and who talked in military-speak: "affirmative," "negatory," and "tango Mike." Once, while we were ordering lunch, Joe asked the waitress, "What is the ETA of a tenderloin?" to which she responded, "Huh?"

Mother continued, "It's still better to have someone here at the helm than to put a notice on the door alerting burglars we've left town on a buying trip . . . announcing that the cats are away and the mice can come in to play."

That would also make our own home across town—filled with high-end antiques, many irreplaceable—a tempting target. Maybe not for mice, but for rats.

Meanwhile, I was half-way through my cookie and Sushi was drooling, so I gave her a piece. Sugar isn't great for dogs, but tell that to a dog.

"What about Soosh?" I asked. Sushi always went with us on overnight trips.

"It's a long journey," Mother said. "And I'm afraid she'd be underfoot once we arrived. Could Sushi possibly stay with Tony? If he has no objection, the little canine will surely jump at the chance."

If there was one thing the little doggie loved more than being with us, it was spending time with Rocky—a male mixed breed with a black circle round one eye—whose master was my fiancé, Tony Cassato, who happened to be Serenity's chief of police.

"I don't think he would mind looking after her," I replied. "But would that be fair to Rocky?"

Sushi was shameless about showing her feelings for the much larger dog, crawling all over him incessantly. The bigger animal's modus operandi was to lay down and play dead.

"Perhaps not, dear," Mother said blithely. "But think of the good time Sushi will have."

That settled, she moved on to other considerations—deciding on a budget (which there was little chance she'd stick to), what types of Western antiques should be bought (which there was little chance she'd limit herself to), and that we wouldn't bring anything back for our own collections (ditto).

Me? I started in on another cookie while Mother's voice faded into the background, which did not hamper at all my thoughts concerning what clothing I should pack, since it would be blissfully warmer in Texas.

Have you noticed how summer clothes seem to shrink in your closet over winter? I'd have to see what still buttoned and zipped, after this bizarre fact of nature.

I was already looking forward to getting out of Serenity and away from the possibility of Mother involving me in another murder inquiry. That would be a relief.

Wouldn't it?

The few days before our scheduled trip passed quickly, business actually picked up a bit, allowing Mother to increase our Texas sojourn's buying budget (which she still wouldn't stick to). And, in anticipation of all the antiques and collectibles we would bring back from Texas, we made room, removing the back seats in the van. Or, I should say, I removed them and Mother supervised.

Wednesday evening my ex arrived to take Jake back to Chicago for spring break. Since Jake's father and my mother mixed like water and vinegar, she wisely remained in the kitchen while I greeted Roger at the door.

Ten years older than me, his brown hair graying at the temples, Roger was as handsome as ever, though his face revealed the kind of lines that came along with a high-powered job, living in a metropolis, and (not the least of it) dealing with a teenager.

As Roger stepped into the foyer, I said, "You're looking better," referring to the absence of the extra strain etched on his brow the last time we'd met.

"I *am* feeling better," he admitted.

"And Laura?"

He knew what I was getting at: the added stress had nearly derailed their marriage. I had nothing against Laura, by the way.

He shrugged a little. "We're fine."

"Good to hear."

He shared the nice smile that had attracted me to him, once upon a time. "And we're really looking forward to spending some time with Jake. We've missed him."

I knew the feeling. The last few years I'd seen little of my son.

"I'll call him down," I said.

Jake's duffel bag, along with a plastic tub containing things he couldn't survive without—laptop, books, and video game system—already waited by the entry.

But I didn't have to raise my voice. Jake came bounding down the stairs, tall enough now that he had to duck the overhang of the landing.

I'd always thought our son looked like me, but—as he matured—I was beginning to see Jake's father in the boy's face. Was this some grand plan to assist a son's close relationship with his mother being passed along to the father? If so, I didn't like it.

Jake gave me a hug, whispering, "Stay out of trouble."

"You, too," I whispered back.

I knew he'd been making plans to have a girlfriend over at times while Roger and Laura were off at work. But I wasn't about to tattle.

Still hugging me, he said, "And keep Grandma out of trouble, too."

"I hear you."

He broke away, calling to the kitchen, "Goodbye, Grandma!"

To which he received, "Have a wonderful time, dear!"

The musical note in Mother's voice told me she knew of his plans to reunite with the girlfriend he'd left behind, too. But then, she was the one—not Roger or me—who had explained the facts of life to her grandson at the tender age of eight, admitting the benefits but emphasizing the drawbacks.

A few quiet embraces with me later, Jake and Roger and Jake's duffel bag went out the door.

My final concern before setting out on our Texas trip was

Sushi, who sensed something was up. When I brought out the suitcases, the little dog got so excited she piddled on the floor. Then, when I began fitting her dish into a certain plastic container—used only for travel—she started a growl that was clearly a run-up to barking.

I had to consider the possibility that she'd rather go with us than even being with the beloved Rocky. So it was with some trepidation that we drove to Tony's on Thursday morning just before seven to deliver Sushi before our chief of police left for the station, Mother in her pants suit and me in jeans and an Iowa sweatshirt, ready for travel.

Tony lived about five miles north of town along River Road, which hugged on the left the mighty Mississippi—a little too closely for my liking, in icy weather. Thankfully, this evening the cold was not accompanied by precipitation.

A narrow dirt lane led to a typical small farm homestead that included a red barn, windmill, and vegetable garden readied for spring planting. But instead of the usual two-story white house was a one-story brown log cabin, smoke curling out the brick chimney to ward off the morning chill.

While Mother waited in the van, I got out with Sushi in my arms only to have her immediately spring from my grasp and run up the three wooden steps to the small porch, where she scratched at the screen door and yap-yap-yapped.

Tony came out in his usual chief-of-police apparel—light-blue long-sleeved shirt, navy-and-white striped tie, gray slacks, and brown Florsheim shoes. Dashing right past him and inside, Sushi disappeared in search of Rocky.

You wouldn't say Tony was handsome in the conventional sense. Approaching fifty, with graying temples, steely eyes, a bulbous nose, and barrel chest, Tony had a commanding presence and self-assuredness that made him so very attractive. Never a man of many words, he made up for it in action. (Take that however you like.)

I asked, "Are you sure about this arrangement?"

"Sushi will be fine," Tony said.

"I'm more worried about Rocky. Talk about the Odd Couple!"

He gave me a half-smile. "My pooch will survive." Then, "What can I bring in?"

I curled a finger and he followed me to the back of the van, where I opened the hatch to reveal the container of dog food and a large tote of toys, treats and, of course, Sushi's insulin.

Mother, twisting in the front passenger seat, said, "Hello, Chief."

I had been working on her to stop calling him "Chiefie," with limited results.

"Vivian," Tony said emotionlessly. "Hope your trip goes well."

Her response was tinged with girlishness. "Thank you, Chiefie."

See what I mean?

Anyway, that was the extent of their exchange.

I don't mean to portray them as adversaries. It had started out that way, due to Mother's interference in police investigations; but a truce of sorts had been silently negotiated, due to her success in solving cases. I think he had gained some respect for her (however grudging) and, in return, she respected him for respecting her.

With Sushi's essentials retrieved, Tony and I stepped inside the cabin, which had a pleasant, woodsy smell. The structure seemed roomier than it appeared from the outside. To the left was a cozy area with an overstuffed brown leather couch and a fireplace with flame-crackling logs, in front of which lay Rocky patiently putting up with Sushi's latest assault.

To the right a four-chair round oak table and corner china hutch announced the kitchen in a small room just beyond. A short hallway led to a single bedroom, tiny bath with shower, and door leading to a back porch. I knew my way around here.

The log walls showcased a collection of antique fishing gear he and I had found while accompanying Mother to various competitor shops and estate sales—rods, wicker creels, nets—including a shadow box of flies (not the buzzing kind) I'd given Tony this past Christmas.

We set the container and tote down, and faced each other, where he placed his hands on my shoulders.

"You promise to drive carefully?" he asked.

"I will."

"You won't be distracted by your Mother's commentary?"

"She's quiet most of the way. Good on long trips."

"Happy to hear that. And you'll stop if you get tired?"

"I will."

"And keep her out of trouble?"

That I couldn't promise, trouble having a way of finding Mother. And vice versa.

"I'll try."

"If you fail, call me on my cell."

"I will."

He lifted my chin and kissed me, and it wasn't the kind of peck I got before leaving his office. It seemed only fair to return the courtesy . . .

When we'd parted, I looked at Sushi, who'd settled between Rocky's stretched-out legs, as if canine carnality might ensue at any moment.

"I'm leaving now," I told her, expecting Sushi to come running to me.

But she didn't.

"Well, Soosh," I said, "goodbye."

Sushi didn't even raise her head.

I felt relieved if hurt.

With a wry smile, Tony guided me to the door. "You know the little mutt'll miss you in a while."

"Don't try to make me feel better."

This time I got an office kiss.

"Go on," he said. He raised a palm. "But stay in touch."

"I promise. Don't you trust me?"

"I trust *you*."

Ah . . . there's nothing like the anticipation of a road trip. Spirits are high. Possibilities are endless. Adventure stretches out like an endless highway, waiting to create memories to be pasted in the scrapbook of your mind.

Well, the first photo in that mental scrapbook would be of Mother and me standing along the highway, surveying a flat front tire before we'd even exited Iowa. I managed to hobble on the rim to a repair shop where the mechanic said both front tires had to be replaced, even though the other was OK, or else the alignment could go out of whack. Our budget had blistered already. (Time lost: one hour, ten minutes.)

The second photo would be of us traveling back along the

same highway after stopping for gas and then me heading in the wrong direction (the van didn't have GPS, nor does my brain), and realizing the mistake only when Mother commented, "Doesn't that look just like that repair shop?" (Time lost: one hour, forty-nine minutes.)

The third photo would be of a detour sign in Missouri, which took us untold miles out of our way. (Time lost: fifty-three minutes.)

The fourth photo would be of the van in a ditch because I hadn't seen any warning that a ramp exit was closed, and went driving through a barricade, requiring a tow truck to get us back on the highway. (Time lost: three hours, forty-seven minutes.)

The fifth photo would be of the van broken down somewhere in the red-clay wilderness of eastern Oklahoma. (Time lost: yet to be determined.)

By now it was approaching midnight, and I was utterly exhausted.

"We'll never get anyone to help us at this hour," I moaned. "We'll have to sleep in the van and wait until morning."

At least the back was empty and we could stretch out.

Mother pointed. "What's that over there, dear?"

"Where?"

"See the lights?"

I squinted. "Looks like a row of cabins."

"Looks like lodging," she said.

We abandoned the vehicle, extracted our two suitcases, then rolled them across a field toward the lights. Soon, we encountered a winding cement walkway illuminated by light poles, leading to various small round huts made of hardened mud with thatched roofs.

"I'm too tired to find the registration building," I grumbled.

"As am I," Mother said. "We can always settle up with the manager in the morning." She nodded to the nearest hut. "See if that one is empty."

I approached a door made of small sapling tree trunks bound together, and knocked. When no reply came, I tried the door and found it, yes, unlocked.

"Anyone here?" I called out.

Silence.

I turned to Mother with a "come on" gesture.

Inside I couldn't find a wall switch, so I turned on my cell phone's light.

While I considered Tony's cabin rustic, this single-room lodging was almost primitive. While there was a decorative rug, it only partially covered . . . a dirt floor! Two crudely made twin beds appeared to have straw mattresses. No windows, only a space for air around where the walls met the roof . . . and no bathroom!

Mother, who tends to see the bright side of anything, said, "Well, isn't this charming! Just look at this decor."

She was referring to the decorative clay pots and hand-woven baskets placed on small tables and arranged in corners, along with an interesting assortment of masks displayed on the walls. Still, a few surprising amenities were provided, like the ornamental robes on each bed, colorful blankets, and even beaded moccasin slippers.

This was better than camping out or sleeping in the van. And there had to be a communal bathhouse nearby.

Safety concerns? All dead-on-her-feet Brandy could think about was moving one foot in front of the other long enough to make it to a bed, not even caring about the *poof* of dust when I flopped down on it. Or for that matter the threat of Vivian Borne snoring.

My last memory before allowing deep slumber to take me was Mother commenting that the complimentary robe and slippers fit her fine.

My *next* memory—and the final snapshot of our trip to date—would be of me, startled awake by the beam of a flashlight, and a gun aimed in my face.

Brandy's Trash 'n' Treasures Tip

Finding fresh antiques and collectibles at prices low enough to make a re-sale profit can be a challenge. Home-moving sales are a good bet because owners want to get rid of possessions they don't want to pack up. I try to get a "sneak peek" a day before when most owners are setting up, by parking the car a block or two away then pretending to be taking Sushi out for a walk.

TWO
Trail of Tears

Startled awake by an intruder in our hut, I called out to Mother, who—though a light sleeper—was already taking action.

Coming up behind the shadowy figure, she raised one of the clay pots high above her head and brought it down hard on his in a brittle crash, the pieces landing quietly on the rug on the dirt floor. The intruder tottered and sat down hard, then crumpled backward, cushioned by the carpet, and lay sprawled on his back.

Shaken but alert, I kicked the gun beneath my bed, while Mother, wearing the ornate robe and beaded slippers, picked up the flashlight.

"Well, now," she said, training the beam on the motionless body, "let's just see who came calling . . ."

The fingers of her free hand flew to her mouth as if something terribly embarrassing had just transpired. "Oh dear!"

Oh dear, indeed. Something *really* embarrassing had transpired!

Our uninvited out-cold guest was a uniformed police officer.

He might have been a slumbering child, so peaceful did he look. Perhaps forty, the officer sported short dark hair buzz-cut along the sides, high cheekbones, wide mouth frozen in a grimace, eye-color unknown because, well, his lids were still closed.

The lawman wore full gear: shoulder mic, ballistic vest, body camera, and a well-stocked duty belt. A patch on the dark blue shirt identified him with the Tahlequah, Oklahoma Police Department, and a name plate on his vest read: YANSA.

Leave it to Mother to attack his one vulnerable spot.

She was saying, "Don't just stand there gawking, Brandy! Find some water to revive the poor man."

Said the woman who put him on the floor.

I reached for an unopened bottle next to my bed, then, gently raising the officer's head with one hand, the other splashed his face, as if watering a plant.

His eyes opened, proving to be dark brown, and he jolted to a sitting position, like a waking corpse in a horror movie, causing me to rear back.

"We thought you meant us harm," I said in an apologetic rush of words. "Are you all right, officer?"

Rubbing the top of his head, the man in blue got to his feet.

"Where is my *gun?*" he asked sharply.

I gestured to Mother's bed, my pointing finger held protectively close to me, as if he might snatch it away. "Under there."

While he retrieved his weapon, Mother began jabbering in a friendly stream. "Officer Yansa—may I call you that?—you see, we left Serenity, Iowa early this morning and really had quite the trip. First, we had a flat tire. Then, wouldn't you know it, we went in the wrong direction. After that, a detour took us miles out of our way. And, finally, the coup de grâce—our van broke down."

I added meekly, "We did intend to settle up with the motel manager in the morning."

Holstering his weapon, Officer Yansa said, brown eyes narrow, "This is *not* a motel."

"Then what in the world could it be?" Mother asked, eyes as wide as the officer's were slitted. I should note that she'd had the aplomb to grab her glasses before getting out of bed to club a cop. This, of course, had a lot to do with how wide her eyes seemed.

His words were as tight as his eyes. "You are in a hut in Diligwa Village. A replica of tribal life in the eighteen hundreds. To be specific? You are trespassing on Cherokee Nation land."

Oh, boy. Talk about Manifest Destiny.

He continued, a cold rage contained, and pointed at her. "And *that*, madam, is not a bathrobe, but what the Peace Chief wore during ceremonies."

"I *did* question the absorbency of the feathers," she said, laying on the charm, trying to redeem herself, "and the long tassel fringe, which does make it quite drafty."

"Please tell me that pot wasn't priceless," I said, abashed about bashing him, gesturing to the shards of clay. Wave goodbye to our home and business. At least we'd have a temporary roof over our heads, even if it did come with bars on the windows.

"No," he replied, and sighed. "We have a museum for true artifacts. Everything here is a replica . . ."

One bit of good news.

". . . but still hand-crafted by the Cherokee people in the old ways."

Mother said, "Of course, we'll pay for all damages. As they say, whoops!"

His smile was not terribly friendly; being clobbered on the cranium can do that. "It's not that simple, ladies. You've trespassed on private land, destroyed tribal property, and assaulted a police officer."

Mother raised a palm as if about to offer an inappropriate "how" in an old Western movie, saying, "Un-in-*tention*–ally assaulted an officer."

I blurted, "Could there be any leniency for stupidity?"

The smile turned into an actual smile, a wry one. "Possibly. But I'll have to take you two women to the station house, anyway."

"Will we have to go before the tribal chief?" Mother asked, suddenly excited about our dilemma. She was always ready for a new experience.

"There *is* a chief you'll be seeing," Officer Yansa replied. "But not our tribal one—you'll be seeing the chief of police." He paused. "Our station operates like most others, except we also have our own laws, and you've broken more than one."

And a clay pot.

"Now," he said, "if you'll just pack up your things, we can deal with this matter."

After restoring the room as best we could—including piling up the chunks of clay pot neatly in one corner—Mother and I, toting our suitcases, were escorted to Officer Yansa's patrol car. We were directed to get in the back seat of the white, blue-striped sedan, the official seal of the Tahlequah Police Department on its side. We sat staring at the wire screen separating us from the officer we'd clouted; at least we weren't handcuffed.

Our luggage was stowed in the trunk, as if a cabbie had picked us up at an airport; with them went our purses, minus our driver's licenses, Mother's having REVOKED boldly stamped across hers.

With the vehicle idling, Yansa used the car's swivel-mounted laptop to check our IDs, then spoke briefly into his shoulder mic, notifying the station he was bringing in a desperate pair. Actually, he said, "Two White females."

As we began to move, I asked through the mesh, "What about our van?" I told him where we'd left it.

"It'll be towed after it's checked," came the response.

Mother whispered in my ear, "It might be helpful if he knew I am a former Serenity County sheriff."

I whispered back, "Best not go there."

She had won the election a year-and-a-half ago, when the other, more qualified candidate dropped out at the last moment. Her short tenure lasted only three months when the city council gave her an ultimatum—retire or be impeached, after having bent several laws bringing a perp to justice.

We rode in silence, the sun just beginning to peek above a flat horizon. On the right we passed Running Bear Casino, where, at the entrance, the lights of several vehicles were flashing, perhaps some patron having had a heart attack losing big.

Ahead, the highway bisected, an overhead sign indicating downtown Tahlequah lay straight ahead; but we swung left, the land barren except for a few small businesses and a farm or two.

I was beginning to worry where the officer might be taking us when the car veered off the highway onto an asphalt road, and a sprawling one-story red-brick building with blue trim came into view, a sign designating it as the Tahlequah Police Department.

Officer Yansa pulled the vehicle up to a back entrance protected by an overhang, got out, and collected his prisoners from the rear.

Inside, the station could have been any modern school—beige-painted block walls, vinyl floors, white ceiling with fluorescent lighting, accentuated by blue doors and trim.

In a booking area, a uniformed female officer logged us into her computer, took our prints and photos, then patted us down. Mother seemed to be relishing the experience. I wasn't.

During our processing, I'd become aware that the department appeared to be in a heightened state of activity, judging by sounds, including loud words, coming from other areas of the station.

Mother, also noticing the noise, turned to Officer Yansa. "What's all the hubbub, bub?"

He just gave her a look. Not coincidentally, so did I.

Her Looney Tunes question not receiving an answer, he instead escorted us along a short hallway to another room, where awaiting us was a row of five holding cells, the doors a blue frame around two panels of thick mesh wire with a slot for food.

The officer ushered us into the last cell.

Only the one next to ours was in use, occupied by a female—she was either a young forty or a hard-living thirty—stretched out on her back on the bench, long red hair a tangled mess, make-up smeared, halter top barely corralling large breasts; she wore jeans so tight they looked painted on, and she had a tattoo of Betty Boop on one arm. At least she had good taste in vintage cartoon characters.

"When can we have our phone call?" Mother asked Officer Yansa, adding, "assuming the Cherokee Nation allows one."

"Soon," was all the officer said, then clanged the door shut after him, locking us in.

As the officer's footsteps diminished, Mother turned to me. "Who should we call, dear?" She seemed to be enjoying herself. "Your fiancé? Or our legal representation, mayhap?"

Our nonagenarian lawyer—long retired except for a few clients like us—usually slept until noon.

"Tony, of course," I replied. "I'll do it, but I don't relish it. He'll find out soon enough the jam we're in." Better for him to hear it from the horse's mouth, even if I was feeling more like a jackass.

The cell was small, with barely enough space for the bench and combination stainless steel toilet and sink. But it was clean, anyway. We'd both been in worse accommodations. Last night had lacked latrine facilities. We'd been upgraded!

Glum, I sat on the thin foam plastic mattress of the bench. "Well," I grumbled, "isn't this another fine mess you've gotten us into."

"Moi?" Mother shot back, pausing in her pacing. "You're the one who led us into that hut."

"After you told me to!"

"I don't recall any such direction."

"You waved me to go in!"

"You must have misinterpreted my gesture. I would have been content to sleep in the van like any good cross-country traveler."

"Anyway," I said, folding my arms, "you're the one who desecrated the tribal robe, and broke that pot over the officer's head."

A female voice called out, "*Ladies!* Good God, I'm trying to sleep off a hangover here! Give a girl a break. If you're in on a pot bust, it's just a misdemeanor."

We were in on a pot bust, all right.

Mother went to the mesh door. "I *do* apologize for my inconsiderate daughter . . . what is your name, dear?"

"Ruby."

"Ruby, what are you in for?"

"Drunk and disorderly."

Mother paused, gathered a thought, and asked, "Do you happen to know what all the hullabaloo out there is about?"

"The *what*?"

"The brouhaha, the ruckus, the commotion."

"Why everybody's pants are on fire, you mean?" Ruby's voice carried a shrug. "A robbery crew hit the casino last night. Running Bear."

Mother blinked at the mesh. "The thieves were unclad?"

"No, lady. Running Bear *Casino*."

So that was the reason for the flashing lights I'd seen as we'd been chauffeured to the station.

"Goodness gracious!" Mother said. "How can that sort of thing happen these days with all the internal and external security?"

"It was outside," Ruby said. "An armored truck got knocked over. So don't expect anyone to get around to you gals anytime soon. Now shut the fudge up."

Only, like Ralphie in *A Christmas Story*, she didn't say "fudge."

Mother, joining me on the bed, said quietly, "Perhaps we should whisper."

"Perhaps we should just shut the fudge up."

Actually, I did say "fudge."

"This is no time to turn on each other, dear."

So I whispered: "Tony is going to be *furious*. I bet he's been trying to contact me."

They'd collected our cells. I wished they'd collect us from this cell.

Mother sighed. "At this rate, I'm afraid you two may never make it to the altar."

Our courtship had had more speed bumps than a school zone, and this time might well break the axle.

I curled up on the bench, allowing Mother enough room to stay seated, then fell asleep. That's one thing I can do anywhere. It's a gift.

Sometime later, Mother shook me awake. "Someone's coming," she said.

Officer Yansa strode into view beyond the mesh. He opened our cell door. "Come with me, Vivian, Brandy."

I sat up, my mouth tasting like an old gym sock, or anyway what I'd imagine an old gym sock would taste like, then smoothed my hair and clothes. Must stay presentable in custody.

Mother and I followed the officer out of the holding cell area through a maze of hallways to a room whose door stood open.

"Wait in there," Officer Yansa said, pointing.

Entering, I whispered, "Mother, I think this is the police chief's office."

"Yes, dear . . . I gathered as much from the name plate on the desk. Really, you must hone your observational skills if you wish to be a skilled writer."

"I don't wanna be a skilled *anything*."

The name plate on the desk said: Chief Douglas Hunter.

Mother lowered herself into one of two visitor chairs in front of the desk. Anticipating a lengthy wait, I gathered some pamphlets from a side table to read, before joining her.

Due to my keenly honed observational skills, I learned that the town of Tahlequah—population around 17,000—was established as the Cherokee Nation's capital in 1839 after the United States government forced all Cherokee Indians to move from their homes in the southeast onto a reservation in eastern Oklahoma. The long and perilous journey on foot became known as the Trail of Tears, so many having died along the way.

The door opened and an imposing man entered. Tall, muscular, with a shaved head and chiseled face, this was a cop any perp would think twice about tangling with.

(*Note to Brandy from Mother:* Dear, please avoid ending a sentence with a preposition. It's a rule.)

(*Note to Mother from Brandy:* That hasn't been a rule for a long time. Maybe it was when *you* went to school.)

(*Note to Brandy from Mother:* Pshaw!)

Dressed in blue, a badge identifying him as the top cop around these here parts, Chief Hunter settled into the swivel chair behind his desk, then studied us with an eagle's eye. A couple of them.

I don't know about Mother, but I tried not to look like a rabbit who'd make the chief's next meal.

Finally, he said, "Vivian Borne. Brandy Borne. I understand you two women are on your way to Texas."

"Yes, sir," Mother replied. "You see, we have the cutest little antiques shop in Serenity, Iowa, and when we heard Tranquility is having a city-wide—"

"I know all about that," he cut in. "I've spoken to your Chief Cassato."

I groaned. No chance I'd get a chance to put a better spin on our incarceration before Tony heard about it.

Chief Hunter went on: "The chief's vouched for your characters . . . such as they are."

Too many chiefs, not enough innocence.

"At Chief Cassato's request," he intoned, "I've decided not to press charges."

Mother asked incredulously, "Not even for trespassing on Indian land or destruction of Cherokee property or assaulting an officer? With a clay pot?"

I side-kicked her foot, the one with the heel spur.

"Owww!" she said.

"No," he said with a sigh. "But I do have a few stipulations."

"Yes? Yes?" Mother said.

"First, you must pay for any damages to Diligwa Village."

"Our pleasure," Mother said, as if we were in any position to negotiate.

Hunter continued, "You will also write Office Yansa a letter of apology."

"A sincere one!" she said. "Anything else?"

"Yes. Leave Tahlequah as soon as humanly possible."

Well, we'd been thrown out of bigger places by larger law enforcement entities, like London and MI6 (*Antiques Carry On*).

"What about our van?" I asked.

"It's been towed to a repair station downtown. You'll have to settle up with them. I'll give you the address. And there's a ride service you can call to take you there."

Mother asked, "Couldn't you have Officer Yansa take us over and drop us off?"

I elbowed her.

The chief said, "We don't provide that service to breaking-and-entering suspects."

Mother raised a forefinger. "Persons of interest!"

"And even if we did," he said, "we are stretched thin this morning."

"Ah," Mother said shrewdly, "the casino robbery!"

A sigh worthy of that other chief, Cassato, ensued. "You ladies need to be going."

He stood.

We stood.

"One more thing," the chief said. "On your way to Texas, you'll be passing through the Creek Nation, Choctaw Nation, and Chickasaw Nation . . . so I'll be contacting the police departments of each."

Mother and I spoke simultaneously, her saying, "That really won't be necessary," me saying, "Good idea," adding, "And any other nation you can think of."

At the front desk, we signed for our belongings—purses, cell phones, and suitcases—and called for our ride with an "on demand" mini-bus service, which happened to have a vehicle in our vicinity at the moment. Then we went outside into a warm day, blinking at the bright sunshine.

"What time is it, dear?" Mother asked. "My phone has gone dead."

I checked mine, which had some life left. "Almost eleven."

She made a face. "We still have a four-hour drive to Tranquility."

"*After* however long it takes to fix the van," I pointed out.

"Let's hope the problem isn't too complicated."

I texted Tony our current situation rather than calling him—after all, I didn't want to interrupt important police business, and also I was a coward.

But he texted back immediately, "Stay in touch," letting me off easy—for now. No recriminations. Somehow that was even more scary . . .

Our transportation rolled into the parking lot and pulled up to the front entrance, a modern white mini-bus with KATS logo on the side.

Mother and I clambered aboard with our suitcases, and having prepaid, made our way past the female driver, who eyed us suspiciously, as did the half-dozen passengers onboard, on their way to work or shopping. They weren't used to making passenger pick-ups at the police station.

As we headed toward the back, Mother smiled and nodded to each person, "Hello, how are you? Not guilty. Released without charges. Only detained. Slight misunderstanding."

She repeated this little speech perhaps five times before we reached the back of the bus.

I took a window seat, putting my suitcase on the empty one next to me so Mother had to sit behind me.

Such small, petty victories were my only defenses against that woman. I never said I was perfect.

As the bus made a left onto Choctaw Street, I turned my face to the window.

The landscape didn't look any less desolate in the daylight, but as the miles rolled by, businesses grew closer together, homes became bigger, and the streets got wider.

This capital of the Cherokee Nation could be Anytown, USA, with strip malls, supermarkets, electric car-charging stations, churches, and such familiar iconic landmarks as Dollar General Store and McDonald's. Entering the city center, signs pointed the way to the courthouse, city hall, library, several museums, and Northeastern State University.

At the corner of Choctaw and Water, the bus came to a halt. The lady driver twisted in her seat, and silently stared back at us, as did the other passengers.

This must be our stop. I thought it odd no passenger had gotten off yet, but maybe she wanted to get rid of the jailbirds first.

Did we look that dangerous? Certainly disheveled after the night we'd been through. And we weren't terribly fragrant, at least not the right kind of fragrant.

Mother again smiled and nodded as we made our way to the front and the exit door. "Goodbye, have a nice day. Again, no charges filed."

This was repeated perhaps a half-dozen times.

I swear a collective sigh could be heard from inside the bus before the glass door closed, and it pulled away.

The repair shop was a red-brick building with four open garage doors, vehicles in various stages of repair, none ours. Instead, our van was parked in a space at the end of the building, in front of a glassed-in office.

Disappointed, I said, "It looks like they haven't got around to us yet."

"Oh, goody-goody," Mother said, a child who'd spotted an ice cream parlor. "I'll have time to go across the street."

Which was not an ice cream parlor, but the Cherokee National Prison Museum, housed in the original limestone jail, which had even retained its backyard gallows.

Mother had an affinity for old jails, having once spent a night in Serenity's ancient hoosegow (now also a museum), which prompted her to crusade for a new state-of-the-art facility, believing even criminals deserved accommodations without cockroaches. Or, perhaps she anticipated being jailed again.

I said, "Let's first find out about the van."

Lugging our suitcases, we entered the main office where a female mechanic with short dark curly hair, in stained overalls, sat at a desk stacked with papers.

"We'd like to speak to the manager," I said politely.

"I'm the manager," she said, adding, "and owner."

"Good for you!" Mother piped up, managing to be both complimentary and condescending.

"Ours is the white van parked outside," I said.

"Chief Hunter said you'd be coming by," the manager/owner replied. She swiveled to a pegboard of car fobs, selected one, then handed it to me.

"You mean it's *done*?" I asked.

"Just a dead battery."

"How much do we owe you?"

"A Mr. Cassato called and took care of the work, and towing, on his Visa card."

I was going to owe Tony big-time.

"Thank you, ma'am," I said.

"Yes, thank you," Mother reiterated, and it would have been nice if she'd stopped there. She didn't. "And should Chief Hunter call, please tell him that, although he told us to leave town ASAP, we're going to do just a smidgen of sightseeing first."

"No," I said. "Please tell the chief we've left town."

I grabbed Mother's arm and pulled her to the door, and out, our suitcases banging against the glass.

Standing next to our van, she huffed, "Well, that certainly was rude of you!"

"Go on, get in," I snapped.

"But I'm hungry and thirsty."

As was I. But in no mood to argue.

"We'll stop somewhere on the road," I promised. Well away from Tahlequah.

I drove two blocks to Muskogee Avenue, then swung south on Highway 62, where the small businesses, boutiques, and bistros of the downtown morphed into a familiar commercial urban sprawl.

We passed the casino, where the parking lot was crowded, the flashing police lights of last night no doubt replaced by a clanging of bells and clinking of coins.

We also passed the scene of *our* crime—Diligwa Village—and a sign designating what it was that we'd missed in the darkness, now clearly visible in daylight. Then I swung west, out of the city limits.

You know those old travelogues from the 1950s that sometimes turn up on cable channels, which always seem narrated by the same sonorous guy? He always ends with, "And so, as the sun sinks slowly in the west, we bid farewell to Rio de Janeiro"—or Peru, or Egypt or a hundred other places most people had never been, back when Germans apparently still wore Lederhosen in their daily lives.

And so, as the sun sinks slowly in the west (actually it was high in the sky), we bid farewell to Tahlequah, Oklahoma . . .

Twenty miles later, in Fort Gibson, we stopped at a cute Mexican restaurant along the highway. The menu was extensive, and because I was starving, I ate too much. I also wanted a margarita in the worst way, but resisted, not anxious for a DUI charge.

An hour later, on the other side of Checotah in the Creek Nation, we passed a woman who was thumbing for a ride.

I slammed on the brakes and pulled off on the shoulder. "What are you doing, child?" Mother asked sharply. "It's dangerous to pick up hitchhikers. Haven't you ever seen *The Hitcher*?"

"I have," I admitted, "but I think that's Ruby."

"Ruby? Oh, Ruby! Our old next-door cell mate! I didn't recognize her."

"I might not have, but for the Betty Boop tattoo on her arm."

"Keen eyes, dear." Mother sighed. "Well . . . I guess we can afford to be charitable. We're not far past our own time of need."

Even if our jailhouse pal *had* told us to shut the fudge up.

I got out and waved, and the woman came running.

It *was* Ruby, although not looking so provocative in a sleeveless plaid blouse, modest-fitting jeans, and white sneakers. Her red hair, no longer a mess, was long and sleek, the make-up minimal compared to last night.

When she reached me, I explained through the window, "We don't have any rear seats . . . you'd have to rattle around in back. So if you want to wait for another ride . . ."

"Naw, that's fine," she said, grinning. Nice smile. "It'll be better than the back of the pick-up truck that dropped me here."

"Where are you headed?" I asked.

"Austin. And you?"

"Also Texas. But Tranquility, which won't take you very far."

She shrugged. "Beats walking. I'll catch another lift from there."

"All right . . . hop in."

Ruby opened the side door, tossed in her duffel bag, then followed it, sitting with her legs crossed, Indian-style.

(*Note from editor Olivia:* That might be considered politically incorrect. Consider omitting it.)

(*Note to Olivia from Brandy:* Glad to consider it!)

After I pulled onto the highway, Mother asked, "When were you released, Ruby dear?"

"Not long after you two. They let me go without a court

appearance or fine since it was my first offense." She paused. "Still, I thought I'd be inside several days at least, anyway. But that's just as well. I'd been in Tahlequah long enough."

"You worked there a while?" I asked, keeping my eyes on the road, hyper-aware she had no seatbelt.

"Yep. Doin' this and that. I'm a bit of a drifter. Just can't seem to settle in one place for very long."

Cue the harmonica solo.

"Where are you originally from?" Mother inquired.

Ruby snorted. "A tiny town called Antler in North Dakota. You could spit across the border into Canada."

Mother said, "But why would you want to?"

Cue the rim shot.

I said, "You *are* a long way from home, Ruby."

"Judging by your license plate," Ruby said, "so are you."

That prompted Mother to tell our passenger all about us—and in excruciating detail: who we were, where we lived, our antiques business, the books she'd written (with my help, she'd said generously), about the murders she'd solved, and why we were heading to Tranquility.

Better she blather at Ruby than at me, which did make the time pass more quickly.

When Mother finally ran out of steam, and to fill a stretch of silence, I commented on the array of tribe-owned casinos we had passed while traveling though the different nations.

"There's well over a hundred," Ruby said, nodding. "But that includes machines in travel plazas and smoke shops and liquor stores."

She'd been around.

I asked, "What kind of profits do the casinos bring in?"

"Oh, billions."

"Of which the US government must take a hefty piece."

"The US gov takes nothing."

"Nothing? Wow."

Ruby went on, bouncing sans seat belt, "But Oklahoma gets its share by way of yearly operating fees."

"Amounting to?" I asked.

"Millions."

Still, an acceptable cost of operating a multi-billion-dollar-a-year casino business, and why the tribes—for the most part—appeared to be thriving.

Ruby was saying, "But that's not the biggest threat the Nations face from the state of Oklahoma."

I asked, "What is?"

"Oil." She snorted. "Can you imagine giving land that was thought to be worthless to these tribes, and then discovering they were pitchin' their teepees on oil fields. I guess the Indians had the last laugh."

Maybe not laughing all the way to the bank, but surely smiling.

We were nearing the border of Texas when traffic began to slow, then came to a complete stop. Ahead I could see multiple flashing lights. "Must have been an accident."

Mother, leaning forward, peering through the windshield, said, "Not an accident, dear. That's a highway patrol check-point Charlie. They're looking for someone."

Or some people.

Brandy's Trash 'n' Treasures Tip

Apps such as Yard Sale Treasure Map make weekend garage sale hunting faster and easier by planning the quickest route to cover an area. It also searches for key words in listings, like antiques, collectibles, furniture, or whatever specific item you might be looking for. So far, Mother's request for a 78 RPM recording of "The Naughty Lady of Shady Lane," sung by Dean Martin, and produced in New Zealand in 1954 (which little Brandy broke) (the 78, not New Zealand) has summoned no results. By the way, the Naughty Lady who has the whole town talking, turns out to be a bawling baby (as our older readers probably already knew).

THREE
Red River Valley

Mother and I, accompanied by hitchhiker Ruby, were nearing the border of Texas when traffic began to slow, then come to a complete stop. Multiple flashing lights beckoned us from about a half-mile ahead.

"It *could* be an accident," I said.

Mother, leaning forward, peered through the windshield. "No, dear. Notice the barricades across the road?"

Ruby said, "They must be looking for those casino robbers. This is the only bridge across the Red River into Tranquility, so we may be here a while."

We were boxed in, cars lining up behind us, dominoes refusing to fall.

Then I did something really, really, really sleazy. You may lose any respect you still have left for me. Blame it on the nightmare of a trip I'd had so far, and the fact that Prozac can only do so much calming. Also, I had to pee. To piddle. Urinate, if you insist.

I swerved onto the shoulder and zoomed ahead of the other cars, campers, and trucks, coming to a stop at the barricades, where ebony Highway Patrol cars lined either side of the road.

A state trooper in wide-brimmed tan hat, bright-yellow vest over black short-sleeved shirt, and brown pants approached, holding up a hand.

I powered down my window. With all the urgency I could muster, I said, "My mother is having trouble breathing and needs to get to a hospital!"

Mother, doing her part, gasped and wheezed. She was the creative director at the Serenity Playhouse, after all.

"I need to see both your driver's licenses," the trooper replied officiously. No mention of Ruby behind us.

"But, she could be dying!" I protested, loud enough to attract the attention of a second trooper who came up behind his comrade and spoke in low tones. But I heard him anyway: "Fred, I checked their plates . . ." And I got the rest of what he said, too.

The first trooper looked at me and said, "You can go," and waved us around the barricade.

"*What* did he say?" Mother asked, having miraculously recovered after I'd sped away.

"You heard him. That we could go."

"No! The *second* trooper, before that."

"'Those are the two idiots Chief Hunter called about.'"

"We've been called worse," Mother said, shrugging it off.

"We've been called worse *today*," I pointed out.

Just before the bridge, a large filling station loomed with a sign saying LAST STOP FOR CHEAPER GAS. Apparently petrol cost more in Texas. With all that oil gushing, you'd think locals would get a better break.

I pulled up to a pump, letting Mother fill the tank while I went in to use the bathroom. When I returned to the van, Ruby was giving Mother a hug that seemed like a goodbye.

"You're not leaving?" I asked our hitcher.

Ruby nodded, her smile a tiny bit sad. "This is as good a place as any to find a long-hauler to get me to Austin."

"If you don't," I told her, "call my cell."

We got our cells out and exchanged numbers.

I said, "I'm at a campground and you could bunk with me." I didn't share where Mother was staying, not wanting to subject Ruby to her snoring. See how thoughtful I am? I'm about more than just lying to police.

Ruby smiled. "Thanks, I'll keep that offer in mind. But I should be fine."

I had no doubt this seasoned road-warrior female could take care of herself.

"Dear," Mother said to Ruby, "do let us know your address in Austin once you get settled."

"I'll do that."

Poor Ruby had no idea she was about to become ensnared in one of Mother's traps—her ever-growing Christmas letter list, out of which a recipient could escape only by death itself. And even then it took a while.

(Unbeknownst to Mother, every year I bestowed a Christmas blessing on a few lucky folks by deleting their names and addresses from the file. And so far, none have ever asked to be put back on. And, until now, Mother had no idea I'd been doing that.)

Mother was saying, "And if you ever find yourself in Iowa, be sure to look us up in Serenity."

Fondly, Ruby looked to me and then back to Mother. "Thank you, girls."

Mother loved being called a girl.

Funny how girls want to be called women and women like to be called girls.

While Ruby walked over to the trucking parking lot, Mother went into the convenience store to use the bathroom, coming out later with some items in a plastic bag. What purchase had she made in there? If it was candy, I hoped she'd bought enough for two.

Moments later we were crossing the bridge over the Red River—so-called due to its reddish-brown silt—where an overhead sign welcomed us to Texas, the downtown of Tranquility spread out before us in all its small-town glory.

"Mother?"

"Yes?"

"Am I hallucinating . . . or does this place look like Serenity?"

"I don't think we could both be hallucinating about the same thing, dear," she said, sitting forward with a curious frown. "Let's drive around a bit first, before making such an outrageous assumption."

As we slowly explored the downtown, the similarity to our little burg was uncanny: a riverfront park with picnic areas, a playground, and bandshell; one long main street for shopping; Victorian architecture; and the clustering of the police department, city hall, and courthouse within a few blocks of each other, the latter nearly identical to our wedding cake structure with one exception—their clock in its tower worked.

While Tranquility wasn't a precise mirror image of Serenity, it was close enough to be unsettling.

Had we gone through Alice's looking glass? Would up be down, and right be left? Truth a lie, and a lie the truth?

Mother said abruptly, "I'm quite knackered."

"You do look tired," I said. "Some food might help." I had spotted several nice-looking restaurants, although it might be hard to get reservations, the downtown already filling up with outsiders like us who had arrived for the city-wide sales. (Well, few outsiders were like us, admittedly.)

"No, dear. I'd like to get to bed early. We'll need to be up well before the ol' starting gun goes off at eight."

North of town lay an old Spanish mission converted into a hotel called the Tranquilo. The main rectangular structure—originally the church sanctuary—had been constructed of limestone with an ornate facade. On one end, an impressive bell tower rose to the heavens or, anyway, to the clouds. On the opposite end stretched a squat one-story wing which (I assumed) once had housed nuns and priests, their holy quarters transmogrified into rooms for guests.

I parked in a space reserved for check-in and retrieved Mother's suitcase from in the back of the van. A heavy wooden ornately carved front door indicated that, along with the thick outer walls, the mission had been built not only for worship, but as a fortress against unfriendly forces.

I followed Mother inside, where we paused to take in the surroundings.

She drew in a sharp breath. "Sacrilege!"

A young woman with long blonde hair, seated behind the check-in counter, asked, "Is everything all right, ma'am?"

Mother approached her. "No, it isn't. Where is the nave, the transepts, the sacristy, and the apse?"

"The, uh, what?"

"The heart and soul of the church, dear!" Mother, spreading her arms and hands like a revival tent preacher inviting conversions, knew all about old missions.

Puzzled, the young woman said, "I could ask management if we have those things. We have standard room service, but . . ."

"She means," I explained, "the original interior."

The blonde unfurrowed her brow and said, "Oh. That stuff is mostly there, behind the dry wall and dropped ceiling tiles."

"Well, thank goodness for the preservation," Mother exclaimed grandly, "of 'that stuff.'"

"Will you excuse us for a moment?" I asked the bewildered blonde, with a forced smile I was used to delivering, and pulled Mother aside.

"Look," I said quietly, "you're not going to find another place to stay in Tranquility, with this sale going on."

She pouted. "You should have shown me pictures."

I had selected her accommodations thinking she'd be happy in a historical setting.

"Well, it's too late now for anywhere else," I said. "You'll have to make do. Most hotels here have been sold out for months."

And I certainly didn't want her to move in with me, nor did I wish to switch places with her. The campgrounds served liquor; these lodgings did not. And a lime margarita (grande) on the rocks (with salt) was calling.

"Very well," she sighed in acquiescence.

After receiving a key card, Mother and I proceeded down a long hallway with an old stone floor, walls, and arched ceiling, giving an indication of what it had been like centuries ago, nuns and priests not included.

But Mother's room had not only been gutted and modernized; a wall had been knocked down to combine two small quarters, allowing for a bathroom and more space.

"Such a travesty," Mother said, shaking her head.

"What did you expect?" I asked. "A board and a brick pillow?"

"Just leave me to my misery."

If a comfy bed, private bathroom, flat-screen TV, and amenities such as a little fridge and coffee station made for misery, then sign me up. I might not get any of that where I was headed.

I asked gently, "What time should I pick you up in the morning?"

"Better make it six. These antique hunters are early risers."

"All right." I was on my way to the door. "Now, call me if you need anything."

She gave me a withering look. "Do you really want me to?"

"Of course." Not.

Outside it was magic hour—the brief time that movie directors love to capture when the sun has just set but there's still light, and the sky is all hues of ultramarine, like one of those magnificent Maxfield Parrish paintings where scantily clad maidens cavort among Grecian columns. I could picture myself doing that, ten pounds ago. Maybe fifteen.

I drove back along River Road, then turned west to my destination, a trailer park (caravan park to you UK readers) turned glamping campground.

You: What on earth is a glamping campground?
Me: Glamorized camping!
You: Isn't that a contradiction in terms?
Me: No, they're completely compatible.
You: How so?
Me: Think of those old movies with a Sheik who sets up camp in the desert. On the outside it's just a tent . . . but inside it's a palace!
You: Doesn't that rather defeat the whole roughing-it aspect of camping?
Me: No. Let me ask you a question. Why shouldn't fashionable women who love the outdoors surround themselves with glamour?
You: You are so wise, Brandy Borne!

A few miles outside of Tranquility a sign announced the glamping ground and I turned onto a gravel road, then down a dirt lane.

In a clearing of flowering cottonwood trees, from which drooped catkins of red and white (depending on the sex of the tree), huddled a small village of trailers.

But not just any trailers—these were of vintage styles from the '40s, '50s, and '60s, many painted on the outside with cowgirl pinups and hand-written slogans, like "GIRL WITH SASSITUDE" and "YOU MESS WITH ME, YOU MESS WITH THE WHOLE TRAILER PARK."

My mood lightened considerably.

The camp's office, set apart from the rest of the park, was a sleek, shiny, turquoise-and-cream-colored trailer, whose tail-end swooped like the back of a duck or a hillbilly haircut. A wide striped awning extended over the entrance, offering protection from inclement weather while doubling as a patio with Adirondack chairs and potted flowers. A beat-up red Ford truck was parked alongside the trailer—a sign of a true cowgirl.

Who would I find inside? Why, the queen of glamping, of

course! I don't know who that is, I'm just saying. But surely someone setting the precedent, a zoftig gypsy lady perhaps, with long black hair, low-cut white blouse, skirt slit up to an ample thigh, wearing more bangles and beads than the character Barbara Stanwyck played in that old black-and-white movie *Stella Dallas*.

A sign on the door read, "Come on in!"

Which is just what I did, going up one step to the interior, where the walls, cabinets and curved ceiling were a lacquered birdseye maple, like my 1930s Art Deco bedroom furniture at home.

To the left lurked a brown leather couch, end table, and an ottoman on a Navajo rug; to the right, a U-shaped kitchen with sink, small stove, and compact refrigerator, and beyond that, a twin-size bed with storage drawers beneath it.

The furniture was modern Western, the decorations items one might buy in a touristy shop, picture frames made of twigs, an end lamp with horses galloping around the shade. And the owner had an obvious fondness for cute little ceramic squirrels, placed here and there, like they had invaded the place in search of nuts. (And, frankly, more than a share of those had likely checked in here.)

Sidebar: once a squirrel had gotten into our attic and had babies. Mother and I couldn't bring ourselves to toss them out, so we let the family stay until the kids could strike out on their own. Many nights they'd play right above my bed, and I'd bang the ceiling with the end of a broom and yell, "Go to sleep!" like a parent whose children had gotten out of bed and were rustling around their room. Then all would be quiet. For a while.

But there were some not-so-cute squirrels among this particular collection, like a pelt of one tacked to the wall (couldn't bag a bear, so ta-da!) and a taxidermy specimen beneath a small dining table, begging for food that it was beyond eating. If my trailer was anything like this, I would be disappointed.

But not as disappointed as seeing who greeted me from behind the extended kitchen counter. It sure wasn't a gypsy lady in baubles, bangles, and beads.

"Well, hello, darlin'," rasped the middle-aged, gray-haired, round-shaped woman reminiscent of Ma Kettle from the comedy movies of the '40s and '50s that Mother so liked to watch. "You must be Brandy Borne from Ay-a-way."

"Yes," I replied, trying not to show my disappointment.

"Welcome to the Glampin' Ground. You're already checked in. You have the Wee Wind."

"Excuse me?" Had I done something rude and unglamperous?

"That's the type of trailer you're in, hon. Airstream Wee Wind. Nineteen-forties."

"Oh." That sounded fine. "How do I find it?"

"Just drive past the Saloon to lucky number seven."

I could use a little luck on this trip.

Margorie Main continued (Google it, young 'uns), "And speakin' of the Saloon, you'll find it worth knowin' that the specialty is Burgoo Stew." She shrugged. "We serve other food, o' course, but that succulent stew is made from my original recipe, goin' back to when the camp first opened up."

I'd never heard of Burgoo Stew, but was hungry enough to eat just about anything. Just about.

Ma opened a counter drawer, pulled out a piece of paper, and handed it to me. "Might as well give you this aforehand. Everyone asks for the recipe once they scarfed the stuff." She frowned. "Funny thing though, folks always seem to leave the paper behind when they go. Wadded up, usually."

I looked at the recipe and got as far as the first ingredient: 6 squirrels. That might explain the pelt on the wall.

Suddenly my hunger disappeared. I thought, *No recipe if this becomes a book!*

"Now, if you need anything, anything a'tall," Ma rasped, "just drop on by."

"Er, what are the office hours?"

"Twenty-four-seven. I live right here, darlin'. My late husband and me bought this very trailer park fifty-odd year ago . . ."

So. No Pa Kettle around.

". . . And then after he passed, I figured I'd have t'sell. But my granddaughter come up with an i-dee-er. These here glampin' camps was becomin' a thing, and she said I could make the park into one of 'em, 'cause I already had these old trailers I been rentin' to down-and-outers. I could get a better rate from the up-and-inners. So Lacy—that's the granddaughter's name—took to decoratin' these trailers we picked up by findin' furnishin's and this and that in thrift shops, and paintin' 'em herself. An' low an' behold, the tourists started a-comin'. And they ain't stopped."

"Is your granddaughter still helping out?" I asked, just making conversation to get the thought of that roadkill stew out of my mind.

Ma shook her head. "Naw. Lacy run off with one of the bartenders that works at the Saloon." She lowered her voice confidentially. "Since it's mostly fillies comes here, I get good lookin' stud muffins to work the bar and keep the gals happy and the drinks a-flowin'." She paused. "But too often these fellers think they're more stud than muffin. Y'know, I really oughta hire geldings."

The conversation was getting too equestrian for my taste. "Thank you, ah, Mrs., uh . . .?"

"Everyone just calls me Ma."

Just what I needed: another eccentric Mother.

But my Airstream Wee Wind was adorable! A miniature blimp on two wheels whose shiny aluminum outside panels were held together by rivets, perhaps courtesy of Rosie herself.

The inside was just as charming. A couch (in the aft) had two fold-out tables for eating or writing, the kitchen (mid-section) contained a little sink/faucet, small microwave, and dorm-room-size fridge. The bed (in the forward) could actually accommodate two people, a filly and a stud maybe, or me and Ruby if she decided to drop by.

Delicate white lace curtains hung on the open windows, a wind chime out there made up of old chandelier crystals providing a soothing cadence in the breeze. Next to the sink were welcoming wildflowers in a white-speckled blue enamel coffee pot.

Two kitchen cupboards above the faucet opened upward, like the storage bins of an airplane, revealing mismatched china plates, saucers and teacups (here a Lenox, there a Wedgwood), while the drawer held a mishmash of orphaned silverware from various eras—from plated to real sterling, others sporting colorful Bakelite handles.

The absent Lacy definitely had an eye for selecting the best that thrift stores had to offer.

Next to the sleeping nook was a tiny closet with a small toilet and wall mirror, but nothing else; you had to use the kitchen sink to wash your hands or the bathhouse for showering.

I put my suitcase on the bed, which bore a patchwork quilt, pink sham with ruffle edges, and pillow with a crisp white case embroidered in fancy scroll with the initials LBJ. Wait a minute . . . the thirty-sixth president of the United States? Couldn't be.

I did my best to devise a scenario where it *could* be: Lyndon's wife, Lady Bird, in a pique over the then Texas senator's decades-long affair with Madeleine Duncan (or was it Alice Glass Kirkpatrick?) packed up any bedroom reminders of her husband and put the box out for the trash where some passerby retrieved it, the pillowcase making its way to a thrift shop where it languished (the former Democratic president no longer popular in this Republican state) only to be plucked out of a bin by Lacy, and put on a bed where I, Brandy Borne of Serenity, Iowa, would lay my head.

Weird!

(*Note to Brandy from Olivia*: While this may all be interesting to some readers, as your editor, I am beginning to wonder when the mystery will begin. We are yet without a dead body.)

(*Note to Olivia from Brandy*: There *was* some excitement in chapter two in the Cherokee hut, wasn't there? An unconscious intruder on the floor? But, OK, I'll pick up the pace.)

My appetite had returned with a vengeance, but before hitting the Saloon, I first wanted to wash off the dust of the road.

I collected my toiletry bag and a fresh set of clothes—black-and-gold Iowa sweatshirt, jeans, crew socks, Superga trainers—then grabbed a rolled-up towel from a wicker basket near the bed. Leaving the trailer, I stepped out into a starry, starry night.

The bathhouse was nearby, a brick structure illuminated by bright security lights, and I entered a door depicting a sexy cowgirl. (*Please help me pick up the pace by reading the following fast.*) Inside I found a clean bathroom with three sinks, three stalls, and three showers, and there were numerous plaques on the wall that said things like TOO GLAM TO GIVE A DAMN, and GOOD GIRLS GO TO HEAVEN, BAD GIRLS GO EVERYWHERE, and I used a stall that had another sign over the toilet: HOLD YOUR HORSES UNTIL SEATED, then took off my clothes and wrapped a towel around myself and deposited both sets of clothes and the toiletry bag on a chair outside a shower which had big dispensers for shampoo, conditioner and body wash, but I had forgotten my washcloth so I don't know how clean I got, then I returned to the same stall and put on my clean clothes, and then while I was standing at a sink mirror applying some make-up, two young women came in, drunk as skunks, both wearing prom dresses and cowboy boots, and I asked one—the least drunk—if my dirty clothes and toiletry bag would be safe left in the bathhouse because I wanted to go to the Saloon, and she looked at the clothes and my open bag and said, "Nobody's gonna want that stuff," and they stumbled out in a fit of laughter, so I took her at her word.

Whew!

(*You can slow down now.*)

The Saloon was rustic, typical of any number of Western bars with beer signs and cowboy decor. Just like the movies and TV. The country music was loud, the air stuffy, and girlie dresses and decorative boots on full display. Every table was taken—the ratio of female to male about ten to one—but there were a few open seats at the bar, which is where I went.

A hunky blond bare-chested bartender behind the counter came toward me in fringed chaps over jeans. There are worse things in the world than stud muffins.

"What can I get you?" he asked politely, his voice mid-range college boy. Did he shave that chest? That sure was a nice tan . . .

I had changed my mind about the margarita. "A glass of white wine—any kind—and something fast to eat, but *not* Ma's Burgoo Stew. I am definitely not in the mood for squirrel, no matter how fresh."

He smiled knowingly, displaying dimples. "We don't make it that way anymore—strictly top-grade round steak."

"Sold."

While I sipped the wine, a pinot grigio, I swiveled in my chair to watch the tipsy gaiety. Once upon a wild old time, I would have happily joined in.

For a split second I thought I saw Ruby—a flash of red hair in the crowd. Had she come looking for me, unable to get a ride to Austin, to take me up on my offer of putting a roof over her head (minus mesh doors)? But that seemed unlikely and too many people were milling around to be sure it was her. No shortage of pretty fillies at the Glam Bar W Saloon.

The bartender set a steaming bowl before me, which I signed to my trailer bill, along with the wine and tip.

Tentatively, I took a bite—*Yum!*—and gobbled the stew down, not caring if it burned the roof of my mouth.

Ma's Burgoo Stew

Ingredients:

6 squirrels, legs and back meat, cut up (substitute with
  2 pounds round steak, fat trimmed and cubed)
1 medium diced onion
2 cups water
1 tbsp. beef bouillon broth
1 bay leaf
6 medium Russet potatoes, peeled and cut into cubes
3 large carrots, peeled and sliced
1 (14.5 oz) can diced tomatoes
2 tsp. Worcestershire sauce
1 tsp. hot sauce
1 tsp. brown sugar
1 (4 oz) can diced green chilies
Salt and pepper to taste

Slow cooker directions:

Heat a skillet over medium-high setting. Add cubed beef and brown for about 5 minutes. Drain off the grease. Add the onion and sauté for 4 more minutes. Transfer beef and onion to a slow cooker. Add all remaining ingredients, and stir to combine. Cover slow cooker and cook on low for 6 hours, or high for 3–4 hours. When done, stir and ladle into bowls. Serves 6–8 people.

I was about to ask for another squirrel-free serving when the room suddenly went quiet.

All eyes turned toward me, or really the bar, as if the women were waiting for something. Then a chant began, growing in volume, "Laredo, Laredo, *Lah-ray-do*!"

The bartender—apparently Laredo—jumped up on the counter. Still bare-chested and wearing the fringed chaps, the jeans had been replaced by a thong. As he began to dance to Billy Ray Cyrus, kicking here, swiveling there, the crowd went wild.

Perhaps if I'd been seated elsewhere, I might have stayed to see if Laredo performed the full monty . . . but this was too up-close for comfort, and the wine and hot stew had made me sleepy.

So it was happy trails time for cowgirl Brandy. (I found out later that the chaps did come off, but not the thong. Ma ran a respectable place.)

Returning to the bathhouse, I retrieved my dirty clothes and bag that nobody wanted, and it was then that my cell pinged.

Oh, no. What did Mother want now?

But the text came from Ruby, saying she had arrived in Austin. I responded, thanking her for letting me know.

Back in my trailer, so tired I left my clothes and make-up on, I flopped onto the bed and went out like a light as soon as my head hit LBJ's pillowcase.

A car alarm jolted me awake, sounding very close. I stumbled out of bed and got to the sink window in time to see a dark figure running away from my van—this had been the source of the disturbance.

The van's alarm had been programed to shut off after a few screeches, going just long and loud enough to scare a person or animal away. I had no desire to run after the prowler, much less wake up Ma, so I turned on a few lights and went back to bed.

My eyes had barely closed when my cell rang.

What now?

Was I ever going to get a good night's sleep on this trip?

The caller ID read: Tranquility Police Department.

I sat up. "Hello?"

"Is this Brandy Borne?" a Texas-twanged male voice asked.

"Yes."

"Is Vivian Borne your mother?"

"Uh . . . yes." My heart began pounding. "Is she all right?"

"Your Mother's fine. But we're holding her in the city jail for questioning."

Now that my worst fear was dispelled, annoyance set in. *Two jail cells in two days? Wasn't that a record, even for her? What had she done now?*

"Questioning for what?" I asked.

"Homicide."

Brandy's Trash 'n' Treasures Tip

Thrift stores are a wonderful resource to find vintage items like crystal, Depression glass, dish sets, and unique handmade items. Often furniture is cheap because it needs refinishing, and if you don't mind the work, can be a good way to make a profit. Who knows? You might even run across a pillowcase once belonging to a former American president.

FOUR
Back in the Saddle Again

Dearest ones! This is Vivian taking over the reins—a most fitting analogy now that we've all climbed onto a buckboard in the metaphorical wagon train and find ourselves in the Lone Star State.

But before continuing with our story, I must first address a few untruths Brandy has passed along about me in her opening chapters.

Despite what you've been told, as if it is receiving factual information, I do *not* snore. *She* is in fact the one who can rattle the windowpanes. And, now that I mention it, *she* is the one who bought those difficult-to-market lighthouses, not moi, who advised against setting sale so recklessly.

Furthermore, I was *not* pressured into "retiring" as sheriff, rather it was a mutual decision between myself and the city council. I requested a release from my elected position when all those legalities unexpectedly hampered my amateur-sleuth standing.

Nor was I "tired" on our first evening in Tranquility—that was *acting*; I needed to break free from my little reluctant Watson because I had places to go, people to see, and things to do, not all of which she might approve of my going, seeing and doing.

And as far as Brandy deleting names from my Christmas letter list—I knew very well what she'd surreptitiously done, and added them promptly back on, and *that* is why no one complained about not receiving one. (Of course I, too, have now tipped my hand, an unfortunate result of my pledge to maintain honesty with you, the reader.)

I think that just about covers everything so far, but I do reserve the right to set things straight in my future chapters—not always easy, as Brandy happened to sign our first book contract, a business practice to which I have been forced to acquiesce, unfairly relegating me to a secondary role in the writing—but not in the crime-solving!

Now. On to another standing concern. My campaign against the appropriation of the word "actor" to describe nefarious or dubious persons appears to have had scant effect upon this continued assault on a time-honored profession—acting! Whether it be on stage or screen, no artistic pursuit is more noble.

So far I have been subjected to "bad actor," "crisis actor," "bad-faith actor," "fringe actor," "political actor," and "lone-wolf actor" (the latter acceptable when referring to entries in the classic *Lone Wolf* film series). Unfortunately I must now add a new one to the list: "foreign actor." Isn't it bad enough to malign American actors without denigrating thespians abroad?

Why, there are many good foreign actors! One of my favorites is Jacques Tati, the French writer, director, and star of *Monsieur Hulot's Holiday* (1953, available on DVD and Blu-ray from The Criterion Collection) about a well-meaning buffoon whose presence at a seaside resort provokes one catastrophe after another. (I don't know why this character resonates with me so deeply.)

And need I mention the great Shakespearean actors the UK has produced? Sirs Laurence Olivier, John Gielgud, Patrick Stewart, and Dames Peggy Ashcroft, Maggie Smith, and Judi Dench? And where would world culture be without Frankie Howerd, Sid James and Benny Hill? Corr! And that's just to mention a few.

I could go on and on lauding the many and varied talents of actors from other countries, but I have a proviso in my book contract that stipulates I cannot exceed a specific word-count in my chapters (currently negotiated to 6,000). (Apparently, the odd reader has accused me of rambling, an outrageous assertion. They're the ones who are odd!) But to keep within my word limit and prevent being cut-off in mid-sentence—which has on rare occasion happened before—I will return to the narrative at hand.

(*Note to editor Olivia from Vivian:* I would request the previous passage explaining inaccuracies that are Brandy's fault, and my simply updating my thoughts on the "actor" front, not be counted against me.)

(*Note to Vivian from editor Olivia:* 6,000 words. Not a syllable more.)

(*Note to editor from Vivian:* Well, these notes surely don't count! . . . Olivia? Olivia?)

Anyhoo, after Brandy left me at my lodgings in a missionary position (see what I did there?), I freshened up a bit, put on a comfortable slacks outfit, gathered my tote bag, and ventured outside to await my mode of transportation, which had been prearranged for seven o'clock.

The night was cool, a gorgeous setting sun filling the horizon with swaths of purple and pink, stars just beginning to appear. Right on time, a blue pick-up truck hauling a trailer pulled up in front of the former mission where I awaited.

Now, gentle reader, I beg your indulgence in explaining my thinking. I could hardly rent a car due to my unfairly revoked driver's license, nor did I care to call for a taxi or use an Uber-type service because both maintained records of the time and place riders went, not to mention that the drivers of either service cannot be properly customer-vetted. You don't know what kind of lunatic you're driving around with! And unfortunately, Tranquility did not have a regular bus route schedule.

This left me with few options.

The stocky, bearded driver, appropriately attired in black cowboy hat, plaid shirt, jeans, and boots, exited the truck, went around to the rear of the trailer, lowered the tailgate, and revealed his passenger: a horse.

I had requested a docile animal, a quarter horse; this beauty was brown with a black mane and a white spot on the forehead. Backing out, the horse did whinny and rear a bit, but then it had been confined in a small space, and I might well have done the same in his (its?) position.

Mr. Garcia, the owner of a cattle ranch who had a side business of renting horses by the hour, approached with the steed, saddled and ready (the horse, not him! I just hate it when writers lack clarity). We had settled all the paperwork—contract, liability form, and fees—a few days ago via e-mails, in which I informed him I wanted to go riding in the countryside at night to commune with nature under the big Texas sky.

Now he and the horse were here in person. Mr. Garcia's expression seemed curiosity-tinged as he doffed his Stetson and asked politely, "Mrs. Borne?"

"Guilty as charged." Good thing we weren't in court!

The horse, larger than expected, eyed me warily.

"I hope you don't mind," Mr. Garcia said, "but after reading your riding qualifications, I felt it only appropriate to provide you with a more suitable breed."

He was referring to my winning the American Dressage Championship in 1982, and competing in the World Equestrian Games in 1987. Speaking of games, that was all horse hockey.

"What, uh, breed is it . . . ?" I asked. I knew a few breeds.

"She. Mustang. Responds to 'Sally.'"

I forced a smile. "Like the song."

"What song?"

I gave him a few bars, and he must have recalled it, judging by his wide-eyed expression.

He let some air out and said, "She's spirited, and, as you requested, no bit."

I indeed *had* asked that there not be a bit, because how would you like someone yanking on a steel rod in *your* mouth? That decision, however, had been made having a gentler breed in mind. But what the hay!

I patted the animal's shoulder. "Sally and I will get along just fine, I'm sure. Pardners all the way."

I hoped.

"Can I help you up?" he asked.

"Wouldn't that be loverly." I put a foot into the stirrup and he gave me a boost, perhaps misjudging a tad, as I nearly went over the other side!

Righting myself, I smiled, exhaled, and said, "It *has* been a while . . . but everything will come back." He looked concerned so I added, "It's just like riding a bicycle!"

"Not really, Mrs. Borne."

"I mean in the metaphorical sense. That some things, you never forget."

Except while I knew how to ride a literal bicycle, I had only been on a Shetland pony as a child, going around in a circle.

He smiled. "Well, I'll never forget you, Mrs. Borne. Anyway, I'm sure you'll be fine. Have a good time."

"Oh, one more thing," I said. "Do automobiles tend to make Sally nervous?"

He frowned. "It's pretty quiet out here in the country, so if you don't venture too far out, I don't imagine you're going to run into many cars."

I smiled down at him from my perch. "Or that any cars will run into us!"

"Uh, that's right." He snugged his Stetson back on. "I'll be back in three hours."

For a moment I thought the man might slap the animal on its hindquarters to get us going, which would have been ill-advised, but thankfully he didn't.

I kept my smile active while he closed the tailgate and returned to his truck; I waved until the vehicle was out of sight.

I stroked Sally's rather coarse mane. How hard could riding a horse be? After all, I had seen every one of John Wayne's Westerns, beginning with his first leading role in *The Big Trail* from 1930, almost a decade before director John Ford put the Duke in *Stagecoach* (not implying I saw either film in the theater!). The Duke hailed from Iowa, by the way, which made us kindred spirits.

Joel McCrea is another superb cowboy rider, who made some terrific westerns like *Wells Fargo* and *The Gunfight at Dodge City*.

Of course, nobody sat taller in the saddle than Randolph Scott, starring in over sixty Westerns (my favorite is *The Tall T*), even teaming up with McCrea in *Ride the High Country*, Scott's last movie, a terrific tale about two aging cowboys, directed by Sam Peckinpah.

War hero turned sagebrush star Audie Murphy was a fine rider, as well (and so good in *No Name on the Bullet*!). He rates a salute!

And then there's Gary Cooper, no slouch on a horse he! I just re-watched the Western classic *High Noon*, although Coop doesn't ride one all that much in the film, mostly driving a buckboard and walking around the dreary Western town looking for help. I'd have pitched in, if he'd asked me!

My point being, one can learn a lot about horses from movies, and not necessarily old ones (movies, not horses). As I've often told Brandy, a great writer is a good observer. (Although I didn't get much from *The Horse Whisperer*, except not to go galloping down icy slopes, and also if you're playing opposite Robert Redford, your character is going to fall in love with him.)

The first thing I did, now that I was saddled up, was lean forward and offer Sally a crisp juicy apple from my tote bag (Gala is my favorite type of the ol' forbidden fruit, although when Brandy and I were in London to meet our publisher, Severn House, I ate a Cox's Orange Pippin that was really a pip! pip!— but hard to find in the colonies.)

Sally swung her neck like a crane, and big teeth snapped the apple from my hand, leaving me relieved to have retained all the fingers. I also had carrots, bananas, and sugar cubes along, purchased at the gas station where we'd left Ruby.

I pulled one rein in the direction of the road, made a clicking sound, and gently prodded Sally's sides with my stirrups, figuring the horse could chew and walk at the same time. I figured right, except Sally did not just walk—she galloped!

Holy guacamole! If I wore dentures, would they be clacking! I tried to employ that technique where a rider will rise up in the saddle to get in rhythm with the horse, but that only made the bouncing worse. Thankfully my hindquarters were sufficiently padded. Nonetheless, I held on for dear life.

Thank goodness Sally knew to keep to the shoulder of the road, and eventually I managed to pull her back to a trot. She seemed unfazed by the cars whizzing by, but I worried that if it got much darker out, the drivers might not see us. I could only hope these Texans knew their way around horses better than I.

Still, this was one of those rare times when I questioned my judgment (the other was using real horses in the Ascot scene while directing the Serenity Playhouse production of *My Fair Lady*—you may recall my use of a "loverly" expression earlier).

But I'd had the foresight to bring a bright flashlight, which was providential, as my first stop was fast approaching—a housing addition outside Tranquility called Manor Ranch, where million-dollar homes hunkered on spacious lots, each trying to outspend the other by way of an impressively different architectural style.

Thanks to my instinctive bridle work, Sally and I slowed, hoofs clopping (hers not mine) on the concrete street while I bounced in the saddle, safely arriving at the address I wanted.

I was due to have arrived at seven thirty, and it was just a few minutes after.

"Whoa, girl," I said, gently pulling back on the reins while applying pressure with my legs.

Sally halted and I dismounted, removing my feet from the stirrups and sliding off one side while holding onto the saddle's horn. Then I wrapped the reins around the post of a mailbox at the entrance of the driveway.

From the tote I gave Sally a sugar cube from a cupped hand. "Stay, girl."

She whinnied and pulled on the reins.

"I won't be long," I promised, patting her head, dispensing another cube.

She settled. We were on the same page.

Two cars were parked in the drive—a white Lincoln and a black Porsche—and I proceeded along a flagstone walk lined with flowerbeds winding to the expansive home. It had a recessed entrance with overhang, the kind of feature I didn't cotton to because you couldn't just stick your head out the front door in your pajamas to see what the morning weather was like, you had to walk out a mite.

I rang the doorbell, which had been programed to play the first few bars of "Deep in the Heart of Texas"—which was not really accurate, as we were *just* over the border and not that deep.

A bright porch light came on, and a man of about fifty opened the door, greeting me with a smile and a Texan drawl. "Vivian Borne! It's nice to finally meet y'all in the flesh."

I didn't know quite how to take that, as it did sound a bit salacious; but I gave him the benefit of the doubt, since we knew each other by way of contact through e-mails and the phone. He gestured me inside.

My host was Wade Stetson, a dealer in Western antiques, who I'd once done a favor. Knowing he lived in Tranquility, I was hopeful the favor would be returned.

Wade reminded me of the actor Tom Selleck—well-built, dark curly hair, thick eyebrows and mustache, hazel eyes, and a tall drink of water. Dressed country casual in a black t-shirt and faded jeans, the man did not quite jibe with the house.

A female voice behind him asked, "Who is it, Wade?"

The way the woman materialized so quickly gave me the impression Wade might be on a short leash. Tall and beautiful, with shoulder-brushing blonde hair (what other kind of woman would this fine male specimen be with?), Wade's wife wore expensive clothes . . . and she *did* jibe with the house.

"This is Vivian Borne, Mary Jo," Wade said, as the woman approached us in the entryway. "You remember—the lady who sold me that matching spur I'd been hunting for?"

The lone spur had been among offerings we'd bought from that Western-themed restaurant's going-out-of-business sale, one of a pair hand-crafted in Cañon City, a prison in Colorado where artistic inmates created some of the most exquisite spurs, because they had the talent. And the time.

"Oh, yes, Mrs. Borne," Mary Jo said dismissively. She didn't offer to shake my hand, but then, hers were holding a stack of papers.

Wade asked, "Aren't you going to your meeting, hon?"

As beautiful as Mrs. Stetson was, Vivian Borne ain't chopped liver, so he had an understandable nervousness about having a well-filled filly at his door.

"I'm on my way now," she replied quickly, stuffing the papers into a large Vuitton bag dangling from one arm.

Wade said, "My wife is one of the organizers of the city-wide sale for the new library."

I was about to say something nice about her charitable endeavor when she slipped around me, in a hurry.

"Just so you know," I said helpfully, "there's a horse tied to your mailbox."

Half-way out the door, she froze, and unleashed big blue eyes on me over her shoulder, as if noticing my presence for the first time. Which was kind of insulting, really.

"There's a what where?" she asked.

"A horse tied to your mailbox."

She looked. Confirmed it.

"Your horse is tied to our mailbox," she said. It wasn't quite a question. It wasn't quite a statement, either.

"It's not *my* horse."

"Not your horse?"

"No. It's a rental."

She shook her head, not disturbing lovely if lacquered hair, and left, without pausing even to glance at Sally before cutting over to the driveway, where she got into the Lincoln and drove off, only narrowly missing the horse, who reared a little.

Wade looked nervous. "Sorry if the wife spooked that steed." A grin happened. "But frankly, you talking to her put a scare into me."

"Why is that?"

"Well, you didn't mention anything about it, but . . . Mary Jo doesn't know about our arrangement."

The arrangement being that I would have a first look at what he had to sell. What did *you* think he meant? But the issue was what Mary Jo might have thought, as after all she was an organizer of the sales event.

"I'd better get Sally off the street," I said.

"Sally?"

"As in ride Sally ride?"

"Oh."

We went out and Wade headed for the garage while I unhitched Sally and led her closer to the house, using a front-walk light post to tie her up, then gave her a banana. She was calm again. Me, too.

Meanwhile, Wade opened the wide garage door, revealing a treasure trove of Western antiques and collectibles.

I walked along the banquet tables where everything was neatly arranged and highly priced (for a good cause, remember), immediately spotting a few items—mostly collectibles—that were within my budget and could easily sell in our shop at a profit.

One was a Hopalong Cassidy white glass coffee mug from the 1950s; another, a reproduction of etched shot glasses from six historic old Western saloons; and a vintage McCoy chuck wagon cookie jar. My final selection was a brass mantle clock with attached horse made by United, mid-last-century. Yippee!

"How much would that come to?" I asked, having pointed out the merchandise.

"One hundred," Wade said.

"Oh, come now, that won't even cover the cookie jar!"

His head shifted to one side. "Vivian, you could have really socked me for that spur, knowing how much I wanted it for my collection."

That had crossed my mind.

"I enjoy seeing paired items reunited," I replied, adding, "and owned by someone who appreciates them."

"Then it's a deal?"

"Would Vivian Borne look a gift horse in the mouth?"

From an inside pocket of my tote bag I pulled out my checkbook (yes, upon occasion, I do still write checks), and paid for my purchases, arranging to return later with our van, by which time Wade would have wrapped up and boxed the whole shootin' match.

Then he proceeded to give me advice on what other Western items I should be on the lookout for, which I appreciated but most likely wouldn't take, since I operate on gut instinct. (My basic rule is only buying things I like for the shop, in case I get stuck with them.) But I listened patiently, nodding now and then.

By the time I managed to extricate myself, Sally was champing at the bit (metaphorically speaking, as I hadn't foisted a bit on her) to get moving. We were again on the same page, or maybe trail, as I was overdue to keep my eight-thirty appointment. Wade had arranged two more meetings for me with individuals willing to provide an early showing.

My host helped me into the saddle, and this time I kept my balance.

"Are you sure you'll be all right?" he asked, concerned about sending a tenderfoot out with dusk fast approaching.

"I have a flashlight," I replied, "and then there'll be the city lights to guide the way."

I gave Sally a nudge and Wade gave us a wave.

My next destination was a chicken farm on the edge of Tranquility, my flashlight bouncing along with me, causing drivers to slow down, perhaps wondering if someone was signaling them or maybe a flying saucer was looking to land. You never know.

Soon I successfully steered Sally down the appropriate dirt road to a modest two-story dwelling, dwarfed by a large, long building with built-in fans along the side where the chickens were kept.

(*Note to Olivia from Vivian*: Is it OK to use the word "dwarfed" in this context?)

(*Note to Vivian from Olivia*: Perhaps "overshadowed" might be preferable.)

(*Note to Olivia from Vivian*: But that could give the false impression the building was close enough to the house to throw a shadow, and I don't think anybody would build an abode close enough to hear all that clucking and squawking while trying to sleep. Hello? Olivia?)

Soon I successfully steered Sally down the appropriate dirt road to a modest two-story home, overshadowed (but not literally) by a large, long building with built-in fans along the side where the chickens were kept.

As my arrival was expected, the yard lights were burning, as were those on the first floor of the house. I'd managed to be on time despite Wade's good-intended but long-winded advice, and I had Sally and the quick pace to thank for that. That and her love of bananas, apples, sugar cubes, and such.

An older-model burgundy Buick sedan was parked in front, with its headlights on, and I was wondering if I should turn them off when they extinguished themselves, so the owner must have just returned home.

I tied Sally to a large metal chicken secured to the ground, giving the horse a few carrots. Taking stock of what food remained in my tote, I needed to start rationing if I wanted to make it back to the mission. Sally didn't run on "Empty"!

Anna Fowler met me at the door, a little out of breath.

Now, a word to two or three about the names found in the Trash 'n' Treasures series. Yes, once in a while, when I can't get a signed release from someone, names have been changed; but most are real, and I can't help it if they often reflect the person's traits or characteristics. This anomaly is called an *aptonym*.

Furthermore, *nominative determinism* is an accepted hypothesis among psychologists, suggesting a relationship based on the idea that people tend to be attracted to areas of work that suit their name. Need some examples? Sara Blizzard, a weather forecaster for the BBC; Margaret Court, Australian tennis champion; Karina DePiano, pianist who toured with Taylor Swift; Ken Miles, English race car driver; Gabe Pressman, American journalist; and Tiger Woods, American golfer (a wood being a type of golf club), just to name a few.

And this does not preclude those who enter a life of crime, like American financier Bernie Madoff, who "made-off" with money from his investment scheme, or Anthony Weiner, the American politician involved in sexting photos of his, well, you get the picture (or perhaps you don't care to). And wasn't Charles Dickens one dickens of a good writer?

Back to Anna Fowler, a plump, middle-aged woman wearing what used to be called a house dress or "duster" (still available through the Vermont Country Store catalogue) and slippers cradling swollen feet.

The house smelled of fried chicken from supper—an irony that is *nominative determinism* adjacent, considering the inhabitant's profession, and we moved into the living room where various card tables had been set up for tomorrow morning's offering, including collections of figurines by Hummel, Precious Moments, Willow Tree, and an assortment of plates printed with roosters.

But I wasn't here for any of that.

She offered me tea. I declined. We sat on a sagging couch in front of a scarred-up coffee table.

I let her talk.

"Our business has always been a struggle," Anna said, "but a few years ago we had to destroy half our flock due to bird flu . . ."

The woman seemed beaten down by the life she'd chosen, or at least had found herself in, each line in her face with its own story.

". . . And then my husband passed."

"So sorry, my dear." My better angels kept me interested and sympathetic, while my lesser demons wanted to see what I'd come for.

Anna sighed. "None of our children had any interest in taking over the farm . . . and now they're grown with their own families and jobs." She brightened. "But I may have found a way to be able to afford keeping the farm. You brought what I wanted?"

"Yes."

From an outside pocket of my tote, I withdrew what has become a rare hardcover first edition of *Antiques Roadkill*, signed by myself and Brandy, wrapped in cellophane because I didn't have one of those plastic covers.

Taking the book, Anna said, "Your series has given me such pleasure, especially *your* chapters."

(*Note to Mother from Brandy*: Oh, come on! Did she *really* say "your chapters?")

(*Note to Brandy from Mother*: Yes, dear. But it *is* odd that a reader of our true-crime books would find them amusing.)

Anna reached for a black binder on the coffee table, and placed it in my lap. "And this is what you came for."

"This" was her late husband's minor league baseball card collection. As a young man in the 1960s, Fred Fowler had played with the Amarillo Gold Sox in the Texas League before being dropped, though he'd never lost interest in the sport.

Hold on! Fowler . . . foul ball hitter. He's an example of double *nominative determinism*!

(*Note to Vivian from Olivia*: Just a reminder that I intend to hold you to the contractual word-count.)

(*Note to Olivia from Vivian*: Yes, ma'am. You're not counting these notes in the tally, are you?)

Among the hundreds of cards encased in protective sleeves, only three were worth real money (according to grandson Jake, who knew his baseball memorabilia); but those three were humdingers, as we say in the Midwest. Produced only from 1909 through 1911 by the American Tobacco Company for insertion into packs of Obak cigarettes, these posed art images of minor-league players included Buck Weaver, Chick Gandil, and Ten Million, who even though mostly unknown today had in a sense "created" cards that could fetch thousands of dollars to avid minor-league card collectors.

And here is a conundrum for many an honest dealer, of which I believe I (honesty being more a guideline than a rule) am: whether or not to inform a seller they have something valuable.

Usually, I at least allude to it.

"Some of these cards could be worth serious money," I said. But not enough to save her farm.

Anna shook her head. "I have neither the time nor the inclination to pursue that." She paused, adding, "And my children have no interest in them, so unless I do something about it, when I'm gone they'll end up in a landfill."

With any guilt assuaged, I made a low-ball offer that she accepted, and—as with Wade—arranged to pick up the card collection later. (Actually, more mid-ball than low-ball. Oh! *Nominative determinism* again!)

Outside, I could see by the bright yard light that Sally had deposited some "apples" of her own on the ground, and not Galas nor Cox's Orange Pippins.

I always picked up Sushi's aftermath with a little baggie; hers were the size of baby carrots, but Sally's dwarfed (overshadowed?) actual apples, something I had not been prepared for. So, from my tote I withdrew a small notebook and pen, wrote SORRY! on a page, then stuck the paper to one of the apples.

(*Note to Brandy from Olivia*: Is Vivian all right?)

(*Note to Olivia from Brandy*: Define "all right.")

But I had a bigger concern than horse doo doo: how to mount Sally without assistance.

I put the leg featuring my best knee in the stirrup, rose up to where I could lay my stomach on the saddle, swung the other leg over and struggled until I was sitting upright.

Sally was patient through this process, receiving a reward of more carrots, which exhausted my supply of equine bribery. And, with the flashlight leading the way, I proceeded down the dirt lane to the highway.

As luck would have it, my final stop wasn't far into Tranquility, and with all the city lights, we could be seen plain as day at night.

Now, a horse with rider in the streets of Serenity would bring stares, but not here in Tranquility, where cars didn't honk at us and pedestrians gave rider and steed nary a glance.

Patrick Cillian Tool (no *nominative determinism* that I knew of, despite the possibilities) lived on a bluff among grand old homes with the best view of the river—similar to West Hill in Serenity, though these near-mansions were built by oil and cattle magnates rather than our lumber and pearl button barons.

As Sally and I began at the base of the hill's incline, these country-fried castles increased in grandeur, fine examples of Baroque, Queen Anne, Gothic Revival, and Greek Renaissance. But numbered among them were examples of a few architectural styles unseen in Serenity, such as Italianate villas and French Second Empire with mansard (flat) roofs—a design unsuitable for the rainy Midwest—displaying a fondness for large porch columns and second-story balconies reminiscent of Southern plantations.

I'd had an internet face-to-face with Tool in the interim before Brandy and I left, and he was a grizzled old coot, looking more like a prospector than the CEO of a bank, which is what he was.

To break the ice on our Zoom call, I'd asked, "Would Tool have once been O'Toole?"

"If you're wondering if I'm related to the English actor Peter O'Toole, I am not. We Tools came from Ireland, and were farmers . . . What are you going to do with the item discussed?"

This was a test question.

"Sell it, of course," I said, adding, "but to someone who will appreciate and care for it."

Which I knew was the right answer; had I—as a dealer—replied otherwise, he'd naturally assume I was lying. In this case the particular someone who would do the appreciating would be me.

"Be at my house Friday night," he said crisply. "Nine o'clock sharp." His square on my screen disappeared.

I quite understood the man's impatience. Time, at his age—at any age—is a valuable commodity.

Tool's home perched precariously on the edge of the bluff, perhaps once having a lawn which had now eroded. The mansion's style was Federal, an austere architecture popular after the Civil War.

I was nearly a half an hour late—the ride up the hill had been slow going for Sally, and both Wade and Mrs. Fowler had been chatty (don't you hate that?)—when I hitched the mustang to a purple sage bush. A light over the front door burned brightly, so apparently Mr. Tool had not yet given up on me for our nine o'clock appointment. Finding the front door partially open was another good sign, and as I crossed the threshold, an antique ebonized grandfather clock struck the half-hour, plaintive tones reverberating in a stark entryway.

The interior I stepped into was as austere as the exterior, the furnishings mostly original Colonial, as if the man wished he'd lived in that earlier time when European settlers were forging their way in the New World.

Straight ahead, a staircase with carved, square-top balusters led to the second floor; to the left was a parlor, to the right, a dining room.

"Mr. Tool?" I called out. "Yoo-hoo! It's Vivian Borne!"

Receiving no answer, I was drawn to the warmth of the fire in the parlor—it was cold inside the mansion, as if Texas weather hadn't found its way in.

Drawing nearer to the fireplace, I could see an arm draped over the side of a high wingback cloth-covered chair—the only modern furniture—facing the glowing logs. The man had not heard me, apparently because he'd fallen asleep.

But, no—Tool had not heard me for another reason.

That lack of response was due to a bullet-hole in the back of the man's head, which I discovered when I touched him and he leaned forward as if taking a bow.

On the slight chance he might be alive—unlikely with such a head wound—I checked for a pulse in his neck, and found none. I estimated Tool had been dead about an hour, judging by the early signs of lividity in his ankles, rigor mortis not yet having begun. This would put the time of death around eight thirty—give or take.

And at this point, any good citizen (not that I wasn't one) would have called the police. But it happens I march to a different drummer. Gene Krupa, possibly.

I did use my cell, not to call, but to take photos of the crime scene, including a Smith & Wesson revolver with pearl handle on the floor below the late Tool's draped arm.

I also put on latex gloves, some variety of which I always carry in my tote—because you never know when they might come in handy—and checked the cylinder of the weapon.

Only one bullet had been fired.

Then I had another matter to take care of—retrieving the item I had come for.

Oh, what's this? You're no longer with me? I've gone too far, have I? First of all, I had already paid for said item, wiring money to Tool's bank at his insistence after our last internet chat. Secondly, I didn't, and don't, consider it fair for me to have what was legally mine tied up in his estate. And thirdly, Tool was dead and the best thing I could do for him, the only thing, was find his killer, and he'd had the good fortune to be murdered when a top-notch amateur sleuth found the body.

Yes, murder, because he certainly hadn't killed himself—no person contemplating suicide would put a gun to the back of his head, which was almost a physical impossibility for a man of his age, and indicated someone had snuck up on him.

Various antique items were arrayed on the dining room's long table. I hoped that rather than put it away for me, Tool might have left the item I'd bought with a "sold" sign tag. The item was an Art Nouveau necklace with a delicate copper chain and large mother-of-pearl pendant. The piece had been made in 1915 by a young artisan named Grant Wood, co-owner of the Volund Arts and Crafts Shop.

Now, Grant Wood may not mean much to Texans, but he was revered in his home state of Iowa (birthplace of John Wayne, remember!), best known for his later-in-life farmland paintings now displayed in the Smithsonian and other notable museums. (His most famous work, *American Gothic*—the stern portraits of a Depression-era farmer holding a pitchfork with his austere wife at his side—can be seen at the Art Institute of Chicago.)

Slowly scanning the table, I clocked mostly primitive antiques, but also some minor jewelry and knickknacks. I did not see my necklace. On impulse I took a few snaps of the table.

Disappointed, I returned to Tool's remains, where, in the pocket of his cardigan was what I'd come for—a successful visit! This I dropped into my tote.

And that—those of you dear readers who are still with me—is when a voice came from the entryway.

"Hands in the air," a male voice barked.

I turned slowly to an officer, who pointed a revolver my way. Didn't he know it wasn't polite to point?

I raised my arms. "Officer, I can explain everything. You see—"

"Save it for the station."

The officer came forward, looked at Tool, and then back at me with narrow-eyed suspicion that I hadn't remotely earned. Well, maybe the necklace rated that, but he didn't know about it!

Nonetheless, I was summarily cuffed, walked outside, and put into the back of his police car, my behind so sore from the saddle I could barely sit. Turns out saddle-sore is really a thing!

That's when I noticed Sally was gone, along with the purple sage bush. Had she beaten me to the getaway?

(*Note from Vivian to Olivia:* I think I have just enough word-count left for the tip! I've been expanded to 6,000, remember!)

Vivian's Trash 'n' Treasures Tip

Estate sales are a great place to get merchandise to sell in your antiques shop or booth. Find local auctions by checking websites of auction houses, or using an app such as AuctionZip or auctioneer. When attending in person arrive early so that you can

(*Note to reader from Olivia*: Unfortunately, Vivian has exceeded her word-count.)

FIVE

The Eyes of Texas

Brandy back at the narrative helm once again. Is everyone all right? I mean, those among you who are still left?

As you recall, my head had just hit the LBJ pillowcase in my Airstream glamper when I received a call from the Tranquility Police Department.

Reenactment:

"Hello?"

I sat up. "Hello?"

"Is this Brandy Borne?" a Texas-twanged voice asked. Might have been male, might have been female.

"Yes."

"Is Vivian Borne your mother?"

"Uh . . . yes." My heart began pounding. "Is she all right?"

"Your Mother's fine. This is Chief Garrison. She's being held in the city jail for questioning."

What had she done now?

"Questioning for what?" I asked.

"Homicide."

Grasping a straw, I considered the police chief might be mistaken about her identity—I mean, couldn't there be another Vivian Borne?

I asked, "Are you *sure* it's Vivian Borne? She should be asleep in her room at the Tranquilo Hotel."

"Attractive lady, late seventies? Thick round glasses? Likes to quote Shakespeare?"

On the other hand, perhaps there was only one Vivian Borne.

Garrison continued in an oddly squeaky voice, "Also, there's a checkbook in her bag confirming she's Vivian Borne."

My heart began pounding again. "What happened?"

"One of our officers found her at the scene, ma'am."

"Scene of *what*?"

"Crime scene. The home of Patrick Tool, now deceased, having been shot and killed."

That would do it. Since the chief had mentioned homicide at the outset, I should have known. How Mother had sussed a murder out so quickly, however, just might be a record.

I sighed. "Where's the jail?"

The chief gave me the downtown address.

Then I called Tony.

When I heard his voice, any control I had left vanished, and I just babbled, then started blubbering.

"Brandy, Brandy, slow down," Tony said. "I'm sure everything will be fine."

I took a deep breath and repeated what Chief Garrison had told me. Slowly this time, wiping tears from my cheek with a fist.

"I'll catch a flight," he said.

"No!" I didn't want that, at least not yet. "Please hold off until I find out more. There may be a simple explanation."

"Brandy, where Vivian is concerned, nothing is simple."

"This is no time to be sarcastic!"

"I'm not being sarcastic, sweetheart. You've gone to Texas looking for antiques and your mother has found another murder."

He did have a point.

"I'll call you," I replied, the sound of his voice soothing me, "after I've spoken to her."

There was a pause, then, "I trust your judgment. I'll wait."

I wished *I* could trust my judgment, but it was nice he did. Or said so, anyway.

"Go see what's up with your mother."

"OK. Thanks. Thank you."

"Just go see what's gone down."

We signed off, leaving me wondering: *Was Mother up or down?* I'd have to find out on my own.

What I *did* want from Tony was that he'd immediately get in touch with the Tranquility chief—which I knew he would do—and at least explain Mother's background before I got there. But would that be helpful or not?

Just before midnight, I pulled the van into the side parking lot of the police station, a modern red-brick one-story not unlike

Serenity's; it even had a plaza with decorative trees to walk through to get to the front entrance.

Inside, the lobby was also small and uninviting, with a female receptionist every bit as sullen-looking as ours, who told me to find a chair, which wasn't difficult as I was the only visitor there. I selected a wobbly one next to a large potted floor plant—a cactus instead of a banana tree, which made it tough to tell if it was equally neglected.

By the way, was I losing my mind?

The receptionist called out, "The chief's coming to get you."

A minute later, a door next to the receptionist area opened, and a short, slender, balding man with wire-framed glasses stepped through.

I almost sighed with relief that he didn't look anything like Tony. But then, wasn't Tranquility opposite-ville? Or similar-*and*-opposite-ville? Or backwards-and-forwards-ville? Or inside-and-out-ville? And shouldn't Tony's flip-side be short and incompetent but with a lovely head of hair?

Absolutely, I was losing my mind.

"Follow me, Miz Borne," he said in that high-pitched voice (it was the only one he had).

As we walked down a corridor, I tried not to notice if the floor was beige-tiled (it was), and if the wall held photos of previous incarnations of their police department (it did), and if the frames were crooked (they were). Only the police chief himself was out of step, a Barney Fife when Andy Taylor would be preferable.

I was led into a small interview room where Mother sat on one side of a bolted-down table. She was already wearing an inmate jumpsuit—but instead of bright orange, it was white. She looked a bit like a demented nurse.

As I sat opposite her, Chief Garrison, lingering near the door, swallowed and his prominent Adam's apple bobbled as he asked me, "Young lady, is this your mother?"

"Yes," I said. "Vivian Borne. We came from Iowa to attend your city-wide sale." I looked at the apparent prisoner. "Mother, are you all right?"

She seemed chipper. "Yes, dear. And I can explain everything . . . except possibly the horse."

"The horse?" I frowned. "Don't tell me you bought a horse?"

"I didn't buy a horse, of course." She chuckled. "Sorry—I didn't mean that to sound like the *Mister Ed* theme."

The chief looked at her, clearly bewildered. It kind of made sense to me.

"Good," I said. "For a moment there, I actually thought you'd bought a horse."

"Don't be silly, dear. It's a rental."

Welcome to Texas. And welcome to my world.

I leaned forward and spoke in low tones, keeping it as confidential as I could in such close quarters. "Mother, I think you need a lawyer before you say anything."

Not that she probably hadn't said plenty already.

"No," Mother said, head held high, no low tones for her. "The innocent have nothing to hide."

Garrison pulled out the chair next to me and rested his skinny behind in it. "Very well, Mrs. Borne, we will begin the interview."

On the table was a rather clunky-looking recording device and, as the chief fiddled with it, Mother leaned forward and pointed. "You press this button first . . . then that one. And that knob is the volume control to keep the wavy lines in the little screen consistent."

"I know how it works, thank you," he said irritably.

"Just trying to be helpful. Not my first time at the rodeo!"

Or in an interview room. Her experience with various incarnations of police recording equipment went back decades.

Garrison got the machine going. "Interview with Vivian Borne. Chief Bernard Garrison speaking. Daughter Brandy Borne in attendance." He noted the date and time.

(For the sake of accuracy, the transcription of the interview was obtained later. CG = Chief Garrison; VB = Vivian Borne; BB = Brandy Borne; FO = forensic officer, who makes a late appearance.)

CG: State your name and current address, please.

VB: Vivian Jensen Borne, Elm Street, Serenity, Iowa. But I was born Vivian Carolyn Jensen in Hackensack, Minnesota to Ernest and Esther Jensen—in a year that is none of your beeswax. I was a lovely, if precocious, child who excelled at everything she did, eventually marrying Jonathan Borne, a world-renowned war correspondent and photographer who unfortunately died shortly before Brandy was born.

BB: That's from her obituary. She has it pretty much memorized. Written in advance, obviously. You're going to have to stop her or we'll be here all night.

(*Brandy to the reader:* There was a pronounced gulp from the chief at this point that was not included in the transcript.)

CG: Mrs. Borne, after your daughter left you at the Tranquilo Hotel this evening, what did you do? In detail, please.

VB: I had made an appointment with a very nice gentleman named Mr. Garcia—I think his first name was Alanzo or Alejandro or Alfonso . . . let's just call him Al.

CG: Go on, Mrs. Borne.

(*Brandy to the reader:* The transcript really should have ended CG's request with an exclamation mark.)

VB: Be that as it may, I rented one of Mr. Garcia's horses having lost my driver's license due . . . lost not in the sense of I-can't-find-it . . . I know right where it is, it just has "Revoked" stamped on it, due to a few trivial infractions that weren't even my fault, with the possible exception of driving down those train tracks in that one instance, but anyone can miss an occasional turn, don't you think? But instead of a quarter horse Mr. Garcia . . . Al . . . provided me with a mustang because I had fudged my history of riding experience a teensy-weensy bit by saying—"

BB: Chief, it's not like you weren't warned.

CG: Please dispense with the fiddle faddle, Mrs. Borne. Where did you go on this horse?

VB: Well, my first stop was at the residence of Mr. Wade Stetson, who lives—

CG: I know where he lives. He's a prominent citizen of Tranquility. Why did you want to see Mr. Stetson?

BB: Now you're getting the hang of it, Chief.

VB: Don't forget whose side you're on, dear.

(*Brandy to the reader:* Again, an exclamation mark missing. Also a throat bobble preceded the next question.)

CG: Please answer the question, Mrs. Borne.

VB: I had made an arrangement with Wade, if I might be so informal, to peek at a few antiques early that would be on offer at the public sale.

BB: Mother.

(*Brandy to the reader:* Again, an exclamation mark missing.)

VB: Nothing illegal about it, dear. More like ignoring a guideline.

CG: When did you arrive at the Stetson home?

VB: At about seven thirty.

CG: And when did you leave Mr. Stetson's home?

VB: Around eight fifteen.

CG: Where did you go then?

VB: A chicken farm owned by Anna Fowler.

CG: Arriving?

VB: Eight thirty.

CG: And the reason for the visit?

VB: The same. Access to early sales.

CG: So you left Anna Fowler when?

VB: About nine.

CG: Next stop?

VB: Patrick Tool's home.

CG: Also for early sales?

VB: Yes.

CG: Arriving?

VB: It was after the appointed time of nine when I walked in the door—I remember because the clock chimed the half-hour.

CG: OK . . . now we're to the crux of the matter.

VB: Yes. And since the recounting here is crucial, I insist on being able to go into more detail.

BB: Careful, Mother.

CG: Pertinent detail is fine, Mrs. Borne. But I will limit your answers if you wander too far off course.

VB: Very well. To reiterate, I was late by the time we made the climb to the late Mr. Tool's mansion—

CG: We? Who was with you?

VB: Sally.

CB: Sally who?

BB: Careful, Chief.

VB: Sally. That's the name of the horse I rented from Mr. Garcia. The porch light was on, so I hitched her to a bush. The front door was ajar and I went in, then called his name. Receiving no response, I continued on into the parlor. There was a high-back chair facing the fire with its back to me, and I could see an arm draped over one armrest, so I assumed my host had fallen asleep. But when I came around and nudged the gentleman, he fell forward, revealing the hole in the back of his head. And that's when the police officer arrived.

BB: Nicely succinct, Mother.

VB: Thank you, dear.

CG: The arresting officer said it appeared you were going through Tool's pockets.

VB: Nonsense! I was taking the man's pulse to see if he might still be alive. He was not.

CG: What about the firearm?

VB: I did see a handgun on the floor near the chair, but the weapon certainly is not mine, and I would have been an idiot to have touched it.

CG: Did you think Tool had shot himself?

VB: Clearly not. You have a murder on your hands.

CG: What makes you say that, Mrs. Borne?

VB: The position of the bullet wound.

FO: Chief, can I see you outside?

I interrupt my annotated (by me) transcript because at this point Chief Garrison was interrupted by a forensics officer who stuck his head inside the interview room, and when the door closed after the chief stepped into the hallway, Mother looked pointedly at the recording device, which was still activated—as was the camera high in one corner—so we sat in silence until our interrogator returned.

CG: Mrs. Borne, Forensics have gone over your clothing and found no firearm discharge residue . . . and there were no fingerprints on the gun.

VB: Then I'm free to go?

CG: Yes. But you're not to leave town. I may have more questions.

VB: May I ask something?

CB: Go ahead.

VB: Am I a person of interest?

CB: Well, you're a person we're interested in.

VB: Next best thing. I'm happy to cooperate in any way I can. Any word about Sally?

CG: When contacted, Mr. Garcia said the horse he'd rented to you had found its way home to her stall.

VB: Thank goodness for that. Do you know if the purple sage bush I tied her to was with her? If so, it can be replanted, otherwise I'd be happy to—

CG: Interview with Vivian Borne concluded.

While Mother was taken away somewhere to be discharged, I returned to the chair next to the cactus plant in the lobby. I texted Tony to tell him that everything had been cleared up.

Since Mother was taking a while, I checked the soil of the plant, and while cactus plants—according to Google—needed to be watered only every two weeks or so, this soil was bone dry. I bought a bottled water from the station's humming soda machine and gave the prickly plant a much-needed drink.

The door next to the enclosed receptionist's area opened and Mother breezed into the lobby; she was back in the clothes that had cleared her, nary a hair out of place, looking as if she'd had eight hours of sleep. Nothing refreshed her quite like a little jail time.

Before even acknowledging me, Mother turned to the female clerk behind the Plexiglass and said, "Ta-ta, Jenny! Don't be surprised if you get an autographed photo of Morgan Wallen in the mail from me! I can't imagine the charismatic young man has a bigger fan than you."

Suddenly the sullen young woman became animated. "Really? That would be great, Mrs. Borne! I just *love* his music."

Which raises the question, when did these two have time for a quid-pro-quo? And what was Mother's quid in return for the receptionist's quo?

"Don't you look dreadful, dear," Mother said to me, approaching.

"Thanks so much." I could feel the acidity from Ma's Burgoo Stew ascending my esophagus. "Let's hit the trail, shall we?"

"By all means, it's back to the mission for me!"

"Oh, no. Not there. You're staying with me tonight."

She frowned. "In your teeny camper?"

"Wee it may be, but there's room enough for the both of us, and I'm not about to let you out of my sight again. Not tonight. Maybe not on the whole rest of this trip!"

"Very well, dear, whatever you say."

Whatever I say? But I was just too tired to realize Mother was merely placating me. Surely even Vivian Borne had done enough for one night.

We didn't speak on the short drive to the campground, but when I pulled up in front of the Airstream Wee Wind, she squealed with delight. She was even more ecstatic after going inside.

"Oh my! Isn't this adorable!" Mother blurted. "You know how I love anything old and well-preserved."

I almost said, "Including yourself?"

But instead I said, "Glad it meets your approval. Have a look around. Knock yourself out. I'm going to sleep." I was heading through the little kitchen toward the bed. "Only . . . leave on all the lights."

Her magnified eyes blinked at me. "Whatever for?"

I turned. "Because earlier this evening, someone tried to break into our well-preserved adorable van."

Mother frowned. "Why on earth would anyone do that? We haven't filled it with antiques yet."

I shrugged.

"Dear?"

"What?" I asked wearily, stopped in my tracks to glance back at her.

She was smiling. Too big. She raised a thumb and forefinger as if measuring an ant. "I may have withheld one tiny thing from Chief Garrison."

"One tiny thing?"

"Maybe two."

I sighed, moved to the little table and sat.

Mother took the other chair. Leaned toward me conspiratorially.

"What I am about to say now, darling girl, may make you an accessory-after-the-fact."

"Accessorize away." I could no longer afford any more surprises. (By the way, my favorite accessory is a Kate Spade novelty bag—like the cute little camper I'm going to send for to commemorate this experience.)

Mother was saying, "I actually *was* going through Mr. Tool's pockets."

"Gee. What a surprise."

"Not even looking for clues!"

As if that improved it.

She explained about the pre-paid necklace.

"I don't think that warrants any kind of charge," I said, adding, "other than lying in your interview."

"I wasn't under oath, remember."

"Fine. What else?"

"I *did* pick up the gun."

When my mouth dropped open, she put a hand up. "But I had my medical gloves on—well, not medical because I ran out of the ones I usually carry—but the kind restaurant workers wear when handling food, which I borrowed from that Mexican restaurant."

"Borrowed" as if she intended to return them. And doesn't every well-dressed woman have medical gloves in her purse, just in case she comes across a murder scene to process?

Exasperated despite my exhaustion, I asked, "Why would you want to touch the gun?"

"To learn how many shots had been fired."

"Is that relevant?"

She shrugged. "Very well could be. I just don't know *how*, yet."

We fell silent.

"Mother, there's a mystery you can solve right now."

"You came to the right person!"

"When did you have time to get friendly with that receptionist?"

Her eyebrows went up so high they escaped her glasses. "Jenny? Never saw her until I went into the lobby to meet you."

"Then how did you know she liked Morgan Wallen?"

"Oh. When I was being booked, I overheard her mention in the break area that she liked his music. 'Last Night' is her favorite song, it seems. I've never heard it myself, or Morgan Wallen."

I pinched the bridge of my nose to ward off a migraine.

She patted the wrist of my other hand. "Dear, you must always be on the prowl for a potential resource with which you might obtain police information."

Many of her "resources" had gotten fired from their jobs at the Serenity Police Department. Or anyway transferred away from dealing with the general public.

"And just how," I asked, "are you going to deliver on your promise to Jenny, since you don't know Morgan from a hole in the Wallen?"

"Now that *would* make you an accessory-*before*-the fact," Mother replied.

But I already knew; she'd obtain a picture somewhere and forge the signature herself.

I got to my feet somehow. Yawned. "I'm going to bed. We have to be up in about four hours, you know."

"Yes, dear. You go ahead. I'm going to sit here for a few more minutes." She began her Nero Wolfe mulling routine of closing her eyes and pursing her lips in and out.

I didn't brush my teeth, didn't remove my make-up, and didn't trade my clothes for pajamas. I just flopped on the rather hard bed and scooched to the wall to make room for Mother.

The last thing I heard before drifting off was her voice coming from the kitchen area. "Garrison! A policing compound. Another aptonym!"

I don't know what that was about. At least I'd get to sleep before she did.

Sunlight streamed through the kitchen windows when I awoke. The space next to me was indented but empty.

I looked at my phone. Eight ten. The starting gun of the city-wide sale had already been fired!

I jumped out of bed. Mother was gone. I checked to see if she'd taken the van, but it was still parked outside. Then I noticed a note on the table.

> Dearest! I'm off to restore my good name, and am counting on you to bring home the bacon—antiques, that is!
> —Mother
>
> P.S. You don't have to go to the community center to pay a fee for a list of places to go, because I obtained one early. It's in your purse.

Why was I not surprised she'd skirted the rules? Or should I say ignored the guidelines, as one thing her personal rule book lacks is rules.

Rather than take time to visit the bathhouse, I used the kitchen sink to wash my face, sponging myself as best I could, getting more water on the floor than myself.

At least I felt better. Putting on make-up and fresh clothes made me feel almost human.

I grabbed my bag—the flyer was indeed inside—then locked the Wee Wind behind me, and went out into a sunny, chilly morning that promised to warm through the day.

My first stop was the campground office where Ma was outside watering her potted plants.

As I powered down my window, she came over. "Ah, if it ain't Brandy. I met your mama earlier, who let me know she would be staying with you for a spell."

Ma's eyes looked puffy and red, as if she had allergies or maybe had been crying. Hard to imagine such a cheerful soul doing that.

"I hope that's all right," I said.

"Ab-so-tively. No charge for the extry towels, and I'm even throwin' in the bicycle fee. I got nothin' but respect for a little gal like you that keeps her mother at her side."

Mother wasn't at my side right now—heaven knew what she was up to.

I winced at Ma. "What was that about a bicycle?"

The woman gestured with the watering can, its contents sloshing. "I have some old bikes behind my camper. We rent 'em out."

Better than another horse, I guessed. So that was how Mother was going to get around. No Sally this time.

Ma went on. "And when she eyed my squirrel collection, she promised me an old squirrel-tail cap Davy Crockett once wore. Wound up belongin' to Fess Parker hisself, for a time."

I was pretty sure Crockett, both the real and reel one, was famous for his *coonskin* cap. And I was pretty sure Mother had no such item—squirrel or raccoon.

"Well, I'm sure you'll get the hat," I said, meaning it. "Mother always finds a way to keep her promises."

By hook or by crook.

Ma nodded and returned to her watering.

Before driving off, my call to Mother's cell went to voicemail, which was her standard MO when out and about on a case. In fact, she probably turned it off.

Once, in order to track her, I'd sent for a little round disc the size of a quarter that I'd read about in her AARP magazine to locate people with Alzheimer's. From my computer or cell, an app showed a map with a blinking arrow of where Mother was at any given time. I had sewed the device inside the lining of her coat, but she found it and put the disc under the seat of Serenity's gas-converted trolley bus, her mode of transportation during cold weather.

Another time I attached one to her Vespa, but Mother discovered that one, too, and stuck it on the underside of someone's car, which threw me into a panic when the vehicle headed south toward St. Louis. I called Tony, who called the highway patrol, who stopped the car, then relayed back it was a male driver. Mother only escaped a verbal lashing from Tony because the man had been wanted in Idaho for three counts of burglary and a gas station holdup.

But now I had her.

This past Christmas, I'd given Mother a special pair of inserts for her favorite shoes because she'd been complaining about her bunions and hammertoes. One insert had a little hidden place on the bottom for an AirTag disc, which sends out a Bluetooth signal of her movements.

I love the app map, too, because instead of a blinking arrow it shows lines of little footprints of everywhere she's been—isn't that cute?

The insoles had come with an extra disc that I tucked away in a drawer, and that she obviously discovered, and hid under the van's driver's seat before we left for Texas; but I kept it there to give her a false feeling of victory.

Running late, I didn't bother to check the app for Mother's whereabouts, but instead pointed the van in the direction of downtown and the Tranquility Baptist Church.

According to Mother, this particular congregation was the oldest (age-wise) and most financially well-off in town, and

Antiques Round-Up 75

therefore retirees were more likely to get rid of years of accumulation as they down-sized from large homes to condominiums.

But the streets were clogged with cars, making my journey frustratingly slow, compounded further by an accident in the middle of a major intersection, which had brought traffic to a halt. Two female drivers were climbing out of their vehicles.

"This wasn't my fault!" one shouted.

"Not *mine!*" the other yelled back.

To extricate myself, I drove up on the sidewalk to an alley, then used other alleys running behind downtown buildings to make my way to the church, which might have been a gothic castle with those large turrets, arched doorways, and stained-glass windows.

A side parking lot was full, but I found a handicapped spot and hung Mother's bunion-operation tag on the mirror, got out and limped—in case anyone was watching—until I reached an open door.

Hey, I never claimed to be perfect.

Considering who raised me, I've had to make an art out of being sneaky. You'd *really* hate me if you knew what I do in long traffic holdups on the highway, which is to ride on the shoulder with my right-turn signal blinking, indicating I was not cutting in but taking the next exit, then I'd get right back on, and repeat the procedure until I'm past the obstruction.

Inside the marbled-floor vestibule, signs pointed the way to the sale, although I could have followed any one of the hordes rushing past me on their way to the lower floor.

The basement was expansive, nicely remodeled to accommodate wedding receptions, with a full kitchen viewed through a large window counter. Dozens of banquet tables held a mélange of items, neatly arranged and tagged; larger items—mostly furniture—were relegated to one area, while in another location was the checkout station attended by three already frazzled helpers, one taking payments, the other two bagging and boxing items.

Even with the sound-absorbing ceiling tiles, the noise was deafening. Elbowing my way through the crowd, I spotted something that made my jaw drop. On one table, nearly obscured by a messy pile of embroidered linens, was a whimsical pair of dancing frogs made by Weller Pottery, identified by the company's distinctive, green-speckled glaze. The price was unbelievably low for pieces worth so much more.

But I wasn't the only one to notice them. An older woman wearing an ill-fitting wig and too much make-up reached for the frogs first.

"Isn't this adorable!" she said to herself, picking the pottery up.

"Yes," I replied, adding sadly, "Too bad they've been glued back together."

She looked at me, unfazed by my attempted buzz kill. "I don't care."

A slightly younger lady with her said, "Lorna . . . don't you have *enough* broken pottery?"

Lorna sighed, and replaced the frogs, which I promptly snatched up the moment the woman turned away.

Had the pottery been broken and glued? Let's just say all is fair in love and war and antiquing. And, anyway, you already think badly of me for my traffic ploys.

I found a few other bargains, like a Golden West Coffee tin, depicting a pretty cowgirl holding a cup to her lips; and an impressive longhorn belt buckle made of sterling. On offer mostly were craft items, and while well-made (or sewn), these were the kind of thing Mother and I did our best not to let infiltrate our shop.

While standing in the checkout queue, I was captive to the conversation of the same two women, neither of whom questioned the frogs now being in my possession.

Lorna was saying, "Wasn't that dreadful about Patrick Tool? I hear he died by suicide."

The friend said, "I just bet it was one of those stepchildren of his who shot him."

Lorna sighed. "I suppose Tool's sale has been called off. And my Harry is going to have to deal with *them* to get that old letter from Houston he wanted."

With my purchases paid for and securely wrapped inside a cardboard box, I went out to the van, forgetting to limp and getting a hard stare from a man hobbling by me with a cane.

OK. No more fake handicapped parking for me. And no more

driving on the shoulder to the next exit and getting back on—*unless* I have to go to a bathroom really bad.

Am I back in your good graces?

While putting the cardboard box into the hatchback, I clumsily spilled the contents. Checking my purchases—especially the dancing frogs—everything seemed intact. On the carpet next to the box was a small silver key that must have been with it. But since it wasn't worth limping back to return it, I tossed the key back in the box.

Then I took care of another matter: disposing of the extra AirTag disc Mother had placed beneath the driver's seat by tossing it into the rear of a truck parked next to me.

Behind the wheel, I took a moment to check my tracking app, and when the map came up, little footprints were all over the downtown area, going in circles!

Was this because Mother's shoe with the insert was moving around and around on a bicycle pedal?

And, disturbingly, the path Mother had taken went right through the very intersection where those two cars had crashed.

That was when my cell pinged with a text from Mother: **Help! Extract me from my ill-fated endeavor!**

Brandy's Trash 'n' Treasures Tip

Church bazaars are a good source for finding unique costume jewelry that has fallen out of favor but has enjoyed a years-later resurgence, such as the chunky Bakelite necklaces of the 1950s, or diamond tennis bracelets like the type Chris Evert made famous during the Wimbledon final in 1978. At a flea market, I borrowed money from Mother to pick up a tennis bracelet that I assumed to be of cubic zirconia only to be told by a jeweler, when I went to have the clasp fixed, that the diamonds were real. Mother wears the bracelet when she's in the mood, pointing out that I had bought it with her money.

SIX
Tumbling Tumbleweeds

Vivian again, ready to giddy up.

But first, regarding what I was *going* to say about my antiquing tip in chapter four, before being cut off for supposedly writing too many words, was . . . well, I don't really remember. Bigger fish to fry! Just be sure you arrive early at estate sales to have first dibs.

Galloping on into our narrative! After one more tiny side-trip . . .

In an attempt to win back Mrs. Earl Peabody of Walla Walla, Washington, as a reader, after she was offended by my joke in *Antiques Ravin'* about an elderly chap whose mates hired a lady of the evening to go to his flat on his 80th birthday, whereupon answering his door, she said, "I'm here to give you super sex," to which he replied, "I'll take the soup." Mrs. Peabody also found offensive my joke in *Antiques Slay Belles*, regarding an elderly gent who lived in a posh part of London, who went for a checkup before his wedding to a nubile young lass, whereupon after the examination the doctor said, "I'm concerned about the difference in your ages and that too much fadoodling on your wedding night might prove fatal," to which the elderly gent replied, "Well, doctor, if she dies, she dies."

And so, good sport that I am, once again I offer Mrs. Peabody another knee-slapper, and if she doesn't approve of this one, then we are just not a good fit, which can happen between author and reader.

Here we go!

An old man is on his death bed with his wife at his side. They have three boys but the last one, Tommy, does not resemble the other two, so the husband has always been a little suspicious. With the end nearing, the old man says to his wife, "Dear, it doesn't really matter at this point, but I need to know if Tommy is my son. His wife replies, "I swear to you, he is indeed yours." The old man dies peacefully. Then his wife says, "Thank goodness he didn't ask about the other two!"

I shall eagerly await Mrs. Peabody's response.

After a few hours of sleep, which seems to be all I need on a case, I awoke in the compact camper next to a snoring Brandy. Since I'd already had a nice shower in my room at the mission the evening before, I merely freshened up at the little kitchen sink, mindful not to rouse the girl.

Do you recall on my visit to see Wade Stetson that his wife Mary Jo was in the process of leaving to attend a meeting of the city-sale committee? Carrying a sheaf of papers? Well, one of those papers fluttered unnoticed to the floor, or I should say unnoticed by anyone but me. I picked it up after she'd left, while Wade was distracted by Sally neighing. You'd think no one had ever hitched their horse to the man's mailbox before!

Anyhoo, this particular stray paper is what I put in Brandy's purse with all the information on the sale locations, freeing the girl from standing in line for it and wasting valuable time, not to mention ten simoleons.

After leaving the slumbering girl a note, I exited the camper to discover the sun was just rising—its warm rays dispelling the chill from the night's air—and walked briskly toward the park's check-in trailer.

Brandy had mentioned that the office was open 24/7, the owner/manager living there. I rapped on the wood of the screen door.

A middle-aged woman came into view, wearing a pink chenille bathrobe and slippers. Though her hair was wrapped in curlers, face puffy and smeared with yesterday's make-up, I could see—even through the closed screen—remnants of a much younger woman who had once been fetching.

"I'm Vivian Borne," I announced. "My daughter's staying here. Do forgive me for disturbing your reverie."

"Oh, we don't blow reveille around here," she replied cheerfully. "We don't stand on ceremony. Hell, we don't even have a bugle. Pardon my French."

Clearly I would need to simplify my vocabulary around this individual, though I could certainly admire her colorful patois.

"Care for some coffee, dearie?" the woman asked, opening

the door wider. It screeched some. "I was just about to have a cup."

"I would love one." The caffeine would come in handy; adrenaline can only take a person so far.

"Come in, come in. Call me Ma. Everybody does."

Since Brandy already described Ma's quarters in her chapter, I won't bother. Plus, I'm watching my word-count.

While Ma poured black liquid into two mugs in the tiny kitchen, I took a chair at a small round table, mindful not to disturb the taxidermied squirrel lurking beneath it.

Handing me a cup, Ma said, "So Brandy's your daughter? Cute little gal staying in the Wee Wind?"

"Yes. I hope you don't mind that I'll be bunking in with her."

Ma sat. "Not a'tall. I'll come by later with some extry towels."

"Thank you." I waited as the coffee cooled. "I suppose you know about the unfortunate death of your local resident, Mr. Patrick Tool . . .?"

"Heard about it on the radio this morning. Shot in the head, they say." Ma took a drink of her coffee, undeterred by the rising steam. "But I can tell you without seein' the remains, that were no suicide."

"It wasn't?"

She smirked. "That old boy thought too much of hisself to pull the plug. Always did. Meanin' no disrespect to the dead."

What else would you call it?

I risked a sip. Strong as it was terrible. But it wasn't just the coffee that was bitter in this kitchen.

Ma went on, "Yessir, that man had more enemies than a hound dog has fleas."

"Enemies? Such as who, dear?"

Her frown made it hard to see the pretty girl this woman likely had once been. "Why go into that? You ain't local, Miz Borne, so it wouldn't mean nothin' to you."

"Oh, I just like to get the feel of any community I visit."

"That's all fine and dandy, and I'd love to sit and palaver with you about that—I like to gossip as much as the next female. But I have chores to do. Place like this doesn't run itself."

"Oh, I understand."

"But if you want the skinny on Tool, I'd suggest you drop by and see the RODEOs."

I squinted over the raised coffee cup. "What rodeo grounds are you referring to, dear? And who should I see there?"

Ma chuckled, nothing bitter about her now. "No, no, no, darlin'—the RODEOs is a passel of old horse thieves—Retired Old Dudes Eating Out!"

They sounded disturbingly similar to Serenity's old-boys' club the ROMEOs (Retired Old Men Eating Out).

"Where might I find them?" I inquired.

"No 'might' about it. The RODEOs will be sloshin' down coffee a damn sight better than mine at the ol' Chuck Wagon, 'bout now. Downtown on Azalea Street."

Her mood had improved, after moving on from the late Tool, and I felt I could risk a request for something I hoped she could provide. "Would you happen to have a scooter around? Either electric or the gas-fueled variety, for rental perhaps?"

Ma shook her head. "No can do. Sorry. But . . . we got some old bicycles around back. You're welcome to pick one from the pack, no rental fee required."

That would have to suffice.

"You're very generous," I said, standing. "And thanks for the delicious coffee."

"I know my coffee is swill," Ma said with a grin. "But at least I don't charge for it."

For her kindness—and perhaps in hopes of future information—I promised Ma a squirrel-tail cap (due to her fondness for the animals) that had once belonged to Davy Crockett. She seemed delighted by the prospect, and did not inquire whether I referred to the historical figure or the lead on a long-ago Disney television show. Not that I had a line on either, but would deal with it later.

Behind the trailer, I found several old bikes and selected the sturdiest one. Wheeling it around to the front, I could see Ma through a window, still seated in the kitchen at the table, staring into her mug. For all her good-natured cheerfulness, something sad hovered over the woman.

Do you remember my comment that once a person learns how

to ride a bike, he, she, they, them (did I miss any pronouns there?) never forgets?

Wrong. I wobbled like a drunken high-wire artist on a tightrope (isn't that a wonderful image?) and fell promptly off, luckily into a batch of tumbleweeds. But then, after a few more false starts, the ol' muscle memory kicked in and I got the hang of it again. Soon I was breezing along the shoulder of the highway, going a good deal faster than the backed-up cars heading into Tranquility.

But now there was another matter to contend with. What to do about the tracking device Brandy had put into one of my shoes?

Foolish girl, thinking she'd put one over on me.

I'd discovered the device almost immediately after Christmas. But since I didn't care at the time if she knew my whereabouts, I didn't remove the disc. If Brandy believed she had fooled me, it would give her a false sense of security that could be exploited later—such as right now.

In retaliation, I'd taken the extra AirTag disc that she had hidden, and tucked it under the driver's seat in the van to track *her*. Two could play this game of "tag"!

But where to dump the disc?

Suddenly a dog ran in front of my bike, and I nearly drove into a ditch, catching myself by dropping one leg to the ground, the heel of my trainer scooting me to a stop.

Afraid the animal might be hit by a car, I withdrew a power bar from my tote, which hung from a handlebar, and waved the treat. "Here boy! Here boy!"

The dog took the bait.

It was a mangy thing, a byproduct of multiple breeds breeding, with crazy eyes as if it had gotten into a patch of peyote and munched down the hallucinatory cactus. Yet someone cared enough about the animal to have tied a red bandana around its neck.

I unwrapped the power bar, feeding little bites to the dog, which gave me time to wrap the tracking disc in the bandana, twisting, then knotting the cloth so it would stay put.

With no more treat on offer, the dog lost interest and ran off, but thankfully away from the traffic. And I continued with my journey.

Zipping past gridlocked cars on my bike, I felt quite smug as I glided through a downtown Tranquility intersection, soon hearing a metallic crunch. Looking back over my shoulder, I took in an unhappy sight: two cars had collided, both female drivers having exited their vehicles, confronting each other. But the accident had not been my fault (shame on you for going there!), instead caused by the mangy hound that I hadn't realized was following me and my bike, the swinging tote a lure of further food.

The women apparently unharmed, I rode on, my only concern being that if my new canine friend continued in pursuit, I'd have to remove the disc from its bandana or lead Brandy right to me! But the mutt had run off again, spooked by the honking horns the collision had induced.

I was starting to feel tranquil in Tranquility. Like Serenity, the thoroughfares were numbered while the cross streets named for flowers (back home it was trees, but we were still in the realm of vegetation).

I wheeled onto Azalea, and immediately spotted the Chuck Wagon restaurant, which turned out to be a real chuck wagon (or I should say a somewhat oversize replica of one), its hooded top covered with white canvas, its back end lowered, acting as a serving station, and supported by a single leg.

I leaned my bike against a large sprawling pecan tree providing shade for half a dozen picnic tables, vacant but for one occupied by four men—the RODEOs . . . my prey.

At the wagon's tail gate a young woman stood, acting as hostess, waitress, and cashier. I walked over to her, a redhead in a plaid shirt with rolled-up sleeves and blue jeans with rolled cuffs over Nikes.

With a musical lilt, she said, "Howdy—how y'all doin' this fine day?"

Even though there was only one of me.

She went on, thumbing her plaid chest. "I'm Calico."

Maybe so, but that was plaid. Anyway, she was cute as a button.

"Here I was expecting Wishbone," I said brightly, "and it's a sweet young dove instead."

She blinked blue eyes at me. "Pardon?"

"Wishbone? Character on an old TV show. *Rawhide*? Never mind. Before your time, dear. What's good today?"

"Today we're servin' up a dandy breakfast special—sausage, egg, and cheese omelet with a side of cornpone."

"As in Jubilation T. Cornpone?"

"Pardon?"

My, that girl could blink. *Li'l Abner* was before her time, too, though you would have loved my Serenity Playhouse production of the Broadway play based on the comic strip, marred only slightly by a passel of pigs running down off the stage and into the audience. Still, some attendees had found that memorable. I told you about the horse and *My Fair Lady*, didn't I? Pretty sure I did.

Where was I?

Ah, yes, at the Chuck Wagon.

The omelet with cornpone on the side seemed to be the only option.

"Sold, Calico, darlin'."

My Southern accent was kicking in. Couldn't help having a good ear, could I? I was lucky Brandy wasn't here, rolling her eyes.

"I'll bring the food to you," Calico said, her smile having gone strangely glazed as she gestured to an old barrel attached to the side of the wagon. "Soft drinks and water are in there, unless you'd prefer coffee."

I somehow managed not to make a remark about Kickapoo Joy Juice . . . or are you too young to understand the reference? Well, what do y'all think Google is for?

As for the lass's offer of coffee, I passed for now. Ma's deadly brew had already set my heart racing, so I instead selected a bottle of H_2O from the ice-filled barrel.

Now, how to approach the RODEOs . . . ?

My usual greeting back home with the ROMEOs was an impression of Mae West's "Helloooo, boooys," which might not play in Texas. So I took a cue from Calico and approached their picnic table with a drawled, "Howdy, partners. Good to be above snakes. Where did y'all get the eatin' irons?"

Too bad I didn't have any chaw to spit-punctuate that with.

But even without it, they laughed heartily, the man closest to me chuckling, "We can talk that way if you insist, ma'am, but we'd rather not."

I smiled feebly. "Whoops . . . Guess I stepped in a cow pie."

Another gent said, "Why don't you join us? Calico'll bring you utensils." A third replied, "And yes, it *is* good to be alive, especially at our age."

They'd completed their meals, empty plates pushed aside, and were lazing over coffee.

While there was room on the end of either side of the table, I chose a place on the bench that put my back to the rising sun. Not because the glare hurt my eyes, but a natural light source is best coming from *behind* a woman of a certain age (some things I prefer men to be uncertain about).

The man across from me made the introductions. "I'm Brock. Next to me is Gideon. Next to you is Milo. And Quentin is on your end."

I'm afraid you young 'uns are going to be scurrying to Google again, because as fate would have it, each RODEO brought to my mind a Western character actor known for playing the lead cowboy's sidekick: Brock was a ringer for Walter Brennan, with his fluffy white hair, white stubble, grooved face, and eyebrows perpetually raised; Gideon resembled George "Gabby" Hayes, sporting a gray beard, floppy hat, and missing two front teeth; Quentin could have doubled for Chill Wills with that weathered face, broad smile, and beige cowboy hat worn back to reveal a nice head of salt-and-pepper hair; and Milo mirrored Native American Jay Silverheels, having slicked-back black hair, high cheekbones, and (pretty sure) real teeth.

"Pleased to meet everyone," I said. "I'm . . ."

"Vivian Borne of Serenity, Iowa," Brock interjected with a good-natured chuckle that seemed to be his trademark. "The tourist who found the body of Patrick Tool last night."

Oh brother, was I in trouble. These men were not pushovers like the ROMEOs. In fact, this group had been waiting for me. Maybe laying in wait for me! Or is that lying?

"I'm no tourist, gentlemen. I have an antiques shop in Iowa with my daughter and we're in Tranquility for the city-wide sale."

Brock seemed to be tasting his grin. "Aren't you a little *more* than that?"

Gideon said, "And didn't you and your daughter have a TV show for a while?"

Quentin said, "Haven't there been stories on the tube about you being some kind of amateur sleuth?"

Milo said playfully, "How about dealing a few cards from the top of the deck, Kemosabe?"

"All right, gentlemen," I said, palms up as if this were a holdup. "I'll put all my cards on the table. Hole card included. No necktie party necessary."

But first, Calico put my breakfast on the table, served in a tin plate, along with some "eatin' irons." She gave me a smile and a wink, as if to say, *You may be a stranger in town, but you move fast.*

When she'd collected the men's empty plates and returned to the Chuck Wagon's chuck wagon, I continued, "You are correct. In addition to being an antiques dealer, I am a former reality TV personality. But no one mentioned my theatrical accomplishments, which I admit are limited to a regional area. What is more pertinent is that I am indeed a well-known amateur sleuth."

"How is it," Brock asked, that grin slanting sideways now, "you just happened to find Pat Tool's dead body?"

"Just lucky, I guess," I said. "I only discovered Mr. Tool at his residence because I was a half-hour late for our meeting for me to make a pre-sale purchase. I found his door open. We amateur sleuths go where fools fear to tread. Also, where fools don't fear to tread."

A lot of wide eyes and raised eyebrows and astonished smiles were trained on me like Matt Dillon's .45 (the sheriff, not the actor).

"So, yes, I did come upon Mr. Tool at his home," I continued. "But I did not shoot him. Nor do I believe he took his own life." I paused. "There's a killer in this town. And what I need from you good men is a list of locals who had a reason to withdraw the banker."

I waited for a response.

It took a while. A lot of expressions got exchanged between these men, and some head shaking and mild laughter followed, until Brock, who seemed to be the leader, said, "Well, what the hell . . . Let's help the little lady."

Nods followed, and serious smiles. I liked these old boys.

"A list of people who wouldn't mind seeing banker Tool dead?" Brock said slowly, then sighed. "That would be a hell of a long one."

"Take your best shot," I said, adding, "If you'll excuse the expression."

Brock's eyebrows climbed again. "I'd start with Tool's stepson—Zeke Norris."

"Norris?" I asked, then answered my own question: "So, then . . . Patrick never adopted him?"

Brock said, "That's right, Mrs. Borne. Nor his sister, Dixie, neither."

"Call me Vivian, please."

Walter Brennan's Doppler leaned forward. "Vivian, there's always been friction between Zeke and his stepfather, especially since Zeke's mother installed Patrick as CEO of her family's bank."

I nodded slowly. "So the new Mrs. Tool held the purse strings."

"That's right. Pat Tool married good. Unless it was one of his stepkids that killed him."

"How did the board of directors feel about their new leader?"

Brock chuckled. "Not thrilled, as you might imagine. But they did as they were told. Irene Tool was the primary stockholder."

"By 'was' you mean . . . ?"

"Deceased."

"Natural causes, or . . . ?"

"Overdose of sleeping pills."

Which could have been suicide. Or murder.

I said, "I imagine her death only made the situation worse between Patrick and his stepson."

"Yes," Brock said. "Especially when Zeke had expected to receive part of his mother's estate at her passing."

"But he didn't?"

"No." Brock shrugged. "No will was ever found."

Possibly not completed, possibly destroyed.

Brock added, "Pat Tool got it all, lock, stock and barrel."

I asked, "What kind of work does Zeke do?"

"Construction, till he hurt his back. But he doesn't do much of anything now."

"Well, I suppose," I said, "Zeke won't have to work now—he'll be flush from his inheritance."

Brook shook his head. "Word is Tool left Zeke and the sister out of *his* will."

I asked, "Where can I find Zeke?"

"Happy Trails Trailer Court."

That seemed to be everything Brock had for me, so I shifted my attention on Gideon, seated next to him. "Do you have any notions about anyone who might've had a reason to kill Patrick Tool?"

The old-timer stroked his gray beard. "My money's on the stepdaughter, Dixie," he replied, the "s" consonants whistling through where his front teeth had once resided. Shyly, he said, "Gettin' a new bridge put in tomorrow."

He wasn't referring to a bridge across the Red River.

Gideon went on: "Dixie hated Patrick as much as Zeke, and made no bones about it."

"And why is that?"

My question clearly made him uncomfortable.

"I . . . I don't like spreadin' rumors," Gideon said, adding, "especially when they're . . ."

"Distasteful?"

He nodded.

"Come, come, now," I chided. "This is Vivian Borne you're talking to. I'm a sleuth, not a rumormonger."

No matter what you may have heard.

Gideon sighed. "All right. But this goes no further, Mrs. Borne."

"Vivian," I corrected lightly. "And my lips will be sealed."

But the knowing expressions of the other men told me the rumor had gone at least as far as them. More than a few lips had been flapping around Tranquility.

His voice hushed, his s's sibilant, Gideon said, "I heard there was some abuse on Tool's part, when Dixie was a minor."

"Verbal or physical?" I pressed.

Gideon shook his head. "That's as far as I feel comfortable goin' with it."

Which seemed to indicate the latter.

I asked, "Where can I find this Dixie?"

Brock responded, "Dixie owns a hair salon on Orchid called The Mane Event."

"Thank you."

Turning my head to Quentin, who was seated on my left, I asked, "And what would your best bet be, in the Tool murder sweepstakes?"

No hesitation here: "Anna Fowler."

Having met that meek bird of a woman, this surprised me. I would have thought her too chicken to be a murderer.

I kept at it with Quentin: "Why?"

He adjusted his beige cowboy hat, moving it forward a bit. "After her husband, Fred, died, Anna needed a bank loan to hold onto the chicken farm. Tool and her husband were old friends and she thought that would carry some weight. It didn't."

So the business Anna and her husband had spent their life building together *was* in jeopardy, as she had indicated.

"Perhaps the loan just was too risky," I said. "I understand her children wanted no part of taking over."

"That's true," Quentin replied. "But with a loan she would have had money to hire help on. Plus, the land itself was becoming more valuable by the day, as the city pushed outward. So, no, I don't believe the loan was a risk."

Perhaps the banker saw an opportunity to acquire the property for a hefty profit in a foreclosure.

I hadn't heard from Milo yet. He'd been mum, seated on the other side of Quentin.

I leaned forward. "Do you have any candidates for murder suspect?"

While the Native American's chiseled face seemed noncommittal, his voice did not. "Wade Stetson."

I could have fallen face-first into my omelet. Which I needed to get to, by the way, before it was colder than Tool, as I'd been focused on the inquiry.

"For what reason?" I asked, astonished.

"Wade lost a lot of money to Tool," Milo said, "in a private poker game. Which as far as I know he has yet to pay."

"How *much* money?" I asked.

"Apparently enough," Quentin said, "that Wade has been trying to raise it."

"How do you know this?"

He shrugged. "Through *my* banker."

So much for bank confidentiality. (I'd been able to breach that wall myself, by way of any number of bribes to employees.)

Feeling sufficiently armed with suspects and motives, I finally turned my attention to the delicious-looking omelet and cornpone, as the conversation among the men turned to benign subjects, like the upcoming Major League baseball season and the chances of either the Houston Astros or Texas Rangers making it into the World Series.

And while my meal wasn't piping hot, it was still sufficiently warm to enjoy to the fullest.

Chuck Wagon Omelet

Ingredients:

¼ cup vegetable or olive oil
12 large eggs
½ cup milk
1 cup cooked meat of your choice
½ cup onion, diced
½ cup bell pepper, diced
½ cup mushrooms, sliced
1 fresh tomato, chopped
4 tbsp. butter, melted
1 cup cheddar cheese, plus extra for topping
Salt, pepper, hot sauce as desired

Instructions:

Coat the inside of a large iron skillet with oil. Break eggs into pan, add milk, and whip until thoroughly mixed. Stir in meat, onion, pepper, mushrooms, tomato, butter, a cup of cheese, and seasonings. Cover and place on a low heat source (campfire, firebox, or stove burner) until fully cooked. Fold in half and remove from skillet onto a big plate. Sprinkle extra cheese on top of the hot omelet.

Feeds four hungry ranch hands or six people watching their cholesterol.

Cornpone

2 cups cornmeal
1 tsp. salt
2 tbsp. flour
2 tsp. bacon grease (or oil)
1 cup milk (more or less to make a stiff batter)

Mix all ingredients together, then form balls by hand and place on greased baking sheet. Bake 12–15 minutes at 425 degrees in oven. Or cook on a high heat source until browned. Makes 12 small or 6 large pones.

The recipe for Kickapoo Joy Juice died with Al Capp, Li'l Abner's creator. There is, however, a regional bottled soft drink of that name.

I was about to take the last bite of omelet when I looked down to my right, where two big brown eyes stared up at me, a certain disc still in its bandana "collar."

Would someone not rid me of this pesky pooch?

Oh, well, what difference did it make if Brandy knew where I was? Just as long as I knew where *she* was.

Feeling antsy to get my investigation under way, I bid adieu to the RODEOs, thanking them for their assistance, and asking the men to keep our conversation confidential. (Had they been the ROMEOs, our interaction would soon be all over town. Old men are the worst gossips!) And when I made a move to pick up my check, Brock beat me to it. (Their Serenity counterparts would also pay my bill on occasion, but usually just covering a cup of coffee.)

Before boarding the bicycle, I checked my app to locate Brandy, finding the van currently parked at the Tranquility Baptist Church. So the girl had taken my advice, for once, and gone there first. (Most of the time, what I say goes in one Brandy ear and out the other.) (I hope you don't mind these very occasional parentheses.)

Orchid Street was but a few blocks away, The Mane Event occupying the street level of a three-story Victorian brick building.

I leaned my ride against a lamppost, trusting the bike's battered appearance would help ensure that it would be there upon my return.

As I entered the salon, a buzzer sounded, usually SOP (standard operating procedure) for businesses having a long boxcar layout, where the owner might be busy at the rear.

I was pleased to see that the shop had retained the original red-brick walls and high tin ceiling, although the floor had been replaced with laminated wood, in a light color to brighten the surroundings.

Otherwise, The Mane Event was a typical salon: appointment counter on one side, waiting area on the other, with stylist stations beyond, all unoccupied at the moment.

I had not expected Tool's stepdaughter to be here, since it had been only a short time since his death, but the woman seated at a computer behind the check-in desk wore a smock with "Dixie" embroidered on the breast pocket. Apparently she was doing her mourning at work.

Dixie appeared to be in her mid-thirties, a curvy cutie, her shoulder-length hair a rainbow of colors, her arms tattooed with flowery designs, which at first I thought were the sleeves of a top.

"I *do* apologize for being a walk-in," I said.

Her smile was pleasant. "No apology necessary. Walk-ins are welcome. And as you can see, we're not very busy."

"I'm surprised you're open at all," I commented.

The smile disappeared. "And why's that?"

I proceeded with caution. "The city-wide sale. One can hardly navigate the sidewalks let alone find a parking place."

Her smile returned. "That is tricky right now."

I gestured to the outside. "But luckily I arrived on a bike," adding, "and knew any businesses not involved in the sale would be less busy than usual."

She nodded. "Very true. Now, what can I do for you?"

"My fingernails need some TLC."

"Glad to provide some. Name?"

"Vivian Jensen," I said, using my maiden name.

"Are you wanting extensions, or just a manicure?"

"The latter."

Dixie handed me a brochure of options, which I gave a slow scan.

Then I said, "I'll have the milk-and-honey procedure."

Which read: *Arms and hands are exfoliated with a honey sugar scrub and wrapped with a milky masque, followed by a hot steamed towel and ten-minute massage. Nails are then soaked in warm milk, shaped to your liking, cuticles groomed, and finally polished with a nail color of your choice. 35 minutes.*

I should be able to learn a lot about Tool's stepdaughter in that amount of time . . . and get pampered to boot!

(FYI: the expression "to boot" derives from "to bote" in Middle English language—the vernacular spoken and written in England from about 1100 to 1500—meaning something extra being added to a bargain or compensation. Just thought you might find that interesting. Too often we use expressions without knowing the origin. Always glad to give readers "something extra" myself at Ye Olde Trash 'n' Treasures!)

"Milk-and-honey procedure is an excellent choice," Dixie said, as any savvy proprietor would have remarked about whatever I'd chosen.

She stood and came around the counter. Good lord, her legs beneath the short skirt also were a botanical garden. Years ahead, as the skin wrinkles, those flowers will look as if they've died on the vine.

(*Note to Vivian from Olivia*: Tattoos are quite fashionable these days, and it might not be wise to alienate younger generations of readers.)

(*Note to Olivia from Vivian*: Quite true. Tats have come a long way from drunken sailors on shore-leave and carnival barkers on the midway.)

Dixie led me to a nail station, where I took a comfy chair in front of a small desk, its top covered with a white towel.

Seated opposite me, in a not quite so comfy chair, Dixie opened a drawer on her side, and withdrew a tube of exfoliating cream. Directing me to place my forearms and hands, palms down, on the towel, she proceeded to cover the skin with the grainy golden sticky mixture of sugar and honey, working in a circular fashion.

"What a darling little girl," I said, referring to a framed photo on the desk of a toddler with golden curls and big brown eyes.

"Yes, she is," Dixie replied, not taking her eyes off her work.

"Your daughter, I assume?"

"Yes."

This was going to be difficult.

"How old?"

"Three."

When a door opens, I go through.

"I have a granddaughter about that age." I paused for a response but got none. "She's named after my daughter, Brandy, but we call the child B.B. so as not to confuse the two."

Dixie pulled back. "Brandy? Brandy Borne who writes that series about true crimes . . . ?"

"Actually, we write them together, although she does have more chapters. It's a contractual thing."

". . . which makes you Vivian Borne, *not* Jensen. And you're here to pump me for information about my stepfather's murder."

My grin may not have been entirely convincing; even Vivian Borne has limits to her acting prowess. "Well, originally we came for the city-wide sale, but then—"

"*Out!* Get out."

I showed a bit of indignation. "You can't send me outside with my arms looking like this."

Dixie pushed back her chair and stood. "Can't I?"

"At least give me the hot towel!"

She pointed to the door. "I said leave."

I got to my feet, my plea—"I was so looking forward to the warm milk soak!"—falling on deaf ears.

I gathered my tote and went outside, garnering pedestrian stares, the scrub having hardened on my arms to a golden crust, making my skin itch like the dickens.

And my *ride* was gone, someone having recognized the value of even a rusty old bike over a stalled-in-traffic car or God forbid anyone in this day and age just *walking*.

The dog had been waiting for me, resting in the shade of the salon's awning, and now bounded over, attracted by the sugary treat on my arms.

Admitting defeat—which I seldom do—I had no alternative but to text Brandy to get me out of this pickle.

Checking my app to see where the girl was, the little footprints led from the church to a bar (saloon?) on the outskirts of town. Was she having that bad of a time?

I just hoped Brandy was sober enough to drive.

Vivian's Trash 'n' Treasures Tip

Online sites are a good place to find antiques and collectibles, especially if you're short on time. Always check the seller's ratings, examine the item's photo and description carefully, and then don't forget to add in the cost of shipping. Buying in bulk can bring down the price per unit, except now Brandy and I are stuck with an excess of vintage Duncan yo-yos that aren't selling very well in this electronic age of video games and interactive toys. You young 'uns don't know what you're missing!

SEVEN
Happy Trails to You

Brandy here. Miss me?

I wish to apologize to Anne Kaufman (Mrs. Ron) of Wayzata, Minnesota, for the recipe "Lobster Curry a la Operakällaren" that appeared in *Antiques Foe*, and which she prepared for the Lake Minnetonka Book Club whose members had been reading the tome, resulting in six hours of hard kitchen labor and ten dirty pans, not to mention the cost of seventeen ingredients, including lobster and a trip to the fish market.

In my defense, I did offer short-cuts, such as not straining the sauce, using Cool Whip instead of real whipped cream, and skipping flaming the cognac.

But, in future, I will not include any more complicated recipes from renowned chefs such as Hans Kegik, who made this his signature dish at the Operakällaren Restaurant in Stockholm.

On the brighter side, the book club members did enjoy the fruits—or anyway the lobster curry—of Mrs. Kaufman's labors, and seemed to like *Antiques Foe*, as well.

Moving on.

Regarding the excess inventory of yo-yos at our antiques store, that was Mother's purchase, not mine. My experience with yo-yos is as such: one day an entertainer who called himself the Yo-Yo Man came to my elementary school for an assembly where he performed such tricks as "walking the dog," "around the world," and "flying saucer," all of which looked really cool. Well, I enthusiastically bought myself a yo-yo that day and it wasn't long before the string got itself tied in knots. Come to think of it, I got the yo-yo from the Yo-Yo Man himself (with my lunch money) who was hawking the toy after the performance. And it was pizza day, too, so I missed out on that.

Some things stick with you. Like elementary-school pizza, but that's another story.

And now, back to this one.

A text came from Mother, directing me to a hair-styling salon on Orchid. As she rarely reached out to me during her solo efforts on an investigation, I figured she must be in a doozy of a jam.

As I turned onto Orchid, in search of the salon, I spotted Mother on the sidewalk, fending off a mangy-looking dog. After double-parking as close to the curb as I could get, I jumped out, and ran to assist (not exactly sure which side I should take). Only then did it become clear the dog was not in attack mode, but merely trying to lick Mother's arms, which were covered in some kind of golden paste.

If nothing else, that was a new twist.

Grabbing the bandana around the animal's neck, I tugged the dog away from Mother and a telltale AirTag disc fell out of the cloth onto the cement. I picked it up. This explained the crazy route the footprints on my app had taken. Score one for Vivian Borne.

"What's going on here?" I asked, holding the dog at bay by the bandana.

"Not now, dear," Mother said. "To the van!"

But what I heard was, "To the Batcave!"

I waited until she'd climbed into the front passenger seat and had safely closed the door behind her before I released the mutt, then scurried around to the driver's side and shut myself in. A horn honked impatiently behind us, so I drove a block into a nearby alley and stopped the engine.

"Well?" I demanded, adding, "And what's that stuff on your arms?"

Mother took a deep breath and proceeded to explain what she'd been doing and what she'd discovered since leaving our Wee Wind early this morning. She'd been a busy little girl.

When she'd completed her breathless account, I sighed and said, "Look, Vivian Borne—we have to start trusting each other."

The eyes behind the glasses grew big. "Says *Brandy Borne* who was supposed to be at a bar on the outskirts of town, but got here in half a tick."

I said, "Listen, if you want to conduct your own investigation without me, that's hunky-dory with, as you would say, moi. You don't have to be so secretive about it!"

"Really? Then stop tracking me with one gizmo after another! A practice that only makes me track you the same way. Do you really think you can outsmart your own mother?"

I twisted into her face. "Where does smartness on your part come in? In case you haven't thought it through, you could be the killer's next victim."

"How so?"

"I'll tell you how. You may have noticed some clue at the crime scene, or maybe even spotted the murderer leaving."

Her chin crinkled into a pout. "Well, I didn't."

"Tell that to the murderer. He—or she—doesn't know that."

I played my ace card with her. "Consider this. You're Vivian Borne, renowned sleuth who has solved twenty murder cases, and must by now have the killer shaking in his or her cowboy boots."

"Twenty-one cases."

"If you want to survive number twenty-two, we should stop fighting each other. Watson and Holmes don't work at cross purposes."

After a moment, she said, "You're right, dear, it's best we stick together. And after a rigid saddle, and a hard bicycle seat, my derriere would appreciate the kinder, gentler form of transportation this vehicle provides."

I pointed out a bitter truth. "That does mean we'll miss out on the rest of today's sales."

Mother shrugged. "It's tomorrow that *really* counts . . . when prices are slashed, and folks don't want to pack up leftovers. That's the big one."

So she had just wanted to get me out of the way today.

"Where to now?" I asked.

"Happy Trails Trailer Court. But, first, I need to get this stuff off my arms."

While I drove, Mother found some wet wipes in the glove compartment. (Isn't it about time to change that name—glove compartment? Nobody wears driving gloves anymore. Nor can it be called a map compartment, as who has paper road maps anymore?)

After using the wipes, Mother marveled, "My skin is so smooth and silky now, and I paid close attention to the mode of application. Now I can do this at home with sugar and honey!"

"Hooray. The flies approve."

She gave me a tilted-head, reproving look. "If we're going to work together, dear, you need an attitude adjustment."

I supposed I did, but oddly enough, it still hurt that she'd ditched me this morning. Was I actually disappointed that she was hogging the crime-solving to herself?

"By the way," Mother went on, "did you make any nice finds at the church?"

"Look behind you," I said, keeping my eyes on the bumper in front of us as we crawled along.

She craned around, rummaged in the box, and brought out the Weller dancing frogs, exclaiming, "Well, isn't this lovely!"

"Pretty cute," I admitted, proud of my purchase.

"Too bad it's been broken and glued together."

My "lie" had been a reality! Curses. So much for my attitude adjustment.

Perhaps noting my sour expression, Mother said, "But whoever mended it did a good job of it. And the coffee tin and silver belt buckle are real finds."

"Thank you."

"*If* you didn't pay too much."

Yes, once again, Mother giveth and Mother taketh away.

A half-mile out of town, a well-worn sign appeared pointing the way to the Happy Trails Trailer Court. I turned onto a dirt road, then traveled another half-mile to a grouping of mobile homes, baking like loaves of bread in the sun.

As we approached the array of haphazardly placed trailers, Mother commented, "I don't believe this is quite what Roy Rogers had in mind when he and Dale Evans sang 'Happy Trails' on his Western TV show."

That was before my time, but I was familiar with the same tune performed by Randy Travis in the 1990s. And Mother's point was well taken.

Happy Trails was indeed a rather low-end campground, although it did have electrical stations. Weeds growing against some of the trailers indicated these homes on wheels had been parked there a long while.

Coming to a stop, I asked, "What's your plan for how we find this stepson?" The electrical boxes had numbers, but no names.

"We ask someone," Mother replied.

"You mean *I* ask someone."

"You present so *well*, dear! We should take advantage of your natural charms."

That's the first time she'd ever called them that.

I powered down my window and waved to a teenaged boy nearby, chugging along on a dirt-bike.

He zipped over. "What's up?"

"We're looking for Zeke Norris," I said.

"*That* creep!"

Mother leaned toward the boy with a smile. "If the creep's name is Zeke Norris, yes we are."

"He's in number five," the boy said, "and you're welcome to him." Our informant roared off in a cloud of dust (but no hearty "Hi-Yo, Silver!") (Not that he'd get the reference.)

"If being a creep is his reputation," I said, "we might anticipate a less than warm welcome."

"I have a plan."

"But is it a cunning one?"

We were both fans of Rowan Atkinson and the BBC's *Blackadder*.

Her eyes narrowed, making big slits behind the glasses. "More a . . . ploy."

She usually did have a planned ploy when making a cold call, such gambits varying in nature depending upon what Mother knew the person might want: a favorite food, tickets to one of her plays, a part in a Serenity Playhouse production (walk-on, no lines), an autographed movie or sports star photo (occasionally authentic, frequently forged) (by her).

But I didn't know how Mother could in any way be familiar with Tool's stepson, and had no inkling of how she might get her bunion-bearing foot in his door.

And, frankly, I didn't ask. Sometimes I prefer being surprised along with her subject (or, often, victim). It's kind of like watching that improv show *Whose Line Is It Anyway?* What will Mother say/do next?

Number 5 was a white single-wide trailer that appeared newer than its neighbors, its owner going to a bit of trouble to make his abode seem inviting on the outside at least, with a brick fire-pit and some nice matching lawn furniture.

I parked next to a green jeep, and we exited the van, Mother lugging her tote.

While I hung back, she ascended three concrete steps, and, lacking a visible buzzer, she rapped on the door, which was immediately opened so quickly we jumped in perfect tandem. Mother had to move quickly down a step to avoid being smacked by the door. A burly man with a dark, close-cropped beard, clad in a t-shirt and jeans, glowered at us.

"Zeke Norris?" Mother asked. "Allow me to introduce myself. I'm—"

"I know who you are," the man answered gruffly. "My sister called and gave me a heads-up. I have nothing to say, so go away."

"That is, of course, your prerogative," Mother said. "But before my daughter and I go—that's my daughter Brandy just behind me—I must first confess something to you."

See? Isn't this exciting? What would she say/do next?

"What's that?" he asked, curiosity piqued.

"Dear," she said to Zeke, reaching for an invisible handrail, "I'm afraid I'm a bit wobbly standing here on these narrow steps."

Frowning, he gestured to the fire-pit and said, reluctantly, "I guess we could sit over there."

Mother, of course, was disappointed at not being invited inside to have an opportunity to spot possible clues, but she didn't push the matter.

She and I took fabric-and-metal chairs in front of the pit, while Zeke sat facing us on its low brick wall, muscular arms folded.

Mother began, "I would guess that you know it was I who found your stepfather's body."

His response was curt. "No guessing about it. The police told me. Is *that* your big confession?"

"No. It's rather bigger." With a phony look of contrition, she said: "While there, I took a piece of jewelry."

Well, of course I already knew that. But I had no idea what his reaction would be.

Zeke's rather close-set eyes narrowed. "What are you talking about? What *kind* of jewelry?"

Mother reached into her tote and withdrew a long copper chain with a mother-of-pearl pendant in an Art Nouveau setting.

"*This* kind of jewelry," she said, dangling it before her, like a hypnotist. "But I can explain."

"I hope so," Zeke said, glowering again.

In excruciating detail, Mother proceeded to describe her transaction with Tool via Zoom, whereupon Zeke said flatly, glower gone, "Sounds like it's yours, fair and square."

She put a hand theatrically to her chest. "That's such a relief to hear!" Then, "I feared you or your sister might question my possession of the necklace during the probate of your stepfather's estate."

His grunt was laugh-tinged. "Neither Dixie or me'll have anything to do with his estate. Patrick bragged about leaving us high and dry."

"Oh?" Mother asked innocently, knowing full well from what the RODEOs had told her, and which she had related to me, that both siblings got nothing from the mother's will—which had either gone missing or been shredded—and was left out of Tool's own will.

Zeke, not rising to her bait, but rising himself, said, "Now, ladies. If that's all . . ."

Which caused Mother to quickly respond, "I was also concerned the necklace might hold some sentimental value to you and/or your sister, since it may have belonged to your mother. That your late stepfather had sold it to me thoughtlessly. In your hour of grief, I thought—"

"Hour of grief!" He sat with a snort. "Bought for Mom by that bastard with her *own* money, after he lost a bundle at the racetrack and wanted to make it up to her. Her own damn money!"

Now we knew that Tool had been a gambler. Seemingly a reckless one.

Zeke waved a hand as if saying goodbye to the necklace and everything it represented. "So no, ladies—that bauble means nothing to either Dixie or me."

Mother, returning the jewelry to her tote, said, "Dear, your frankness encourages me to level with you. This visit was not entirely about the necklace."

Another snort. "I was wondering when you were going to admit that. And I'll give you the same cooperation Dixie did—none."

Mother was batting 0-2 on suspect cooperation.

Zeke stood, his burly frame looming. "You should go. Now."

I reached over and touched Mother's arm. "We really should."

Nonetheless, she stayed put.

Gazing up at the man, Mother said sternly, "Mr. Norris, *please sit down!*" Just short of a Nero Wolfe bellow.

Surprisingly, he did, his head going back as if he'd taken a punch.

"Now," she continued in a lecturing manner, "you surely must realize that you and your sister are prime suspects in the murder of your stepfather. I'm here to offer my help."

"What, to the gallows?" he replied with a sneer.

"No, it's lethal injection in Texas," Mother corrected, "but that's irrelevant, as I believe you both to be innocent."

That was a bunch of baloney—she couldn't know that!

Mother went on, "So it would be in your best interest to be cooperative. I have an impressive record, as a helper to law enforcement—and a one-time sheriff of Serenity County—as regards to nabbing the guilty and exonerating the innocent."

His forehead tensed; he was listening.

She hurried on. "Let's start here. Where were you last evening, between the hours of seven and nine?"

"'Here' is right. I was *right* here."

"Elaborate."

She was the one with folded arms now. In full command. Had to hand it to her.

Zeke gestured behind him. "I cooked myself a steak . . ."

The fire-pit did have a grilling grate.

". . . and then went in and watched a basketball game—Duke against Houston—on CBS at seven thirty."

Mother didn't pursue who had won, or what team was ahead each quarter, as Zeke could have recorded the game and viewed it later.

She arched an eyebrow well above her glasses. "Did anyone see you during that time?"

He shrugged. "Maybe while I was out grilling, but after that, no. I went inside and stayed inside."

"I understand you and your sister were not in line to receive a single thing from your stepfather's estate . . . not a *sou*."

"My sister's name isn't Sue, it's Dixie . . . but yes, my stepfather got it all."

"When did you become aware of this?"

Zeke hesitated. Then: "After our mother died, I approached Patrick about Mom's will, because she had told me she'd left Dixie and myself substantial amounts of money, including giving *me* control at the bank."

I gave a low whistle.

Mother said, "Well, since neither money nor control of the bank came to fruition, I gather her will was either never written or destroyed."

"Wouldn't a lawyer have a copy?" I interjected.

Zeke looked at me. "Her lawyer was also my *stepfather's* attorney, who has a questionable reputation."

A crooked lawyer could have helped Tool make sure the document was never found—if it ever existed at all.

Our reluctant host was saying, "Anyway, none of this would be a motive for killing my stepfather, since neither me or my sister will be inheriting anything."

"No," Mother said slowly, "but blaming him for your mother's death would be."

Zeke's expression indicated she had struck a nerve.

Now he glared at her again. "All right, it's no secret I thought Patrick was responsible, either purposely giving my mother too many sleeping pills, or having made her life so miserable she herself swallowed them down." He sat forward. "But if so, why didn't I take my revenge sooner?"

"Sooner" would have made Zeke the prime suspect. If revenge was what he had in mind, it would be better to let time pass and his accusations die down before enacting it. And time enough, too, for Patrick Tool to have made fresh enemies.

Mother, side-stepping his question, asked, "Did your sister feel as you did about your mother's death?"

Zeke shrugged. "She may have, but she never expressed as much to me. I think she just kind of swallowed it. Anyway, Patrick wasn't as tough on her . . . although, I know she had no love for the man and couldn't wait to get out on her own."

Moving on, Mother said, "The gun I observed on the floor by the body was a Smith & Wesson revolver with a pearl handle."

Zeke nodded. "That would be his. One of several handguns he kept around."

"All the same?"

A head shake. "No. A SIG Sauer in the study, Kimber in the kitchen, Beretta in the bedroom."

What about a Luger in the living room, or a PPK in the pantry, or a Glock in the garage, or stop me somebody . . .

"And this particular gun?" Mother was asking. "Where was it?"

"He kept his Smith & Wesson stowed in the grandfather clock in the entryway. Patrick said he was worried about a kidnapping."

Mother frowned. "Of you or your sister . . .?"

"Neither one! Patrick wouldn't have paid a dime for either of us. He thought someone might force him to open the bank vault, or worse, kidnap him for a ransom he'd have to pay with his own precious money. Or, I should say, my mother's money, which was precious to him."

"So then the guns," Mother said, "would have been loaded?"

"Yes." Then came a surprise admission: "Don't think using one of them on him wasn't a temptation for me." And a retraction: "But I never followed through on it."

I asked, "Do you think he may have killed himself?"

Zeke's answer was sardonic. "That's a laugh! The question is not who in Tranquility wanted my stepfather dead, but who *didn't* want him dead." Our host abruptly stood, signaling the end of his cooperation. "Now, I have business to do."

Whatever business there was for an unemployed construction worker with a bad back.

We returned to the van and he disappeared inside his trailer.

Starting the engine, I said, "Zeke doesn't know, does he?"

I was referring to the rumor of abuse Dixie had suffered, as told to Mother by one of the RODEOs.

"No, dear. Otherwise, Zeke would likely have killed his stepfather long before yesterday."

"Do you believe his alibi?"

"I'll accept it for now. Although, he could possibly know of the abuse his sister suffered at Tool's hands, and is merely hiding that knowledge from us."

I frowned at her in thought. "Do we really know Irene Tool's will was destroyed? Couldn't she have hidden it away in the house somewhere and her husband never found it to destroy?"

She raised a forefinger. "Good thinking, dear. In which case, the house not being turned upside down, by someone looking for the document, does further indicate Zeke's innocence."

"Unless Zeke hadn't had time to search for it because of your arrival." Head spinning with the possibilities, I began wheeling out of the trailer park. "Where to now?"

"Where you picked me up."

At late afternoon now, and with the five o'clock deadline of today's sale approaching, traffic into Tranquility had thinned, and I easily found a parking spot in front of the salon.

As we were about to enter, a teenaged girl wearing ripped jeans and a Taylor Swift t-shirt came out, her long tresses colored pink.

"Ah," Mother said, "it would appear Dixie's day wasn't a total waste."

Whatever that meant.

Inside, a woman about my age, seated at a desk, her shoulder-length hair not limited to the color pink, took her eyes off the computer.

The attractive face scowled. "I told you to leave me alone, Mrs. Borne!"

Mother shut the door, turned the sign on the glass to CLOSED, and approached Dixie confidently. "Yes dear, but this is *important*. I've just come from seeing your brother."

"Yes, I know," the salon owner replied curtly. "He called."

Choosing her words carefully, Mother went on, "And it became clear to me that Zeke is unaware of the . . . manner . . . in which you were . . . mistreated . . . by your stepfather."

But not carefully enough.

Dixie sprang to her feet. "What are you *implying*?" she demanded.

"Merely stating what I understand to be the truth." Mother raised a silencing palm. "Dear, you must consider this: if a perfect stranger—like myself—can hear such a troubling rumor when

I've only been in your community twenty-four hours, how much longer is it going to be before your brother hears it? And my stirring the pot, I'm afraid, will only help to bring it floating to the top. Apologies, but murder takes precedence."

Dixie leaned against the desk.

"Brandy! Get this poor woman some water."

I hurried to the back of the elongated shop where, behind a curtain, I found a small kitchenette. When I returned with a glass filled with tap water, Mother had moved Dixie to a chair behind a manicure table.

"Here, dear, drink this," Mother said to Dixie, taking the glass from my hand.

But the young woman waved it away, and the glass was placed on the table.

Mother and I waited.

After several moments, Dixie said, "Back then, and even now, I never told Zeke. I was afraid . . . afraid he might have killed Patrick."

Mother nodded. "So you moved out, instead."

"Yes. Ran away was more like it. I was only fifteen."

I said, "That's young. What did you do to stay alive?"

Her eyes flashed. "That's none of anyone's business!" Then, to soften her outburst, she said, "Anyway, nothing I was proud of, until I met a man a few years ago who was very kind and patient with me, and helped me buy this salon." Dixie paused. "But I was still hurting too much to make a marriage work—we *tried* to make it work, then eventually . . . I hurt him." Another pause. "At least what we had together wound up producing something . . . positive."

"Your daughter," Mother said, gesturing to a photo in a frame on the table.

The woman nodded. "Kaylee. Her father stays involved with the child, and sees her when he can."

Mother asked, "Did he know *why* you had left home?"

"Yes."

"May I ask who this man is?"

Mother's question brought an immediate, eye-flaring response. "No! I don't want him being pestered, much less persecuted. He's remarried now, and lives in Arizona."

Mother backed off. "That's a relief to hear."

But I knew what she was thinking: Arizona was a plausible drive for whoever-he-was to exact revenge over the perceived root cause of his marriage's collapse.

I had been staring at the photo of her little girl, and said softly, "You were worried for her."

Dixie's body stiffened, eyes expressing fear . . . then hatred.

"Yes. I have a very reliable woman named Ulla who lives a few blocks away, in the Olson Building, which makes it convenient for her to look after my daughter when I have her here at the shop. But mostly she takes care of Kaylee at my home. Anyway, I gave Ulla strict instructions that Patrick Tool was never to see my daughter. Never!" Dixie's voice took on a tremor. "But one day last week, he suddenly showed up at my house while I was here, demanding to see his granddaughter. Ulla threatened to call the police, so he finally left, but that was enough to . . ."

Mother finished Dixie's sentence. "Believe Kaylee was in danger, too."

She nodded.

"Where were you last night, dear?" Mother asked gently.

Dixie looked at her with wet eyes. "At home with my daughter. I would *never* leave Kaylee alone." The watery eyes froze. "Mrs. Borne, I didn't shoot that bastard . . . but I'm damn well happy he's dead. Somebody deserves to be congratulated."

In the van, I delayed starting the engine. "Well?"

"Dixie wouldn't leave her daughter alone, but she could have called for the sitter, Ulla. It should be easy enough to check on later."

Traffic was congested once again, folks now scrambling to find a seat in a restaurant or barstool in a pub.

"I'm starving," I complained. "And every place will be full."

"Perhaps Anna Fowler has some cold chicken in the icebox," Mother suggested, using that old term for a refrigerator, even though the latter had replaced the icebox long before she was born. (It's up to each generation to eliminate such antiquated terms. And antiquated ideas.)

I happened to like cold chicken. With sweet pickles. I knew

Mother probably had some fresh questions for the Fowler woman, but my mind was on a cold chicken sandwich.

Before long we were driving down a dirt road on the outskirts of town, where soon I pulled up in front of a typical two-story clapboard home with a porch, situated near a poultry building.

I parked next to a burgundy Buick and we got out.

"That's odd," Mother commented.

"What?"

"The chickens are upset."

There *was* quite a cacophony of clucking and screeching coming from the building, but maybe we had disturbed them.

"Where are you going?" I asked.

Mother started moving toward the long building. "Something's out of whack. Those chickens didn't greet me that way when I was here before."

"Maybe they're hungry, like me," I said irritably.

She ignored my remark, so I followed her.

Entering the building, I saw thousands of chickens flapping their wings, feathers flying in the air, like it was snowing plumes.

But that's not all I noticed.

Hanging by rope from a metal catwalk was the source of the disturbance: a woman who most surely was Anna Fowler.

Brandy's Trash 'n' Treasures Tip

This is a tip on finding new merchandise that I don't recommend. But it's something Mother will do, often to great success. Because she knows everyone in Serenity, Mother will show up on the doorstep of a bereaved citizen after a funeral with a condolence dish (usually a tuna casserole) (ick). After getting invited inside (if she isn't, she will ask for a glass of water to gain entry), Mother will take stock of what antiques are worth pursuing in the upcoming estate sale. I'm only mentioning this because some day you may be on the other side of the doorbell that she rings.

EIGHT
Bury Me Not on the Lone Prairie

Inside the poultry building where Anna Fowler hung from a central catwalk, Mother turned to me.

"Be a good girl and go into the house and see if there's a suicide note." She said this casually, as if asking for a cup of coffee, or the morning newspaper.

But I couldn't take my eyes off Mrs. Fowler, swaying ever so slightly, wearing a colorful house dress and only one slipper, her knee-high support hose scrunched down around each ankle.

"Brandy . . ."

I desperately wanted to pull up the stockings and find the other slipper to make her look more presentable.

"Brandy, dear, look at me."

I did.

Her voice was firm: "We can no longer help that unfortunate soul. Now, do as I've asked. Please."

"OK," I responded rotely. But my feet seemed stuck to the ground.

She took one of my dangling hands and squeezed it and released it. "You'll be fine. Be strong."

I nodded.

She clasped her hands before her and advised gently, "And don't touch anything, even the note, should there be one. Go on and do it now."

"OK."

I willed my legs to move, but don't remember walking toward the house, or going inside . . . only standing in the modest living room where the odor of fried chicken had been baked into the fabric of the window curtains and furniture upholstery.

Several card tables displayed various items carefully arranged and tagged for the city-wide sale. Things that had once given the woman pleasure, her life meaning, but that she had no longer wanted, and now no longer needed.

Was she a suicide?

Not finding a note here, I wandered into the kitchen, where no missive was visible on either the table or counters.

But I did have the presence of mind to notice several oddities.

First, the table had one place set for dinner. Second, the glass had been filled with water. Third, a plate of chicken was warming in the oven, as seen through its glass door.

So, in the midst of making a meal, had Anna Fowler suddenly decided to go to the poultry building and hang herself? Did that really seem likely?

No other room in the house gave up a farewell note, nor did anything seem disturbed. A few larger items were tagged for the sale in several of these other rooms and appeared to have been made more than just presentable for any buyers who might come around. If anything, this indicated Mrs. Fowler had taken time to straighten the rooms up after having her home invaded during the day's influx of collectors and bargain hunters, and readying for tomorrow's sale.

Upon hearing the faint sound of a siren, I left the house and stood on the front porch.

Mother, obviously having phoned in on her cell, was stationed by the door of the poultry building waiting to meet the police car. It rolled to a stop. One male officer disembarked and Mother went to him.

I was too far away to hear their conversation, but when the officer rushed inside the poultry building, Mother came toward the house in a steady stride.

After she'd joined me on the porch, I informed her I'd found no note in a thorough tour of the house, then detailed my kitchen observations.

"Very astute, dear," she replied. "Which only confirms my inspection of the crime scene."

"Then you don't think she took her life either?"

"No."

"You told that to the officer?"

"No."

"But—"

She touched my arm to silence me.

A black sedan had come swiftly up the dirt drive, abruptly halting next to the police car. Chief Garrison exited the vehicle, shutting the door with a gun-shot-like sound that seemed to echo in the emptiness of the coming night. Moving quickly he went into the poultry building.

"Mother, why *didn't* you tell the officer you suspected murder? He might contaminate the evidence if he assumed otherwise."

"Because," she replied, calmly firm, "I have all the evidence we'll need on my cell-phone camera."

I wasn't as calm as she was. "But surely you'll share your homicide opinion with Garrison when he questions us."

"No. I have little faith in the Tranquility Police Department in general, and their chief in particular. This isn't Anthony Cassato we're dealing with. Plus, I want the killer to think he or she got away with it."

Though she seemed steady, Mother's train seemed to have gone off the rails. Our reputation as amateur sleuths had preceded us, and she was putting a target on our collective back. I started to say what a chance she was taking, when Garrison came out of the building and walked briskly in our direction.

(By the way, Mother's favorite railway line is the Atchison, Topeka and Santa Fe; she's a fan of the 1946 movie *The Harvey Girls* starring Judy Garland and Angela Lansbury.)

"I'll handle him," Mother said quietly.

When Garrison, a mini scarecrow in a business suit, badge on his belt, planted himself before us, Mother pre-emptively said, "Chief, may we *please* go inside to sit down for the interview? My poor daughter here is feeling rather faint."

For once she wasn't exaggerating.

The balding man in wire-framed glasses replied in his high-pitched voice, "All right, but let's confine ourselves to the living room."

"*Thank you*," Mother said, over-playing her deference.

A few minutes later, she and I had settled on a well-worn couch while Garrison stood facing us, next to a table of ceramic chickens, several of which seemed turned to look at him.

Obviously none too happy, he began, "This is the *second* death where I've found you at the scene, Mrs. Borne. Do you have an explanation for your presence at this one?"

"Well, Chief," Mother responded, "as you will recall in my interview at the station—which you did record, so you have that for reference—last night I visited Mrs. Fowler for a sneak preview of her city-wide sale offerings, whereupon we arrived at terms for some minor-league baseball cards. My daughter and I, with the sale over for the day, dropped by to retrieve them."

Garrison began to pace a small area in front of where we were seated. "And how did Mrs. Fowler seem last night?"

Mother sighed. "Quite melancholy. She spoke emotionally about the inevitability of losing this farm, which was all she had left after her husband's passing."

Garrison stopped pacing and squinted at her. "Then you think she took her own life?"

"Indubitably."

"What?"

Mother gave him a Mona Lisa smile. "Absolutely. Certainly. Definitely. Undeniably. Without a doubt."

He frowned in thought. "Oh."

Perhaps later he'd realize she'd been mocking him, but right now he didn't seem to see it.

"OK," he said. "You can go." His voice rose in volume to make his point but only gave it a less-threatening higher pitch. "But I'll need a statement later, so don't leave town."

You'd think a Western lawman would *want* the Bornes out of Dodge by sundown.

"Wouldn't dream of it," Mother replied. "Not with the final city-wide sale tomorrow."

Some dry sarcasm came into his reply: "I'm glad you're enjoying your trip to Tranquility."

"We've been doing very well in our efforts to re-stock our shop back home. We made a real killing today. Oh, sorry . . . poor choice of words."

The chief gave Mother a look that said, "Are you messing with me?"

But Mother's only response was a sweet smile.

We followed Garrison back onto the porch when Mother

suddenly asked, "Would it be all right if I used the bathroom before we go? I'm on a thiazide diuretic."

Garrison looked at her like he was trying to bring her into focus. Good luck with that. "Huh?"

"A water pill," she said, and added cheerfully. "When a gal's gotta go, a gal's gotta go."

When he hesitated, she said, "It's not like this is a crime scene. And it's only number one."

I groaned inwardly.

"Be quick about it," he said, his irritation and embarrassment mingling.

As she headed toward the facilities, the chief looked at me as if all of our sanities were in question.

I smiled weakly. "She's also on bipolar medication."

"Oh."

Or was she? It had been a while since I'd counted Mother's pills to make sure.

Garrison left me and rejoined his officer. As I waited for Mother, the yard light went on, triggered by deepening dusk, the rooster vane on the poultry building turning with the wind. The farm's life went on, even without Mrs. Fowler.

Mother returned. "I didn't really have to go."

"I guessed that. You aren't on any water pill. But what made that trip necessary?"

"I thought we might need some photos of the kitchen, among other rooms."

I hadn't had the presence of mind to do so. And she'd guessed, correctly, that I'd been thrown enough by discovering Anna Fowler that I wouldn't think of it.

"What's that?" I asked, pointing to a blue binder in her hands.

"The baseball cards."

"Oh, Mother. Are we robbing the dead now?"

"No, dear, I'd already compensated her for them. But I couldn't take the binder with me last night."

"Why not?"

"I was on a horse, remember?"

I had to ask. "What did you give her?"

"A modest amount, and a valuable first-edition book. Signed."

"What book?"

"*Antiques Roadkill.*"

I closed my eyes and shook my head.

"Open your eyes, dear. It's time we skedaddle."

Note to self: check her pills.

She put the binder in the back of the van with our other purchases, and we climbed aboard.

"I hope you know what you're doing," I said.

"I do too, dear." A rare admission for her. "But these are uncharted waters. We're not in Kansas anymore. Or Iowa, either."

Driving back along the lane, I had to move over for an emergency vehicle, the paramedics racing to their unpleasant task.

When the lane led us to the highway, I stopped the van and asked, "Which way?"

"Left." She thrust an arm with a pointing finger on it in the right direction. Which was the left. "We have one more suspect to interview—Wade Stetson."

"Now?" I moaned. "Must we?"

"Yes."

"Can I wait in the van?"

"No. I need your gifts of sharp observation."

Which seemed pretty unlikely to get unwrapped at the moment.

"I saw Mr. Stetson last night," Mother said to me, "as you may recall."

"I recall."

"Well, I'd like to have your insights, your input, where this particular suspect is concerned."

Now she was just buttering me up.

At her direction we arrived at the Manor Ranch housing addition, where Wade Stetson lived in a sprawling modern manor, one among a number of monuments to wealth.

I pulled the van up the concrete driveway and parked next to a black Porsche. The huge garage was open and the lights were on, now that night was descending.

"That's Wade," Mother said, referring to the man straightening and rearranging what remained of sale items on the tables.

Wade, wearing a Texas Longhorns sweatshirt, jeans and sneakers, noticed our presence, and exited the garage as Mother and I climbed from the van.

"Sorry, ladies, I'm closed till tomorrow morning," he said politely, then added, "Oh, it's you, Mrs. Borne!"

Tanned, ruggedly handsome with a trim mustache, he might have stepped off a Hollywood set.

"I didn't recognize you without your horse," he joshed with a smile.

Mother chuckled politely. "No horse today. I'm here with my daughter to pick up my purchases—that is, if you don't mind."

Did it matter if he did mind?

"Of course," he said. "Come into the garage."

We did.

"Looks like you did quite well," Mother said, observing the spaces on the tables.

"Very. I should be able to rid myself of the rest of this stuff tomorrow. I'll be slashing prices, so if you spot something now, let me know."

Mother said, as if answering a question Wade hadn't asked, "We just came from Anna Fowler's farm."

"Nice lady . . . she's had it rough lately. How did she do with her sale?"

"I don't know. I couldn't ask her."

Wade frowned. "Why's that?"

Mother might have been a waitress reading off the specials. "We found her hanging from a catwalk in her poultry building."

Wade's eyes got big. "What did you say, Mrs. Borne?"

Mother repeated the news with no inflection at all.

Some of the tan left his face, invaded by a pinkish white. "That's . . . that's terrible. I knew Anna'd had it rough lately, but . . . how horrible."

Mother asked, "Then you knew Mrs. Fowler was going to lose her farm?"

Wade sighed sadly and nodded. "Anna told me Pat Tool had turned down her request for a loan, and her children didn't want to take over the business. She coulda sold out, but as I understand it, all she wanted to do was keep the farm going for a while. I had no idea she felt so . . . so desperate."

"Indeed," Mother said. "I saw her as frustrated and sad, but not a candidate for taking her own life."

A white Lincoln pulled into the driveway and parked behind the black Porsche.

"Ah, Mary Jo is home," he said, the news of Anna's demise fading, color returning to his face.

The woman, not much older than I, wearing a patriotic combination of long-sleeved silk red blouse, navy slacks and white tennis shoes, was a real knock-out. She looked like she might have made it in Hollywood as well, though as she drew closer some lines showed in her face—too much sun?

Approaching Mother, Wade's wife said, "I do wish to apologize, Mrs. Borne, for my rude behavior last night, when we first met. I was putting out so many fires with this city-wide sales event. As I was all today." Her laugh had tiredness in it. "I'll actually be glad when this is over."

Mother responded graciously, "No apology necessary. And I quite understand about fires."

Like the time she directed *You Can't Take It with You* at the Serenity Playhouse and used real fireworks that set the curtains ablaze. And when she burned down an outdoor stadium to summon help. And . . . well, you get the point.

Mother acknowledged my presence. "This is my daughter, Brandy."

"Pleased to meet you," Mary Jo said with a nod.

"And you," I replied.

Wade said, "Honey, bit of a shock. These two little ladies just found Anna Fowler dead at her farm."

"How awful!" Mary Jo said. "I did see flashing lights in the direction of her farm on my way home. Knowing she has . . . had . . . a problem with diabetes made me wonder if that's what it was about."

"It wasn't diabetes that killed her, dear," Mother said. "She hanged herself."

Mary Jo raised one hand momentarily to red-lipsticked lips. "That poor woman!"

"'Hanged' is correct," Mother said. "But most people say 'hung.'"

"Mother!" I said, giving her a look.

"Darling," Wade said to his wife, "I was telling them about Anna being unable to keep the farm going."

Mary Jo nodded. "I know that strong possibility was weighing heavily on her. So sad. So very sad." She paused, then added cheerfully, "On a brighter note, the sales have been going so splendidly, we're assured to get our new library."

"That is wonderful news," Mother said with a phony smile.

"Yes! But I'm just one of many who made this happen. Now, if you all will excuse me, I have *so many* phone calls to make before tomorrow."

Mary Jo swiveled on her white tennies to exit the garage and access the house via the front entrance.

Mother faced Wade. "On a *less* bright note, since I was the one who discovered the deceased Mr. Tool and am inescapably involved, I'm conducting my own investigation into his murder."

Wade looked confused. "But didn't he shoot himself?"

"No gun residue was found on his hands. And he was also shot in the back of the head."

"I see. Well, I'm not sure what I could tell you."

"*I* can tell you it's unlikely that two suicides would happen in two days in a town the size of Tranquility, particularly when the two individuals who took their lives were intertwined."

Wade shook his head. "That's nonsense, Mrs. Borne. Tool was a banker and Anna Fowler was just someone he turned down for a loan, at least that's what I understand. What are you saying— that Anna killed Tool, then a day later killed herself? Isn't that a little far-fetched?"

"But not impossible. It's true that Patrick Tool had more enemies than Anna Fowler alone. For example, I understand *you* owed Tool a substantial amount of money over certain poker losses . . . involving one big game?"

His face turned a darker color. "I repaid that debt."

"In cash?"

"No. Not cash. I parted with something that was worth more than what I owed."

"Which is?"

"An historically significant letter from Samuel Houston himself."

This must have been what I overheard those ladies at the church sale speak of, though at the time I thought they meant the city of Houston, not the man.

I said, "I heard Tool was offering the letter for sale this weekend. If he wanted it so badly, why would he part with it?"

Wade looked at me, possibly surprised I had the power of speech. "I was surprised to hear that as well." He shrugged. "Perhaps having the new library named after him had something to do with that. He gave a considerable amount to the fund to insure that happened."

"Some men do care about putting their imprint on buildings," Mother commented, adding, "It looks like you contributed quite a bit to the library yourself with this sale."

He laughed once. "Nothing to compare with the late Pat Tool. But my bride has really made it happen. As for me, holding down the sales fort is the extent of it."

She asked, "You didn't enlist anyone to help you?"

How obvious could Mother be, trying to find out where he'd been all day?

But Wade seemed to take no offense. "No. Just yours truly. Even had a sandwich and soda out here for lunch, and if I took a bathroom break, well, that's what the honor system's all about. We're all friends in Tranquility."

Did that include a murderer?

Wade was saying, "But I'm going to have Mary Jo take over tomorrow, now that most of her work with the event is done."

"Splendid idea," Mother replied. "Brandy and I may drop by to see what's left. The Borne girls are unashamedly bottom feeders!"

That got a grin out of him. "Look forward to it. Come late enough and I'll practically give the stuff away."

Since this dance was getting painful, I said, "Would you mind getting my mother's items now?"

"Glad to." Wade gestured to a door in the garage leading into the house. "I'll be back in two shakes."

As soon as he disappeared, Mother turned to me. "Dear, in the future *I* will end my interviews."

"He was on to you."

"Perhaps. But one can learn important details during a cat-and-mouse game."

"But who's the cat and who's the mouse? After this, we're going back to the glamping ground."

"I'm all for that," she said, chipper. Nothing like a second murder to get her juices flowing. "We'll drop by the Saloon for a tête-à-tête—compare notes! I'm famished. I could eat a horse, apologies to Sally. Why, I'm so hungry I'd eat Ma's stew *with* squirrel meat."

I groaned. "I can't even *think* of eating."

But my stomach contradicted me with a Sushi-worthy growl.

While waiting for Wade to return, I wandered around the tables when something on the garage floor caught my eye.

"Mother!"

"What, dear?"

"Have a look at this."

She came quickly over. "It's a white feather."

"A white *chicken* feather," I whispered.

Entering from the house, Wade said, "Here's the box of things you had me put aside."

Mother went right to him while I knelt pretending to tie my sneaker, when what I was after was that feather . . . only the motion caused it to flutter away!

Mother was asking our host, "Would you be a dear and put the box in the back of our van?"

"You bet, Mrs. Borne."

This diversion—thanks, Mother!—gave me another chance to nab the evidence, which I managed to do, tucking it into a jeans pocket.

Moments later, as I backed the van onto the street, Mother said, "Did Wade track the feather into the garage, after . . . smile, dear, he's looking!"

I did. "Or maybe his wife?"

Mother waved. "Or one of us?"

As I drove away—my big discovery's importance floating off like a, yes, feather—Wade Stetson was still visible in the rearview mirror, standing in his driveway watching us go.

By the time we reached the Saloon, a full Texas moon had begun its ascent, twinkling stars gradually appearing as if the night were just waking up.

Inside, the bar-cum-restaurant was more raucous than ever, country music blaring, the majority of women again in colorful prom dresses and boots and glittery cowboy hats. A generous sprinkling of local studs were on hand on this weekend night. There wasn't an empty table or barstool to be found.

"Let's get our food to go," I shouted to Mother over the noise.

"Good idea. I'll be in the van."

The same hunky blond bare-chested bartender was serving behind the counter and I asked for two orders of Ma's stew, knowing that would be quick. The evening seemed to call for a beer while I waited. But the place was rowdy enough, and my order took long enough, to get bumped and have my beer spill on my blouse.

Ensconced back at the Wee Wind, Mother and I sat on the couch making use of the two pull-out tray tables for our meal. (I had changed blouses.)

No more beer. For libation we substituted tap water from the sink, having yet to find time to stock the little refrigerator.

I didn't think I could eat, but the stew was so delicious I could have had another serving.

In between bites, Mother told me she found small blood splatters just inside the poultry building near the door, suggesting Anna had been hit on the head when she entered, then dragged up the metal steps, which explained the crumpled knee-high support hose around the dead woman's ankles.

Mother also posited that the pooling of blood in the body's lowest area (liver mortis) indicated the likely time of death was between two and four hours *before* we had arrived.

Taking a big bite of stew, like a morgue attendant on lunch break, I said, "So someone had been waiting for the poor woman inside the building."

"Yes, dear. Please don't talk with your mouth full, it's unbecoming, not to mention disrespectful of the departed. I surmise that while Anna was busy making her dinner, the killer sneaked inside—or is it snuck?—the poultry building and riled up the chickens, causing her to leave the house and check on the flock. Then, as Anna stepped through the door, *wham!*, she's knocked out and hauled up the steps to the catwalk, where a rope noose is slipped around her neck, and the unconscious Anna rolled off."

My stomach lurched and I ran to the tiny bathroom and threw up what I had eaten. Those morgue attendants had stronger stomachs than yours truly.

After rinsing my mouth at the kitchen sink, I returned to the couch.

"Quite all right, dear?" Mother asked.

"*No*, I'm not all right! This was supposed to be a working vacation, with the emphasis on vacation, and working on antiques, not murders!"

"Well, that can't be helped, dear. We're in the stew, so to speak, turning up at two crime scenes somewhat suspiciously. And we have to get ourselves out. Of the stew. The metaphorical stew." She stood. "I'll be back."

Alarmed, I asked, "Where are you going?"

"To the van."

"Why?"

"To get something I just acquired."

While Mother retrieved whatever that was, I put the dishes in the sink, wiped the little trays, and returned them to their hideaway. Well, my appetite was satisfied anyway, and few calories had counted. I supposed that was something, at least.

Mother returned carrying a large whiteboard.

"Where'd you get that?" I asked, helping her in.

"From the Saloon." The board had a hand-written list of beers available.

"Mother! That's outright theft!"

"Not if we return it when I'm done, dear, which I fully intend to do. But it's high time we devised a suspect list on this case."

Mother kept an old wooden schoolroom blackboard on wheels in our library at home, tucked behind an ancient stand-up player piano that she would roll out to compile her suspect list on in white chalk. But this was a whiteboard.

"There are two murders," I pointed out. "Do we need two lists?"

The old schoolroom blackboard at home was double-sided in such an event.

"Valid point," Mother replied. "But I'm going to assume the same killer committed both homicides."

"You know the old adage about assume," I said, "which makes an ass out of you and me."

"Dear, negativity is hardly helpful at such a key juncture. We'll use the victim's initials to indicate which suspects are applicable."

That made sense. That's how long we'd been at this kind of thing: Mother was starting to make sense to me.

She rested the board against the couch and we knelt before it. Then Mother picked up a marker she must have also "borrowed" from the Saloon and began to write in block letters. The finished board looked like this:

SUSPECTS IN THE MURDERS OF PATRICK TOOL AND ANNA FOWLER

NAME	MOTIVE		OPPORTUNITY
Dixie Norris	(P.T.)	abuse	TBD*
	(A.F.)	?	TBD
Zeke Norris	(P.T.)	mother's will	TBD
	(A.F.)	?	TBD
Wade Stetson	(P.T.)	gambling debt	TBD
	(A.F.)	?	TBD

* P.T. = Patrick Tool
* A.F. = Anna Fowler
* to be determined

I said, "I think Anna Fowler should be added."

"Why is that, dear? After all, she was a victim."

"She could have shot Tool, and some other person killed her for an unrelated reason."

"What kind of unrelated reason?"

I shrugged. "Like Anna's children who wanted her land and were tired of waiting for her to die."

"While that theory does have some merit," Mother replied, "I'm going to discount it. Or at least table it."

"Why?"

"For one thing, we don't even know the names of Anna's children. We can add them, if it becomes appropriate later. For another thing, it's possible that Anna knew who killed Tool and was blackmailing some unknown person, who might have killed her."

I snapped my fingers. "That could be the *other* option Mrs. Fowler was referring to last night, when you spoke with her. When she indicated she might have another way to save the farm."

"Indubitably."

"Please stop saying that. All right, but you really should add Mary Jo Stetson, because of the feather."

She shook her head. "Not until I can come up with a motive for her."

Not just anybody could get on one of Mother's suspect lists. She had standards.

This suspect list, however, seemed to have a notable flaw.

"Wade claimed he'd paid his debt to Tool with the Sam Houston letter," I pointed out, "which eliminates his motive."

"*Unless* the letter merely kept Tool at bay until Wade came up with the rest of the money. We have no information as to the size of that debt. I need to determine how much cash was owed and how much that letter was worth. Until then, he stays."

I stared at the board. "Wouldn't it take a man, a strong man, to haul Anna's body up to the catwalk?"

"Not necessarily," Mother said. "A woman can be quite strong when motivated. And whoever it was might have carried Anna up the steps, eliminating the telltale scratches on the back of her legs and the loss of a slipper."

"OK. What's our next move?"

"Not ours, *mine*. *You*, Brandy, will be doing your best to fulfill the purpose of this trip, the promise of it . . . which is finding merchandise for our shop."

I shook my head. "I don't think splitting up is a good idea."

She touched my arm. "Dear, you've been through quite enough on this little adventure. As it is, Chief Anthony Cassato will never let me hear the end of it, getting you involved in all of this."

"It'll be even more stressful for me," I said, "wondering if you're all right."

"I'll willingly wear my shoe tracker."

"And you'll keep your cell phone on?"

"Yes."

"And text me every hour on the hour?"

"You have my word."

"You've given me your word before."

"This time I'm not kidding."

Reluctantly, I agreed. In addition to acquiring stock for the shop, we had to pay for the trip's expenses, which were mounting.

Mother struggled to her feet. "Now let's get some shut-eye. I'll even let you fall asleep before I do."

Which took me no time at all. Within seconds of my head hitting the LBJ pillowcase, I was out . . .

. . . until the shriek of a car alarm startled me awake!

Mother was dead to the world, and I had to climb over her to get out of bed, in the process knocking us both on the floor.

"What in heaven's name!" she exclaimed.

"I think someone's trying to get into our van again . . ."

Untangling myself, I got to my feet, but by the time I'd reached the door, the alarm and blinking car lights had ceased.

I stepped outside into a night cold enough to see my breath, and walked around the vehicle.

No windows had been broken, and the doors remained locked. And everything we had collected from the city-wide sale so far remained in the back, visible through the back window.

Drunken squeals and laughter came from the direction of the Saloon. Perhaps some reveler had bumped into the van, or mistaken ours for theirs.

When I returned inside, Mother—apparently unconcerned—had taken over the bed, her snoring rivaling the alarm. I took my pillow and curled up on the couch, feeling uneasy.

One attempted entry to get in the van could be rationalized.

But two?

That might be considered a coincidence, but not in a murder investigation.

Brandy's Trash 'n' Treasures Tip

Other antiques booths are often a good source for obtaining merchandise, especially if that booth is having a sale or closure. An item that had been languishing unwanted in one place can suddenly seem attractive to a buyer in a new setting. This was not true, however, for a bright yellow smiley-face wind-up alarm clock I'd gotten from another dealer, even after showcasing it in our shop placed on a Heywood Wakefield bedside table, on a lace doily, and in a spotlight.

NINE
Don't Fence Me In

Vivian once again. While midway in our narrative—a great mystery writer once said, "Nobody reads a book to get to the middle"—I would like to address the use of the term "unpack" to describe assessing a complex topic.

First and foremost, "unpack" immediately throws a negative cast upon whatever is about to be discussed. After all, who likes to unpack? (Or pack, for that matter.)

I'm reminded of the Andy Hardy movie, *You're Only Young Once* (1937), in which the family arrives on Catalina Island for a two-week vacation, and poor Mrs. Hardy is stuck in a sweltering cabin unpacking all the suitcases and trunks, while husband Judge Hardy goes off fishing, son Andy chases after a pretty girl, and daughter Marian sets her sights on a handsome lifeguard. Then, after a day of misadventures—the judge falls overboard trying to reel in a swordfish, Andy decides the young girl is "too fast" for him, and Marian discovers the lifeguard is married—they all return to the cabin to ask a worn-out Mrs. Hardy what's for dinner. This is what cast-iron skillets are made for—to throw, not cook with.

P.S. Mrs. Hardy never did get outside—by the time she unpacked and made three meals a day, it was time to pack to go home.

Personally, I live out of my suitcase whenever I travel. Dirty clothes go in that plastic bag found in the closet for the purpose of dry-cleaning—which I never use. Just because a label says "dry-clean only," it doesn't mean you can't. That's mainly for the manufacturer's protection. Just use cold water and a mild detergent and gently rub or let soak. Wrap the item in a towel and press out the water, then hang to dry. Only once did that not work—a blouse made from viscose that shrunk to the size a toddler would wear.

(*Note to Vivian from Olivia*: Vivian, Brandy mentioned that you might not be current on your medications.)

(*Note to Olivia from Vivian*: I may have missed a pill or two.) Or three or four.

Dear reader, at my age—which is on a need-to-know basis, and, meaning no respect, you don't need to know—I cannot summon energy I no longer have. Nor can I go without much sleep. Therefore, to catch this killer, I knew I must rely on the "high" I first receive from my bipolar disorder, hoping to do so before the "low" kicks in, when (for example) I think aliens have landed, and Sushi can talk. I mention this only that you might understand why I may seem a little "off" in these later chapters. Those of you who feel I am "off" in the earlier chapters, and are unhappy about it, are probably reading the wrong book.

Where was I?

The following morning, Brandy and I showered at the communal bathhouse, then partook of a continental breakfast offered at the Saloon—strong coffee, weak orange juice, stale cinnamon rolls, and something that was meant to pass for scrambled eggs. The bar/restaurant had been half-heartedly cleaned from last night, windows opened to bring in fresh air to make the food seem more palatable and banish the scent of stale beer.

Brandy looked better today, the naturally pink cast having returned to her face, eyes bright and clear, appetite clearly restored, as she was onto her second helping when one helping was quite enough.

I picked at my plate, mind in overdrive, thinking of what I needed to accomplish today.

Brandy was asking, "Where do you want me to drop you off?"

"Dear, there's a napkin there for your use."

"Sorry." She wiped the roll's white frosting off her upper lip.

I couldn't fault the girl's manners too much. After all, she had mostly grown up with the bipolar version of Vivian Borne, before my diagnosis and subsequent treatment.

I said, "Downtown."

She frowned. "It's Sunday. Aren't stores closed?"

"Some are, like law firms and insurance agencies, but the retail establishments and restaurants are open to take advantage of the influx of visitors. After all, the city-wide sale is taking no day of rest."

"Oh. So that's where you'll be? Just downtown?"

"Yes, dear."

She was looking at me through narrowed eyes, much as little Brandy had years ago when I'd said I would be home in an hour, then boarded a bus to Boston for no reason other than I'd always wanted to go to the fish market there.

I said, "I'll have the tracker in my shoe and keep my cell phone on, texting you every hour on the hour, as promised." I was well aware of trying to sound normal, like a tippler pretending to be sober.

"All right," Brandy replied, then checked the wristwatch Tony had given her the prior Christmas. "The sales will be starting soon, so we should go."

We went.

Traffic in the center of town was nonexistent at this hour, making our journey smooth, and I told Brandy to drop me at an empty lot that had been transformed into a rest area with wrought-iron benches and a gurgling fountain.

"You can pick me up here," I said, climbing out.

"When?"

"I'll let you know after I get what information I can," I replied, then, to turn the focus off myself, said, "Remember, I'm counting on you to bring home the bacon."

"I'll do my best."

I hoped Brandy's bacon would be better than the Saloon's this morning.

She drove off.

What's all this obsession with bacon, anyway? Bacon in chocolate, brownies, popcorn, you-name-it. Consuming bacon in moderation for breakfast now and then is acceptable, but really, all that fat is not good for one's cholesterol, much less the arteries. And just because it's fried crispy doesn't make it any more healthy.

On the other hand, as I write this, I really could go for a BLT right now.

Apologies! I can't stop my mind from going places it wants to go. (Notice I did not say "My bad!" My bad what?)

Let's get back on track.

The downtown of any city, big or small, can be compared to the vital organs of the human body.

For example, the brain would be city hall, representing through elections the thinking of the people and how they want their town to function. The lungs are the courthouse, breathing life into the rules and regulations set by the city, state, and federal government. The heart is the police station, pumping blood throughout the body, carrying out law and order, for without these the other organs would die. The liver is the city jail, breaking down what the courthouse has given it, passing those sentenced along to the kidneys, which determine what is worth absorbing back into the body (society), and what must go on to the intestines (prison), and you know where that leads.

I'm not sure how the stomach and pancreas and spleen fit into this analogy—I understand the liver can take over the duties of the spleen if need be—but the appendix is totally worthless, only causing trouble when you least expect it. Certainly the male and female reproductive systems make the town grow, but maybe I shouldn't talk about that. And then there are lesser organs like the gall bladder, tonsils, and adenoids. My goodness, it certainly does take a village (of body parts)!

If I might interrupt myself, I would like to formally grant permission to any teachers of creative writing who wish to make use of the above passage to instruct their pupils in the art of the extended metaphor. You're welcome!

Moving on.

This being Sunday, all the organs were shut down except the heart, which continues beating day and night, so I hoofed it over to the police station, where I found an unhappy-looking Jenny on duty behind the Plexiglass.

"I see you have to work today," I said, approaching.

"All hands on deck this weekend," she said with a sigh, sounding miffed and muffled.

"Many disturbances?"

A shrug. "Not really. A few bar fights, a report of pickpocketing, but that's to be expected with such a large influx of people."

"Oh! By the way. I have a line on someone who can get you a personalized autographed photo of Morgan Wallen."

Jenny brightened. "That would be *so* cool!"

I smiled.

And stood my ground and gave her a steady stare. Wasn't the young woman on the ball enough to understand the way quid pro quo works?

Jenny glanced over her shoulder to see if anyone was around. "I heard you found Mrs. Fowler, Mrs. Borne."

"Yes, dear. I did. It would seem she had taken her own life."

The receptionist leaned closer to the little holes in the Plexiglass. "Only, she didn't."

I feigned surprise. "Didn't what, dear?"

"Take her own life." She leaned even closer to the Plexiglass barrier. "Mrs. Fowler was *murdered*. I overheard the chief talking about it to someone when I was in the breakroom."

"Hmmm," I said, showing interest but not overdoing. "What do you suppose made the chief come to that conclusion?"

She came so close to the glass she bumped it. Her whisper seemed to ooze through the nearest little hole. "He found blood splatters at the scene."

Garrison was hot on the trail—the killer's trail and mine.

"What else did you hear, dear?"

Again, Jenny checked to see that she was alone and unobserved. "There was *skin* under her fingernails."

Good lord! Poor Anna had been conscious enough to struggle before being rolled off the catwalk. But that was good news (not for the late Anna), as it indicated the murderer must have at least superficial scratch marks.

When Brandy and I saw Wade after finding Anna, he had been wearing a sweatshirt, arms fully covered; his wife wore a long-sleeved blouse. That kept them both on my list for now. Regarding the other two suspects, I hadn't seen Zeke since *before* Anna's death, and how could one detect Dixie having a scratch hiding among the floral garden on her limbs?

Jenny was saying, "There'll be a DNA test, of course, but that will take time."

Which I didn't have in abundance. By tomorrow Brandy would be wanting to get back to Serenity and the shop, and I couldn't blame her. But I had an itch to find who had those scratches.

"Did you want to see the chief?" Jenny asked, adding, "He's in today."

"Oh, no, no," I replied. "I just wanted to let you know about the Morgan Who's-It's photo. And I'd appreciate it if you didn't tell Chief Garrison I came by. He has enough on his mind."

"Certainly." She gave me an exaggerated wink.

This girl could make a very useful contact in the Serenity PD administration. She was efficient, personable, and putty in my hands.

I asked, "Have you ever considered relocating out-of-state, dear?"

There was no hesitation. "Nope, I'm a yellow rose of Texas all the way."

"Well, if you ever change your mind, look me up. I believe a similar position could be found for you in my little town, Serenity, Iowa, which isn't so different from Tranquility—things always seem to be popping there. Do you mind telling me how much you make a year, dear?"

She told me with just a touch of hesitation.

"Not too shabby," I said, "but not near what you could bring in, in Serenity. And I have sway with the chief."

At least until Tony discovered why I'd recommended her.

My next stop was the Owens Apartments, where Dixie had mentioned her daughter's sitter, Ulla, lived.

The building was located on Begonia, a side street, and I was pleased to find that the turn-of-last-century brown-brick Italianate-style structure with bay windows had been well preserved, on the outside, at least. So many of these lovely old buildings, designed expressly for renters back in the day, had been torn down to accommodate the more modern expectations of tenants. Latter-day renters did not take to a living room that shared space with a small kitchen, or a tiny bedroom with an infinitesimal bathroom—if there was one at all; in bygone days, a renter might have to tread down the hall to a communal lavatory.

The horror!

I entered the past through a lovely old door with etched glass. The compact vestibule still had its original black-and-white tiled floor, wall of brass mailboxes, and authentic hanging light fixture.

Taking note of the last names on the boxes, written on cardstock and slipped into little brass holders, I figured "Svensson" made the most likely match with "Ulla" and took my chances and pushed the little button on 205.

I pushed it again.

A female voice crackled over the ancient speaker. "Yes?"

"Ulla?"

"Ja?"

"Vivian Borne. You don't know me, but I'm a friendly acquaintance of Dixie Norris's." With luck the hairdresser hadn't mentioned me to the babysitter. "I need to speak to you."

The voice became guarded. "About vhat?"

"The murder of Dixie's stepfather, Patrick Tool."

Silence.

"My dear, it's very important I talk to you. Or must I call my good friend Chief Garrison?"

The door leading into the interior clicked open.

My tour of the past continued. To the left and right of a central staircase, narrow gleaming hallways led to the first-floor apartments. Since Ulla lived on the second, I climbed marble steps that had indentations in the middle created by decades upon decades of use. For better footing I kept to the right, holding onto an elaborately scrolled hammered-iron railing.

Those were the days! Of course, I wasn't nearly old enough to have experienced them first-hand.

Apartment 205 was at the top of the stairs. Bathed in light cast from a wall sconce made of Murano glass in the shape of a seashell—how lovely!—I knocked on the oaken door.

Imagining what someone you've never met might look like is usually a mistake, but I couldn't help thinking of Ulla in terms of the Ulla in the 1967 movie *The Producers*, starring Gene Wilder and Zero Mostel, with Lee Meredith embodying (so to speak) their dishy Swedish receptionist.

The door opened almost immediately.

This Ulla was a matronly middle-aged woman with steel-gray hair braided in a bun at the base of her neck, wearing a plain navy dress and orthopedic-type shoes. She had never resembled the Ulla of *The Producers* at any stage of her life. And yet, I could see why Dixie had hired the sitter: the eyes seemed kind, and the ample bosom and expansive lap were the perfect place to console a little girl who'd hurt herself.

Ulla said preemptively, "I go to church soon."

"This will only take a minute," I replied.

She hesitated, then—reluctantly—stepped aside and gestured me in.

This was where my visit into yesterday ended.

Looking past my hostess, I said, "Oh, dear! The apartments have been remodeled."

Probably around 1980—bland modern furnishings, pale pebbled walls.

"Ja," Ulla said. "Now vhat you vant?"

Since I was stuck just inside a door that was still open, I trotted out a tried-and-true old routine. "Those steps tuckered me! Might I ask for a glass of water?"

"Nej. Vhat you vant? I go to church."

Since feigning faintness wouldn't likely work either, not with this no-nonsense woman, I asked, "Let's cut to the chase. Did you look after Kaylee the night Patrick Tool was killed?"

When I received no answer, I had no other option than going for the jugular. "I imagine you're here on a green card working as a nanny. Withholding information in a murder investigation could have consequences. Would you like to see my badge?"

I had one in my tote—honorary deputy sheriff of Serenity County. No real authority to it, of course.

But she didn't ask to see any ID. Ulla closed the door behind me and said, "You vill sit."

And we sat. On a small sofa next to the bay window, angled toward each other (us, not the sofa and window).

I repeated, more or less, what I'd asked before: "Were you looking after Kaylee the night Mr. Tool was killed?"

When no reply came from my stony-faced reluctant hostess, I said, "I'm not recording this conversation."

Ulla took a deep breath, exhaled. "Ja. I vent to vatch Kaylee that night."

"Vhat time—I mean—what time did you arrive?" I couldn't help being a compulsive mimic; once I spent a week in Savannah and didn't lose my Southern accent for two months.

"Just before seven," Ulla replied. "Dixie left a few minutes later."

"How long was she gone?"

"I vould say . . . half an hour, maybe less."

"Did Dixie say where she was going?"

"Ja. To tell *him* to stay away from Kaylee."

"Patrick Tool, him?"

"Ja."

I smiled graciously. "Thank you, Ulla. Now that wasn't so hard, was it?"

Having gotten what I wanted, I stood. She didn't seem in the mood to chat.

But Ulla pulled me back down; she was strong. Maybe she *vas* in the mood!

"Dixie vouldn't kill that man." Tears formed in her light-blue eyes. "She vould never do such a thing. She is a good person. Please. I do not vant to loose this job. I love that little girl."

Loved the child enough to remove any threat to her?

Holy moly, did I have another suspect?

Ulla was pleading now. "You vill find the one who did this, please? This mörda?"

"Ja," I said.

Every town has a barfly or two—someone who hangs out at a drinking establishment from opening to closing. From when the lights go on till they go out and come on again at last call.

Usually this person is a long-time resident who knows the town and its denizens inside and out, and where all the bodies are buried, and who buried them. He or she are not to be found in any bistro bar, or hotel watering hole, but a lowly pub, frequented by like-minded patrons who know each other's names. Not a self-conscious one called the Saloon at the glamping ground.

A tavern.

Back home, this place was called Hunter's, a business that hadn't changed in one hundred years. The front end of our tavern sold hardware while the rear peddled hard booze to soft men. A patron might stop in to purchase, say, a battery-powered nail gun or electric saw, have a belt or two or three at the bar, then go home and affix his hand to a wall, or lop off a spare finger. No one seemed to question this questionable business practice. I suspect it was because a husband could say to his wife, "Honey, I'm going out to get a screwdriver," and not be lying.

Tranquility had a similar establishment—hardware in front, bar in back—but their "hardware" was guns and ammo. (Did I mention they always did things bigger in Texas?)

It didn't take much detecting, however, to find the aptly named Shooters and Shots, located at the end of the downtown grid, in a patched pink adobe single-floor structure that could have harkened back to when the town was just a cattle stop on the Chisholm Trail.

Entering through swinging doors, I was immediately confronted by locked glass cases displaying various kinds of firearms.

A burly bearded man in a t-shirt bearing the store's name stood behind one of the cases, showing a formidable-looking weapon to a potential male buyer.

"Yes, sir," the seller said, "this puppy can fire eighty rounds in twenty seconds."

"Just what I'm lookin' for," the buyer replied.

The burly man noticed me. "Be right with you, ma'am."

"Just here to wet my whistle," I replied and kept moving toward the back where the bar took over.

The burly clerk lost interest in me, returning to the sale at hand.

An authentic old tavern must have several common attributes: dim lighting, small tables with mismatched chairs, sticky floor, scarred bar, older male bartender with mottled nose, and, of course, the ubiquitous barfly. I assessed Shooters and Shots. Bingo!

Today being a Sunday, the bar was expectantly empty of customers, except for my mark at the end of the scarred counter. A window on a small short-order kitchen was in back, enabling the bar to be open on a Sunday by serving food.

The barfly at Hunter's, whom I regularly called upon for information, was Henry, who sat quietly by himself, year after year, ignored by others, soaking up conversation like a bartender's rag. He'd once been a prominent surgeon whose career came to an abrupt end after taking a shot of whiskey to steady his hands before an operation, then removed a kidney instead of the intended appendix. The patient survived, and the kidney found an appreciative donor, but Henry lost his license (and will) to practice, which was probably for the best. So I was a little surprised to see a woman hunched over a tumbler of golden liquid.

I took a barstool in the center, its split plastic seat duct-taped, and held my tote in my lap.

"What'll ya have, honey?" the bartender asked. His nose wasn't mottled, but it was red.

I gestured to the only other patron, of a type of female who might once have unkindly been called "blowsy," which I guess makes me mentally unkind. Let's just say the lady had a lot of miles on the odometer.

"What's she having?" I asked.

"Bourbon, straight."

Yikes. I'd been off my medication long enough to safely consume alcohol, but would have preferred something diluted.

"I'll have the same," I said, making us kindred spirits (pun intended—creative writing teachers take note!). "And get another for the little lady."

The woman's head turned toward me with an appreciative nod. The bartender poured two drinks, delivered them, and she and I picked up our glasses in a toast. Good lord, that bourbon was strong!

Feeling entitled now, I relocated, keeping one stool between myself and my new friend.

"Allow me to introduce myself. I'm Vivian Borne."

She responded, but her words were too slurred to understand. I could have used Henry to translate. But who would have translated Henry's translation to me?

I looked to the bartender for help.

"Name's Maddy—don't know the last, or anything else about her. She came with the bar when I took over a few years back. Pays for her drinks and doesn't cause no trouble."

The perfect tavern customer.

I'd often been able to decipher the hapless Henry, so I gave Maddy another try.

"I'm investigating Patrick Tool's murder. What can you tell

me about the man?" I leaned closer so the bartender couldn't hear me whisper, "Secrets, I mean."

Maddy's slurred words were impossible to understand. She was worse than Henry—and I hadn't helped . . . I'd just given her another drink!

Again, I looked at the bartender, now polishing a glass. He gave me an elaborate shrug. "Don't ask me."

As mentioned, a town can have more than one barfly, and it appeared I'd have to find another, but one less lubricated.

I slid off the stool, "Well, thank you, dear. If you sober up, I'm staying at Ma's campground."

Suddenly Maddy grabbed my arm.

"Something about the campground?" I asked.

She shook her head no, then yes, and made a sound I thought I recognized as a name.

"Something about . . . Ma?"

She nodded.

"And Tool?"

Another nod.

But how to proceed from here?

I removed my cell from the tote, brought up the keyboard as if composing a text, and placed it in front of her. Thick fingers took their time.

So it took a while before one word appeared: Affair.

I was astounded.

"How many years ago?"

Maddy's bloodshot eyes rolled upward as if searching through the few brain cells left, then typed: 50.

"Did they ever get married?"

She shook her head, and typed: Baby.

Ma had mentioned a granddaughter named Lacy who helped her start the glamping ground . . . so this baby conceived with Tool had to have been Ma's daughter, or possibly son.

"Where is the offspring now?" I asked.

Maddy typed: Dead.

Which explained why Lacy had been living with Ma. And now made Ma a suspect.

"Thank you my dear," I said. "You've been most helpful."

I paid for our drinks.

"You're nice," Maddy said.
Clear as day!
What a good judge of character.

Authentic Prints and More was located on the main drag in a Greek Revival building, whose symmetry—sash windows and two half-columns sandwiching the entrance—was at odds with its Victorian-style neighbors. Gazing farther up the two-story edifice, the words FIRST NATIONAL BANK were chiseled into the stone facade, announcing its previous grander existence.

The current business specialized in historical documents and letters, old maps and train schedules, defunct stock certificates and old paper money. The "more" included autographed photos of celebrities (according to its website), which gave me an opportunity to fulfill my promise to Jenny while also pursuing another matter.

The interior was a large square area with wide-plank hardwood floors and plaster walls, the ceiling moldings its only ornate features.

Back in the day, a row of cashier cages would be ready to collect and dispense money . . . but any remnants of the former financial institution were gone, except for a large iron vault in the back that I imagined came in handy for storing the more valuable documents.

Glass cases took up most of the space, displaying items for one to gaze upon, as if in a museum, only these paper artifacts were for sale.

The gentleman approached me, his brown tweed suit going well with the historical and literary surroundings. He was portly, with salt-and-pepper hair, wire-framed glasses and a little goatee, and might have once been a professor, or played one on TV.

"How may I help you?" he asked pleasantly.

Coyly I said, "I'm afraid I'm not going to be your most lucrative customer of the day."

He had a nice smile and his teeth looked real. "Let me be the judge of that." His dark-blue eyes had a nice twinkle.

I could be interested in such a man . . . but the goatee would have to go.

"I'm in need of an autographed photo of the country singer

Morgan Wallen," I replied, adding, "Not for me—I prefer big band music—but a friend for whom I owe the pro of a quid. Or the quid of a pro. Never quite sure which is which!"

"Pardon?"

Get it together, Vivian!

"A gift," I said. "I owe this person a gift."

"I do have one of Wallen," he said, adding, "but the photo isn't signed."

It would be after I got my hands on a Sharpie.

The gentleman was saying, "If you'd wait here, I'll try to find it in the back."

While alone, I perused the cases, taken with the historical merchandise, but not by the expensive prices. How much would this photo set me back?

"Here it is," the man said, returning, showing me an eight-by-ten glossy of a handsome young mustachioed man wearing a green baseball cap backwards, white t-shirt (not worn backwards), and gold necklace.

I said, "Thank you very much . . . ah . . . I didn't get your name."

"Sebastian."

"Are you the owner?"

"I am."

"Isn't it unusual to have such an exclusive business in so small a town?"

"I'm a people person who enjoys having a shop," he said. "Though admittedly, ninety percent of my sales are done online."

Brandy and I had so far avoided moving in that direction. Packaging up items is right up there with packing a suitcase.

Sebastian asked, "Is there anything else I might help you with?"

"Yes. I noticed a letter signed by Samuel Houston in one of the cases . . . Can his signature really be worth what you're asking?"

"It's not the signature alone, madam, that determines the price, it's what the signature is attached to. In this case, it's a letter Houston wrote to the Secretary of War, Lewis Cass, in 1834."

"And the one Patrick Tool offered for sale?"

His expression turned hard-eyed. "Quite a bit more. Really a museum-quality piece. Tool's is a dispatch sent from Samuel

Houston as commander of the Texan Army, to Lieutenant Colonel William Travis at Alamo, telling him help was coming."

I gasped.

"You didn't know the contents?" Sebastian asked.

I shook my head. "Just that it was something Houston had signed."

"Only one other dispatch between the two officers has survived, and it was written by Travis to Houston, begging for troops." Sebastian paused. "Of course, help did not arrive in time before the Alamo fell to the Mexican army."

"I suppose the one Houston signed is the more valuable of the two."

"Actually, no. The Lieutenant's dispatch contained a heart-wrenching account of conditions at the Alamo while under continuous attack, demonstrating the bravery and patriotism of the troops."

Especially heart-wrenching, knowing the outcome.

"What kind of money would Tool's letter be expected to fetch?"

"Not as much, but still quite a sum, especially to the right collector."

A savvy dealer always played the game with their cards close to their vest.

Then Sebastian included a shocking caveat. "That is, if Tool's dispatch is real."

"You doubt its authenticity?"

"I'd like the chance to examine it . . . but no one seems to know where it is."

I intended to remedy that.

"Well, thank you, Sebastian, for the photo," I said. "How much do I owe you?"

"Nothing."

"Nothing?"

The twinkle was back. "Nothing. But if you find Tool's dispatch, Mrs. Borne, will you bring it to me? I could discern its authenticity immediately if I could see it."

I hadn't given Sebastian my name. Of course, wherever I go, my name does get around.

"Certainly," I said. "Oh! If I might impose on you for one more thing . . ."

"Yes?"

"Do you have a spare Sharpie I could take with me?"

Outside, my mind began buzzing. I needed some strong coffee to clear my head. Recalling a little bistro one block over, I cut through an alley to get there faster.

Apparently that's when I was struck from behind.

I can't report it, because I didn't see it coming.

Vivian's Trash 'n' Treasures Tip

Auctions are the least efficient way to stock your store due to the time spent bidding on something you are not assured of getting. I will bid absentee on interesting items through a service, setting my high (not to be exceeded) bids ridiculously low. That way, if I do happen to win something, it will be a bargain even with the service's commission. So far my strategy hasn't worked all that well.

TEN
The Great Roundup

When I hadn't received my on-the-hour text from Mother, I called her cell and it immediately went to voicemail.

Furious, and not just a little alarmed that she had broken her promise to stay in touch and available, I checked her AirTag on the app, fully expecting Mother to have thrown it into the Red River.

But that fury and alarm turned to fear and dread when the footprints led to the Tranquility Hospital.

Driving recklessly enough to get a ticket, though thankfully I didn't, thankful too that the Sunday traffic en route was still light, I arrived at the modern facility a few minutes later. My vehicle's wheels squealed as if imitating my inner state of mind while the van made its turn into the emergency entrance.

After abandoning the van at the patient drop-off area—but somehow having the presence of mind not to block the ambulance lane—I burst into the waiting area, where perhaps a dozen people were seated. At the check-in desk, I muscled in on a man giving insurance information to a female receptionist.

"Vivian Borne," I asked, out of breath. "Where is she?"

The receptionist responded with barely perceptible irritation. "I'm sorry, you'll have to wait your turn."

No way would I do that.

I whirled and hurried through a set of double doors into the ER as the receptionist called out behind me, "*Hey!* You can't go in there! That's strictly—"

I didn't hear the rest, moving quickly down a corridor that led to individual treatment rooms. Once in that area, I slowed and stalked, opening doors, startling patients and physicians alike. Not finding Mother, I could only wonder if my destination should be the basement where most morgues were located.

Then I heard a familiar voice that for once I was ecstatic to hear.

"Dear! I'm quite all right!"

She was seated on the edge of an examination table, her hair mussed, clothes the same if a little dirty, her glasses sitting cockeyed on her nose. But, overall, she appeared all right, if slightly more demented than usual.

"This is my darling daughter!" Mother said, overly animated. "Brandy will tell you how clumsy I am, always tripping over my own feet! I had bunion surgery a while back, and I'm still battling hammertoes."

The male physician attending her seemed surprisingly young for the horrors of the ER. His identification tag read DR HEALEY.

"What happened?" I asked.

Mother said, "Well, dear, I—"

"I was asking the doctor."

Dr. Healey responded, "Your mother was found unconscious in an alley, although by the time the EMS arrived here with her, she had come to." His voice turned exasperated. "I've recommended a CT scan due to the lump on her head, but she has refused."

Mother looked at me. "I'm fine. I merely stumbled while taking a shortcut through an alley, and must have hit my head on the cement. Not the first time!"

"All the more reason, Mrs. Borne, that—"

"She'll have the scan," I said.

Something in my face or voice told Mother it would be best to comply. "Little" Brandy didn't put her foot down often, but when it did come down, it did so with a boom.

"I'll have the scan," Mother said.

While her brain was being assessed, at least as much as medical science could manage, I sat fuming in the waiting area. The crisis having passed, my fury built.

After what seemed like hours but was probably at most forty-five minutes, Dr. Healey entered and approached me with a paper in one hand.

"The CT didn't show anything concerning," he said. "Certainly not enough to keep your mother overnight, but she'll have that lump for a few days, which will be tender." He paused, then continued, "Naturally, the first twenty-four to forty-eight hours after a head injury are crucial, so if you see any signs of these symptoms, call the emergency number right away. You seem to be in charge."

Appearances can be deceiving.

The doctor handed me the paper.

"Thank you," I said. "Where is she?"

"At the check-out desk. She'll have to wait for a wheelchair, which is protocol."

I nodded.

With the release work concluded, and the wheelchair provided and utilized, and with Mother secured in the van's passenger seat, I started the engine and pulled away.

But I didn't drive very far. In fact, not even out of the parking lot, pulling into a legitimate spot, where I let my frustration and anger loose on her.

"'Stumbled' my ass!"

"Dear! There's no need for offensive language." She leaned toward me with a confidential and very inappropriate smile. "Did you notice the doctor's last name was 'Healey'—as in to heal people? Turns out he comes from a long line of Healeys who were physicians. Of course, the most famous Healy I know of is Ted, who discovered the Three Stooges."

"Don't change the subject! Someone hit you! Tried to kill you!"

She tossed that off with a hand gesture. "Dear, if this individual had wanted me dead, they'd surely have finished the job. It was merely a warning."

"Well, the best thing to do with a warning in a murder case is heed it!"

She gestured again, this time with her thumb almost touching her forefinger. "Brandy, I'm *this* close to solving these murders! We could do it together."

"No."

Her hand went to her chest and her expression was one of mock shock. "Don't you even *care* who clobbered your poor old mother?"

My upper lip curled into a smirk. "That baloney might have worked years ago on little Brandy, but I'm great big Brandy now."

"Pish posh. You're still a delicate creature. Anyway, I'm certain Dixie is our killer."

She tossed that off as casually as she had the threat to her life. I had to ask—we'd come this far. "Why?"

Mother recounted her conversation with Ulla, who had admitted staying with the child Kaylee while Dixie went to see Tool the night he died.

Finally, one of the suspects had been caught in a lie! I have to admit I was interested. Enough, anyway, to ask her, "What if Ulla called Dixie after your visit, and she's who hit you in the alley?"

"Quite possible, dear."

"We should go to the police. Right now."

"With what evidence? Your precious Tony would take us seriously, but not Chief Garrison! And Ulla would most likely deny what she had said to me, and I'd promised the woman not to record our conversation in order that she might talk more freely. And I actually *kept* that promise, for once." Mother paused. "I'll call Dixie and ask for a meeting. I have a card from the salon with her cell number."

"All right," I said reluctantly. "But we should meet her somewhere safe."

Mother raised a forefinger as if testing the wind. "I know just the place."

We set sail.

The Chuck Wagon served only one option for lunch each day, and today it was tamale pie. Mother and I sat on one side of an empty bench and, to justify taking the whole table, Mother ordered two extra meals in addition to ours from an attractive young woman named Calico, for "friends who were coming."

As the waitress walked away, Mother asked, "By the by, dear, did you make any purchases for the shop?"

"Yes." I didn't feel like going into it now.

"Well?" Mother persisted, probably to take my mind off meeting with a murderer.

"A Frankoma boot vase, and a pair of brass cowboy bookends."

"Not bad! Not bad! Anything else?"

I might as well give it all to her. "A tin gold-mining pan, a turquoise-and-silver bracelet, a Navajo horse blanket, and a board game from the 1950s called Cowboy Checkers."

"A very good haul! Tell me—the board game, it came with its box?"

I nodded.

"Good girl!"

What was I, Sushi? If so, where was my treat?

I didn't mention, among the listing of my haul, the branding iron with the initials BB that I was keeping for myself.

Calico appeared carrying a tray with four individual-serving pies, and still no sign of Dixie. Not one to wait, I dug into the casserole, which was delicious. (Mother got the recipe later from Calico.)

Tamale Pie

1 pound ground beef
½ cup onion, chopped
⅓ cup green pepper, chopped
2 cloves garlic, minced
1 11-oz. can chili beef soup
1 16-oz can Mexican-flavored diced tomatoes
⅓ cup ripe olives, sliced
2 tbsp. chili powder
3 cups water, divided
1 cup cornmeal
½ tsp. salt
Butter
1 cup cheddar cheese, grated

Brown beef in skillet. Add onion, green pepper, and garlic, cooking until tender. Drain fat. Stir in soup, tomatoes, olives, and chili powder. Cook over low heat 15 minutes, stirring occasionally.

Meanwhile (back at the ranch), bring 2 cups of water to boil. Mix cornmeal with salt and remaining 1 cup of water. Pour cornmeal mixture into boiling water, stirring constantly. Cook over medium heat until thickened, about 15 minutes.

Butter bottom and sides of a 2-quart shallow baking dish, and line with cooked cornmeal. Fill with beef mixture. Bake at 350 degrees for 30 minutes. Top with cheese and continue baking until cheese melts. Serves 6.

I was contemplating eating a "friend's" serving when Dixie sat down across from us.

The first thing I did was check out her exposed tattooed arms, and I'm sure Mother was doing the same; but I couldn't detect any scratches Anna may have made.

"Well?" Dixie demanded. "Let's hear this 'damning' evidence you have that I killed my stepfather."

That's what Mother had said to the woman on the phone, to encourage her presence.

But before Mother could answer, I blurted, "Did you hit my mother on the head an hour ago?" Possibly emboldened by the spicy tamale pie.

Coldly, Dixie replied, "I have no idea what you're talking about. Your Mother looks fine to me."

"Well," Mother said cheerily, "the bump doesn't show. It's hidden by my hair, I'm pleased to say."

I pressed our guest. "Then you deny getting a call from Ulla this morning?"

Unlike Mother, I'd made no promise not to record my conversation with Dixie; my cell phone in my lap was catching everything.

"I haven't talked to Ulla since Saturday," Dixie said. "Now, what's this about? And what does Ulla have to do with it?"

Mother told her.

After a moment, a deflated Dixie said, "All right . . . all right. I *did* ask Ulla to watch Kaylee while I had it out with Patrick about staying away from my daughter."

Mother prodded, "And how did that confrontation go?"

"It went nowhere. There was no confrontation. Once I got to the house, I just sat in my car on the street. I never even went up to the door. Never saw him at all."

"You want me to believe you just lost your nerve?" Mother asked. "That you didn't do anything about the threat that evil man presented to your little girl?"

She snorted. "Lost my nerve? Hardly. I was afraid I'd shoot him with one of the loaded guns he kept around."

So Dixie knew about the various weapons, and where at least some of their hiding places were.

Mother's eyes were narrow behind the big lenses; she, and her mission, were in focus. "Let's say for the moment I believe your story, Miss Norris. When did you arrive at your stepfather's home?"

A shrug. "Around seven."

"And how long did you sit stewing in your car?"

Dixie thought about that briefly. "Maybe ten minutes. That's when I decided that rather than confront my stepfather, I'd finally bring charges against him. Because as long as I continued to keep quiet, I'd always be a victim. And even if it didn't go anywhere, it would be enough to curb his appetites. He did care about his public image." She added glumly, "The ironic thing? Apparently the whole town already knew."

Mother asked, "Were you worried that your brother Zeke, after you told him about the abuse, might show up and exact his revenge?"

Dixie's response was fast and emphatic. "No! I did talk to my brother, after I *almost* confronted our stepfather. Zeke promised not to do anything that wasn't *my* decision."

Mother changed the subject. "So you left about ten minutes after seven?"

"Yes, but . . ."

Dixie seemed to catch herself.

"But what, dear?"

"I don't want to get someone in trouble."

Mother asked, "Someone you saw?"

"Yes."

"Exiting Tool's home?"

"No. Not, uh . . . not coming out."

"Going in?"

Dixie nodded reluctantly.

Mother's expression seemed kind; maybe sincerely so. Maybe. "Dear, it's a crime to withhold evidence. It would make you an accessory after the fact, and in a murder case that could have extreme consequences. Think of Kaylee."

Dixie sighed. "It was a woman driving an old red truck. I don't really know her *real* name."

"But you recognized her?"

"Yes. Everybody knows her. Everybody calls her Ma."

The Texas sun was blazing high when Mother and I arrived back at the glamping ground. Ma's red Ford pick-up, parked next to her trailer, indicated the woman was there.

On the way, Mother had told me about her encounter with barfly Maddy, prompting me to say, "If Dixie really did see Ma that night, then the story about Ma and Tool having a child must be true."

Mother pointed a finger at the trailer. "That, dear, is what we're going to find out."

We found Ma seated at the little table, keeping company with a bottle of Wild Turkey. She wore a sleeveless white blouse with denim jeans—with no visible scratch marks on her arms. So if Ma did shoot Tool, she hadn't murdered Anna, which seemed to put a hole in Mother's theory that we were looking for a single killer.

Before Mother had a chance to speak, Ma said, "I been waitin' for you gals to come around and have a serious chin wag."

Mother took the other chair at the table, while I stood by, cell recording at my side.

Ma finished what was left in her glass, then poured herself another. "Figure you musta finally found out I paid that no-good S.O.B. a visit the night he got shot by somebody doin' the world a favor."

"Yes, dear," Mother said. "And aren't you known for doing favors? Dixie was there before you came around, and recognized your truck. When would that have been?"

"Long about ten minutes after seven."

Which jibed with the time Dixie said she'd seen Ma.

Mother continued: "What was the purpose of the visit?"

"My granddaughter. *His* granddaughter."

"Lacy," I said.

"Not a strong resemblance to either you or the late Tool," Mother said, "but I should have thought of it sooner."

Ma looked from her to me. "You think I always looked like

this? A party can change over time." She gestured toward the kitchen. "Go to that first top drawer . . ."

I did so.

Ma shook her head. "No, not that one, the one next to 'er . . . That's the one."

I rummaged around and pulled out a formal portrait taken of a beautiful young woman with a blonde pageboy and dazzling smile.

"Once upon a time I was quite a looker, wouldn't you say? Had that taken when I turned sixteen. That's when I met Patrick Tool. This part of the world, sixteen wasn't so young. And he wasn't as old, just a feller unhappy with his wife, and me? I had dreams of marrying up in the world. Can't blame Tool a hundred percent. Takes two to tangle, but only one gets knocked up, right, girls? And I admit it—I didn't see this as a tragedy but my ticket to somewheres better. Oh, not outa Tranquility, but to a nice house in a good part of town, married to a respectable feller. But instead, Tool turned me away . . . well, he paid for me to go, I should say. Paid for me to get rid of the child, too. But I didn't, as you well know."

She took a slug of Wild Turkey, let out a satisfied sigh.

"After the child come, I figured I was back in the game, so to speak—it was a son, and seein' as Pat Tool didn't have no son, no offspring a'tall from that wife of his, I figured he might reconsider. But makin' a baby with me was one thing and havin' an offspring by the likes of me was somethin' else entirely. So he married that second wife of his, that rich woman with two kids . . ."

Zeke and Dixie.

". . . who he treated just horrible. Which made the missus unhappy. So maybe it was for the best we didn't get hitched. My boy deserved better than bein' raised by the likes of Patrick Tool."

"Where is your son now?" Mother asked.

"Danny got hisself killed in a head-on crash 'tween his motorcycle and a big old Lincoln. His wife was ridin' on the back, and she went to her rewards 'longside my boy. Lacy, a chile of eight at the time, come to live with me."

"I'm sorry you suffered such a loss," Mother said in a rare show of compassion to someone she suspected of murder.

Ma shrugged. "That was hard. But it were long years ago, and

Danny he was a wild child who took too many risks. Maybe he was lucky to live as long as he did, with all the booze and pills he put in hisself. But Lacy's been a real sweetheart, blessed with her daddy's best qualities and none of his downside. I just hope she hasn't turned out like me, runnin' off as she done with some bartender I hired. And both of 'em with no money."

I asked, "Is that why you went to see Tool, Ma? Money for your granddaughter?"

Ma nodded slowly. "I wanted to know if Mr. Patrick Tool was leavin' his granddaughter *somethin'* in his will. But he said he had no 'tension of doin' such for no bastard offspring of a bastard offspring. So I tell him I'm goin' to spread the word all over Tranquility about how I was just sixteen when we was together, and how it led to our son, Danny, and Lacy, his granddaughter. But he just laughed and said nobody would pay any mind to trash like me. And, anyhow, he was old and rich and the world could kiss his bee-hind. Right then and there I wanted to kill him."

Who wouldn't? I thought.

"Did you?" Mother asked. "Kill him?"

"No. I did not. When I left around seven thirty, he was alive and well. If you don't believe me, just ask the feller I seen showin' up after me, drivin' a green jeep."

Mother asked her who that was, and Ma told us.

Zeke Norris.

We sat around the firepit again, Zeke in sweatshirt and jeans on its wall, Mother and me in the same metal-and-fabric chairs as before.

Annoyed by our sudden appearance at his trailer's doorstep, he snarled, "What's so damn important we couldn't do this over the phone?"

Mother said sweetly, "I didn't have your number, dear. And you can't look up someone's number in the phone book because nobody's in the phone book these days, since everyone's on cells. Isn't that bothersome?"

"Well, you're bothering *me* some, lady." He heaved a sigh; weight of the world. "Well, what do you two want, anyway?"

Mother's hands were folded in her lap. "Just to ask for some clarification about what you were doing at your stepfather's house the evening he was shot and killed. You were seen arriving there, so let's not bother with a denial."

Mother's accusation hit him like a glass of water splashing his face. "OK, I was there—so what?"

"Was your stepfather alive when you left?"

"Yes! Look, if you're asking did I kill him, I did not. Maybe I *wanted* to, after Dixie told me what he'd done to her years ago, but I'm not the one who killed that old bas . . . old bum."

Mother's tone was butter-wouldn't-melt. "Bums are not known for their monetary wealth. What time did you arrive, Zeke? If you'll pardon the informality."

Red was crawling up his neck. "About seven thirty. But Patrick wouldn't let me in."

"A strapping lad like yourself couldn't push his way in? That seems unlikely to me."

"I don't care how it seems to you. I banged on the door, yelling that I wouldn't go away till I talked to him. Took a while, but he opened the door all right . . . and stuck a gun in my damn face!"

"That Smith & Wesson with a pearl handle? The handgun he kept in the clock in the entryway?"

Mother's questions seemed to let the air out of him. "Yeah. That one."

"Then you just . . . left?"

Zeke shrugged. "I just left. He said I was threatening him and no jury would convict him if he shot me." He paused. "There was a witness to me leavin', but it won't do a damn bit of good."

"Who?" Mother asked.

"That lady with the chicken farm who also got herself killed."

"*Anna Fowler* saw you leave?"

"Yeah. She was sitting at the curb in a burgundy Buick when I got run off the place."

I said, "Clever of you to invoke someone who can't say you actually *did* go inside."

As before, I was recording.

"My daughter here is correct," Mother said. "I'm afraid nothing you've shared with us absolves you of either murder."

His eyes showed white all round. "Either murder? You think

I strung up that poor woman? Get the hell out of here! Both of you!"

"Happy to," Mother said. "But we really can't go until we've had a look at your arms."

His face scrunched up like a wadded-up sheet of paper. "*What?*"

Mother gave our very reluctant host an impatient wiggled forefinger. "Push up your sleeves, dear. Let's get this out of the way."

He was wearing a sweatshirt.

"What the hell for? Lady, are you some kind of lunatic?"

"Don't change the subject. Anna Fowler scratched her killer's arms. If you have been scratched in that manner, it will only be a matter of time before law enforcement connects you to that tragedy. Your DNA under the victim's fingernails would spell your doom."

Melodramatic, I thought, *but accurate.*

He bared his teeth. "Well, nobody scratched me, so get the hell out of here! Both of you! Right now."

Mother didn't move. Neither of us did. She said, "Perhaps you should just humor me first. Or do you have something to hide?"

"Of course I don't!" He shook his head, astounded by us. "You think I killed this woman because she saw me go in the house?"

"That's right," Mother said, firmly triumphant. She went into full Perry Mason mode: "I put it to you that you took that gun away from Tool, forced him inside, marched him over to the chair, sat the man down, put that gun to his head, and fired."

Zeke sprung to his feet. "That's a damn lie!"

"Well, then, why not humor me? Roll up your sleeves!"

His irritation spread. "If it'll make the two of you leave any faster!" He pushed up the sleeves, one at a time, and turned each arm over.

Nary a scratch. Not even a tattoo.

"Satisfied?" he asked archly.

"It's a start," Mother replied. "We can't rule out that you had an accomplice on the second murder!"

Things were getting out of hand.

I touched Mother's arm. Whispered, "We should leave."

"You damn well better!" he shouted.

We did.

As I drove away, Mother said crossly, "Why did you stop my interview? I was just getting somewhere. He might have confessed!"

"He was only going to get madder. Besides, I believe Zeke was telling the truth. You can't really think there's an accomplice! Or do you have some idea you haven't shared with me about who his accomplice might be in the Fowler killing?"

Her arms were folded; she was on the verge of pouting but too keyed up to go there. "I do not. Have we hit a dead-end, dear, do you think?"

"No. There's a pattern here. So let's follow it."

Suddenly Sherlock gave Watson full attention. "I'm listening."

"Let's say Zeke doesn't have his confrontation with Tool, and leaves. But Tool lets Anna in for some reason—maybe she's offered to sell him her land."

Mother was nodding. "Tool puts the gun back in the clock, which Anna notices."

"Or maybe he just sets it down."

"They go in by the fire to talk. Anna tells him she'll see herself out—but *doesn't* leave."

"And Anna knows where the handgun is."

Mother continued, "He sits in the chair by the fire, she sneaks up behind him and—*blam!* Then leaves the gun on the floor to make the murder look like a suicide."

I frowned. "If so . . . who killed Anna and why?"

Mother shook a finger at the air. "Let's go back to what you said—follow the pattern. Say Anna *didn't* kill Tool. Whether she spoke to him inside or not is inconsequential—the important thing is she was around long enough to witness who arrived next."

I snapped my fingers. "That's it!"

"Dear, I would most likely have figured this out sooner, except . . . I'm off my meds."

"I know."

"And there's something else you should know."

What now?

"I think we may be being followed."

"Followed! Who by?"

"A flying saucer."

* * *

We returned to the Wee Wind, where Mother erased what was on the whiteboard, and instead made a timeline for the suspects who paid Patrick Tool a visit the evening he was murdered.

SUSPECT	ARRIVED	DEPARTED	OBSERVED
Dixie	7pm	7:10pm	Ma
Ma	7:10pm	7:30pm	Zeke
Zeke	7:30pm	7:45pm	Anna
Anna	7:45pm	8:15pm	?
?	8:15pm	?	?
Vivian	9:30pm		

Mother said, "Some of these times may be off, give or take a tick—but I know for certain Anna barely made it back to her farm before I arrived at eight thirty. So that much is set in stone."

"Anything else?" I asked.

"Only assumptions," she admitted. "But I believe they have merit."

I waited for Mother to gather her scattered thoughts, hoping she wouldn't bother picking some of them up.

"Since Anna did *not* go to the police," Mother said, forcing herself to speak slowly, "she must have decided to blackmail whoever she saw. She needed money, after all."

I nodded. "There certainly wasn't any love lost between her and Tool after he denied her a bank loan."

"*Correctamundo!* And blackmail must have been the other opportunity to save the chicken farm that she mentioned."

"That makes perfect sense," I said. Not always the case with Mother, especially off her meds. "So whoever it was had to have money—or *appear* to have money, at least to Anna." I paused. "We're talking about Wade Stetson here, aren't we?"

"Yes we are. But his motive has changed."

I was staring at the whiteboard. "You mean the money he owed Tool from that poker game? I thought that Houston letter, or dispatch, took care of that."

"It did. I learned it was quite valuable. But now he needed that missive back."

"Why?"

"My assumption? It was a forgery."

I hadn't considered that.

Mother went on, "You see, Wade was safe as long as Tool held onto the dispatch . . . but then it was offered for sale."

"For the new library."

"Correct again. And if the document is false, a routine authentication would mean exposure for the phony letter *and* the phony who sold it to Tool. Perhaps Wade thought after Tool died, he'd buy it back from the estate—or maybe he was always planning to kill Tool and destroy the dispatch. Either way, he suddenly had to move fast."

"And you came conveniently along."

She took a half-bow. "Indeed. The perfect patsy. Remember, he set up my meeting with Tool for early buying, throwing himself and Anna into the mix to disguise his real intent."

"But he never expected Anna to trip him up."

"Nor to encounter the great Vivian Borne in full detective mode! And her assistant Brandy, proving even a lesser light can cut through the darkness."

I let that pass. "How can we prove Wade committed both murders?"

"By first finding that dispatch."

I opened a hand. "But what if Wade got it the night he killed Tool, and destroyed the thing?"

Mother's smile was unsettling. "I have a way of finding out, dear."

Of course she would.

Mother retrieved her cell from the tote.

"Sebastian? Vivian Borne, here. How would you like to see that dispatch, and catch a killer in the process? . . . No, you won't be in any danger . . . Now, this is what I'd like you to do . . ."

Brandy's Trash 'n' Treasures Tip

Don't dismiss craft shows as a source for finding antiques and collectibles. Often treasures can be found among the homemade. It's wise to remember that folk artist Martha Nelson Thomas provided the genesis for the Cabbage Patch Kids craze of the 1980s by creating her similar Doll Babies first. I found an original Doll Baby at a craft show and stored it away in the attic knowing its value would increase, only to discover later a family of mice had made a home in its soft body. C'est la vie.

ELEVEN
Pistol Packin' Mama

Mother had called Dixie Norris next, letting me in on both sides of the conversation by way of her cell phone's speaker option.

"Might we borrow a key to your former residence, dear?"

Dixie replied, a good connection making it seem like she was in the Wee Wind. "What former residence is that?"

"The family homestead. I am hopeful that you may have retained a key. In fact, I would strongly assume you would have done so, though admittedly it's been some years since you lived there."

Dixie sounded wary. "Why do you want to know, Mrs. Borne? How does that factor into this unofficial investigation of yours?"

"It's only unofficial because I am not operating in my jurisdiction as an honorary deputy sheriff of Serenity County."

Neither was Serenity County her jurisdiction. She didn't *have* a jurisdiction!

"I don't know . . ." Dixie said, quite reasonably.

Mother went on, filling the silence: "I am assuming you may have, from time to time, entered the Tool mansion to get something of a nostalgic or even practical nature from your former digs. Perhaps you stopped by to see your mother when your stepfather was away, now and then. Time to time."

What was she up to?

"You aren't wrong, Mrs. Borne, in those assumptions. But I still don't see—"

Cutting in, Mother said, "My daughter and I would just like to have a look around the crime scene. We're examining some clues and a visit would provide context."

She really was off her meds.

Dixie said, "There's . . . understand I haven't been in that place in several years . . . but when I did go there, when my mother was still alive, there was a rock key—that is, a key in a fake rock—in the potted plant on the back porch."

"Thank you, dear!"

"Whatever you do, Mrs. Borne . . . I don't want to be part of it."

No one did.

"Understood, dear. And if we find your mother's missing will, we'll be sure to let you know!"

A sigh came over the line. Or was that me?

Dixie said, "You do that," and clicked off.

So did Mother.

"Are you kidding?" I demanded. "You expect me to accompany you, breaking into a crime scene!"

She summoned patience for her wayward child. "First, I rarely kid. Second, we have a key and permission of a family member. Third, we've come this far, haven't we?"

Right on all three counts.

"But," I said, "we're attempting to flush Wade Stetson out and confront him as a killer, which it appears he is, on at least two occasions. And we're doing it in a house full of guns!"

She smiled, shrugged. "Well, it *is* Texas, dear. Anyway, would Wade kill two women at the scene of a previous murder of his, and have to deal with the messy aftermath?"

"Well, that's reassuring."

She stood and put superhero fists at her waist. "Anyway, I intend to arm myself with the firearm hidden somewhere in the kitchen, no doubt in an easily accessible hiding place. I'll do that promptly after we enter."

"So we're doing this."

"Yes, darling girl. We're doing this."

The paint-peeling Federal-style edifice on the edge of a bluff displayed little of the wealth the banker had accumulated over the years, through business and marriage, casting the murdered man in a miserly light.

We waited until after midnight before dropping by, when most neighbors would likely be asleep. I parked the van out front since the point of our visit was not really to hide our presence, rather to draw Stetson out. Since Mother's new friend Sebastian was aware of our whereabouts, Mother felt confident we'd be safe.

I felt something, but confidence wasn't it.

The front door was barred with yellow police tape, hardly a welcoming sight, and the rear door up a small open porch bore the same yellow tape with black letters. We were holding our flashlights, beams crisscrossing like in an *X-Files* episode. *The truth is out there*, they used to say on that show. But the truth, if it was anywhere to be found, was in here.

I found the rock key in the potted plant as Dixie had said (and I was relieved, because otherwise Mother would have been producing her two lock picks, making us break-and-enterers). I removed the key from the fake rock and Mother worked the key in the lock.

She gave me a girlish grin. "Let's hope there's no alarm on!"

Yes, let's hope.

"Not likely to be," she said, latex-gloved right hand on the knob, about to twist it, "as the occupant with the code is deceased."

I followed Mother into a mud room, which contained only a primitive bench for removing boots and a simple wooden coat rack. The one modern feature awaiting us in the mud room was indeed a security alarm panel. But since it was not beeping, nor any red lights flashing, it was not armed, just as Mother had figured.

A door led to a kitchen, my beam exposing gleaming white appliances, and relatively modern cabinets, most likely at the insistence of Mrs. Tool, installed a few decades ago no doubt at considerable expense.

"Should we turn on some lights?" I asked.

"No, dear. We want to provide limited illumination, as if intruders had broken in."

"Well, isn't that what we are?"

"No, Brandy. We had a key."

"What about our flashlights? Can they stay on?"

I wasn't crazy about proceeding in the dark.

"Those we can and should use," she replied. "We want to project a limited invasion."

Maybe by that flying saucer she thought she'd spotted.

"Any *other* instructions? Like don't cross the beams?"

She held her flashlight under her face to show the displeasure in her expression. "Sarcasm is not helpful. I'll begin searching here, in the kitchen . . . You take the main room with the fireplace."

"To be clear, we're just *fake*-searching for the Alamo dispatch."

"Yes, dear." Her flashlight was still under her chin, invoking a seance somehow. "That document is probably long gone, either in collector hands, a safe deposit box at Tool's bank, Wade's own safe, or shredded, all of which are sad prospects. And the latter is almost certainly what became of the second Mrs. Tool's last will and testament."

"What *are* we looking for, then?"

"Nothing! If you run across something pertinent, so much the better. What we *are* doing is killing time—if you'll forgive the expression—until Wade arrives." She paused. "Now, since Wade is a dangerous, perhaps desperate individual, get to work. I hope to arm myself with a handgun concealed in this kitchen."

Mother *would* assign me the murder room, where the sparse colonial furniture only added to the gloom, casting strange, distorted shadows in my lowered beam. Tool had given himself the only comfortable seat in the room—the winged-back chair in front of the hearth, where he'd been shot, dark dried blood visible on the headrest.

The couch was made of wood, with spindles for the back and arms, and no cushions to look under. Other pieces included a drop-leaf walnut table with two chairs, a three-drawer writing desk with lift-up lid, and a solid oak five-shelf lawyer's bookcase.

The only impractical items were in a corner: a spinning wheel and crude wooden cradle. Perhaps Tool had purchased them as an investment, or maybe a statement of the role he thought women should play in society.

I crossed a round hook rug that looked new to look old, to the secretary, checking the drawers, which were empty, then lifted the lid, the inside also empty. It seemed the room was meant to epitomize what colonial life had been, and Tool had been born too late.

The glassed-in shelves of the bookcase caught my attention, as its top shelf was given over to several models of the Alamo itself. I went over for a closer look. Volume after volume of Alamo-related books were packed in—*The Gates of the Alamo*, *A Time to Stand*, *13 Days to Glory* and dozens more. DVDs and

Blu-ray video discs with Alamo themes, including John Wayne's, were turned face-out to provide imagery.

Next to the bookcase was a folk-art painting, obviously old, of the Alamo's commander, William B. Travis, looking resolute and young. It wasn't much bigger than a sheet of typing paper, and maybe that was what compelled me to pluck it off the wall.

The back of the framed picture did not have the usual brown-paper seal—little nails held a piece of cardboard in. The nails were loose enough to pop off with a fingernail, and hidden between that cardboard and the little canvas painting itself was a nine-by-twelve-inch manila envelope.

A beam entered the room, followed by Mother. "Shall we move on to the study—it's through that open door behind you."

When I didn't answer, she asked, "What's wrong, dear? What's that you have there?"

Numbly, I said, "I think I've found the dispatch. I think it may be in this envelope."

She came over, excited. "What are you waiting for, child? Open it!"

I held my flashlight between my knees and opened the envelope.

Mother spotlighted the contents with her flashlight beam: a stained yellowed paper with fold creases, protected in a clear plastic sleeve.

The dispatch had no heading, just a date of 4 March, 1836, addressed to *Lt. Col. Comdt. William Travis*, written in formal cursive. The content was brief, saying troops were on the way, and to hold out as long as they could. The dispatch was signed, with an elaborate flourish, *Major General Sam Houston*.

Mother, looking over my shoulder, said, "You've found it!"

Somebody turned on the lights!

"Thank you, ladies," a female voice said.

We turned to it, in admirable tandem. You couldn't have rehearsed it better.

Mary Jo Stetson stood in the connecting doorway.

"We're happy," Mother said, acidly sweet, "to help out such a good civic-minded citizen of Tranquility."

"Not as happy as I am," the lovely blonde said. "I thought the document would be somewhere in this house. Old Tool wouldn't trust a wall safe, and he wouldn't put it in one of his deposit boxes at his bank, either. An Alamo buff like him would want to take the thing out and look at it when the mood struck him."

A hand at her side came up with a gun.

She went on: "And wasn't it thoughtful of the old boy to leave all these weapons around—the one in the clock, which I used to put him out of his miserly misery, and this SIG Sauer from the study."

"Don't forget the Kimber from the kitchen," Mother said, dropping the flashlight and yanking a black pistol from her waistband. No Western gunslinger could have done it better.

"It's like a game of Clue, dear," Mother told our surprise guest. "Only it's Mrs. Borne in the kitchen with a gun."

Mary Jo had been shocked enough not to immediately shoot, but the weapon in her hand was steady, and pointed our way.

Mother went on, "I would guess this is what folks in Texas calls a Mexican stand-off." She tilted her head toward me without taking her eyes—or her handgun—off Mary Jo. "Is it all right to say that, Brandy? Mexican stand-off."

"Might be considered racist," I said. "Bad taste at best."

"Well, what can I call it, then? This is a specific situation."

"Call it a stalemate."

Mary Jo's laugh was casual; she had regained her poise. "Not accurate, Mrs. Borne. Not really." She called out, "Wade!"

Her husband appeared from the shadows of the entryway, in a black short-sleeve shirt and black jeans and black shoes. A regular Texas ninja.

"Don't tell me," Mother said to him. "You have the Beretta from the bedroom. This Clue is a tricky game."

Wade came forward and aimed the gun and its barrel right at Mother. "That's right, Mrs. Borne. But the Beretta is in the living room now."

I blurted out: "Sebastian knows where we are, should anything happen to us."

Mary Jo's reaction was not what I expected. She laughed. "Who do you think forged the Houston dispatch?"

"Then it *is* a fake," Mother said.

"Yes, and a damn good one. I followed you into the alley after he called me while you were in his store. And I should have finished the job. Now drop the Kimber."

"No," Mother said.

Mary Jo seemed confused now. So did her husband.

She sounded a little too much like Clint Eastwood when she said, "This is no less a Mexican stand . . . stalemate with one gun against two. I'm an expert pistol shot, and at least one of you will take a bullet-with-your-name-on-it. So, ask yourself—do you feel lucky?"

"Nobody has to die here," I said. Mother had taken this far enough. "Take this document and go. And then it'll just be your words against ours."

"My daughter does have a point," Mother said, still steadily training the weapon on them. "I have a history of mental illness. There's an argument to be made that you can take this document, destroy it and leave no evidence, and as witnesses? We two are questionable at best."

Well, she wasn't Clint Eastwood now, but that was pretty well-played. I tossed the document in its plastic sleeve to the floor. Wade looked at it but his wife didn't.

Mother, stalling for time, said, "I must admit I didn't figure you and Wade for working together. He frankly doesn't seem like the murdering type."

"No," Mary Jo said. "He doesn't."

I spoke and everyone, including Mother, seemed surprised. "Why did you kill Tool?"

"He had to go when Wade admitted to me that the dispatch was a forgery. I wasn't part of that stupid scheme." She sighed. "And then, of course, I had to silence Anna Fowler, after she saw me leaving here. The foolish old witch thought she could squeeze me for money."

Mother looked at Wade. "Something you might want to consider, Wade."

"Yeah," he said flatly, Beretta not quite as steady now. "What's that?"

"You didn't commit either murder. A jury might be convinced your wife acted on her own accord."

"You're in this as deep as I am!" Mary Jo said to her husband. "Don't listen to her. Are you with me, baby? Are you with me?"

"I . . . I . . ."

That hesitation was all it took. Or maybe she had planned it this way all along . . . but suddenly the SIG Sauer's barrel swung his way. The blast reverberated in the sparse room.

Mother's handgun barked and—I could hardly believe it!—shot the gun out of Mary Jo's hand! Like the Lone Ranger! Which made me Tonto, not a bad gig, and I can't believe how happy it made me, seeing that Mother had shot Mary Jo's thumb off. This isn't the kind of book that reports the spurt that ensued, or the blood-curdling scream she emitted.

I could move faster than Mother, so I was the one who went after the gun the blonde dropped, and snatched it up and pointed it at her.

I needn't have bothered.

Mary Jo was kneeling, holding her damaged hand with the remaining good one. Whether she was crying for herself or her dead husband, to whom she'd performed a Wild West shot between the eyes, I couldn't say. Maybe both.

On second thought, she was crying for only one person: Mary Jo.

"Mother," I said, returning to her side. "Since when are you a crack shot?"

"Since never, dear."

"But . . . you shot the gun out of her hand!"

"I wasn't aiming at her hand."

Brandy's Trash 'n' Treasures Tip

A good place to look for new merchandise is in your own home! Our garage is stuffed with antiques and collectibles Mother has found over the years but refuses to part with. When our stock gets low, I sneak things out of there. So far she hasn't gotten wise, although sometimes she wants to keep an item I "found," so back into the garage it goes.

TWELVE
Git Along Little Dogies

And so it was that the Borne girls again found themselves in a holding cell, though with separate accommodations this time around.

The moment I entered my cell, I stumbled to the padded bench, flopped down, and either fell asleep or passed out.

The next thing I knew a forty-something female guard with a covered tray roused me. Her eyes had seen everything, including—judging by her close-cropped coiffure—an occasional hair-pulling inmate.

I asked, "What time is it?"

My watch had been confiscated.

"Seven."

I groaned. Four hours of sleep at best.

"How's my mother?"

"She's already eaten. Seemed to enjoy herself."

"I'm not surprised. I don't suppose I could have a shower?"

"No. But there's a kit on the sink for your use."

At least that was something. My mouth tasted like the inside of a dirty sneaker. Well, what I'd imagine the inside of a dirty sneaker would taste like.

"Thanks," I said. "What happens next?"

"Chief Garrison will interview you both in an hour," the guard replied, then left me alone with my tray, the sink, and what little was left of my dignity.

The food looked (and smelled) like the kind of free breakfast that came with a low-end hotel reservation: weak coffee, rubbery scrambled eggs, dried biscuit, and something the prison system thought passed for hash browns.

But no meal in recent memory ever tasted so good.

Afterward, I opened the kit, which contained a small soap (not big enough to carve into a phony gun for a real break-out), a tiny toothpaste tube, a mini-brush, half-size comb, scrap of washcloth, and small towel perfect for drying dishes.

I did what I could to look presentable, pinching my cheeks for color. Then I sat on the bench/bed to await my interrogation. Yes, I know it's called an interview now. But I knew an interrogation situation when I saw one.

Just imagine—Patrick Tool, Anna Fowler, and Wade Stetson would still be alive, and Mary Jo would have two thumbs, if her husband hadn't gotten himself into that poker game, losing more than he could afford and cooking up the dispatch scheme.

In something less than an hour, the same reasonably human guard returned to walk me out of stir and on my way, I expected, to a cold interview cubicle to be shackled to the wall or maybe a table; but instead I was escorted into a conference room.

Mother was already there, seated at the near end of the oval table, appearing relaxed, hair neatly arranged, her clothes looking pressed, unlike mine. Had she put her blouse and slacks under the plastic mattress and slept on them in her underwear? These were the kind of thoughts rattling around in my head while in custody.

In contrast, Garrison, standing at the head of the table, his face weary and drawn, looked as if he'd slept in his clothes, like me.

Mother said cheerfully, "Ah, there's my darling daughter. So we can begin!"

It was like a meeting she'd called.

I sat across the table from Mother to keep from strangling her. Always good not to commit a new crime when you're waiting to deal with whatever we'd been booked for.

Garrison, in an even higher-pitched voice than usual, began angrily, "Never in my entire career, never in my wildest dreams or *nightmares* have I ever encountered two such disruptive, meddling—"

"How *is* Mrs. Stetson?" Mother inquired.

He sighed. "She is in the hospital wing of the Tranquility County Jail, under guard."

"Were the medics able to save her thumb?"

"No. It was too badly damaged by you."

"Allegedly by me," Mother insisted. "And I'm already being

more forthcoming than I should, as we have no legal representation. You recovered my cell phone? And were able to play back the recording of the incident?"

She had no cell-phone password—a simple swipe would take you into the world of Vivian Borne. Exiting it was rather more demanding.

Garrison nodded. "We know what transpired at the Tool home is recorded there. But we have some things still to clear up."

Mother folded her hands as if about to say grace. "Dixie Norris has told you that we were there with her knowledge and permission? And a key she'd provided?"

Another nod.

She added brightly, "And the forged dispatch? Has it been taken in as evidence?"

"It has. And we've picked up Sebastian at his home. He's currently in a holding cell in the County Jail, and we intend to charge him."

"On fraud by way of forgery? I don't believe he should be held as an accessory to attempted murder—I don't think he had any idea how far the Stetsons would take this matter. Of course, I'm not an attorney, but—"

"Mr. Sebastian is refusing to answer any questions until his lawyer arrives, but I have no doubt he'll eventually cooperate to save his own neck."

"Satisfactory," Mother said, invoking Nero Wolfe again. "Would you mind answering one more tiny question?"

"Would it matter if I did?"

Ignoring that, Mother went on, "What about the skin found beneath Mrs. Fowler's fingernails?"

Garrison's eyes tensed. "How did you know about that?"

"An elementary deduction, my dear Chief Garrison."

A defeated sigh. "DNA test results won't be back for several weeks, but Mrs. Stetson has visible scratches on her arms."

"That's good to know!" Mother said. "I've not seen her in short sleeves since the murder."

Garrison leaned forward, apparently having deduced the location of his backbone. "There's a little matter of you not being licensed to carry a firearm in the state of Texas."

"First of all, that's hypocritical considering firearms can be purchased at convenience stores in these parts. And second of all, I wasn't 'carrying' a firearm—I had confiscated one in the Tool home. As a good citizen of these great United States, as well as an honorary deputy sheriff of Serenity County, I was merely doing my civic duty."

"Mrs. Borne," Garrison said tightly, eyes so watery he might have been near tears, "your interference in this case may well have you facing obstruction of justice charges."

"We did not obstruct justice," Mother said, chin up. "We *brought* justice. Do you *really* want all the paperwork and bad publicity incurred in charging two famous authors for solving these murders for you?"

Garrison seemed knocked back by the weight of her words.

I finally spoke up. "Or would you rather be given," I said, "full credit for the apprehension of a murderer?"

At least till this book came out.

"What say you, Chief?" Mother asked innocently.

His eyes were closed. Was he praying?

"All right," he said finally. "But on one condition."

I said, "Get out of town before sundown?"

An emphatic nod. "Sooner, if possible."

One more locale to add to our "not wanted" list.

Mother was saying, "Naturally, we'll need to come back for the trial."

"I doubt there'll be one," Garrison said.

Mother frowned. "And why is that? The woman does have a path to a reduced sentence by claiming the murders were her husband's idea, and she was protecting his image."

"I know something about Mary Jo Stetson," the chief replied. "She's a vain woman who'd rather plead guilty and get this over with than appear in the media for weeks on end wearing an orange jump suit."

"Not a good color for her," Mother said, not joking in the least. She swore by her color charts back in Serenity. "And that bandaged hand would hardly be the ideal fashion accessory. There's a good chance a jury would throw the book at her. Of course, if you need us, we could always attend via Zoom."

Mother was not about to be left out. She did love a juicy trial, especially when she was the star witness. And the thought of a jury and courtroom gallery leaning forward to watch her perform on a TV screen rivaled an actual in-person performance.

Me? I never wanted to come back.

In the flesh or on TV or otherwise.

Our van had been transported to the station's lot, and after Mother and I were signed out and our confiscated items returned (except Mother's cell phone, as evidence), I drove us back to the glamping ground to pack up our belongings in the Wee Wind for the long trip home.

Stepping into the small trailer, we knew that someone had been there in our absence. Our clothes and personal items were strewn about, suitcases opened and linings ripped out.

"Who did this," I whimpered, "and what do they *want*?"

Mother frowned. "It can't be something we bought because those items were in the van parked at the police station. And I don't see how this would have anything to do with the Tool situation. I say we pack up and leave immediately and drive straight through until we get home."

"Then I need a shower first." I'd rather face further danger smelling clean than settling for having washed up in a jailhouse sink; some things are non-negotiable.

"Very well," she said. "But take a knife along! Better safe than sorry. Meanwhile, I'll pack up while you're gone."

Take a knife along! Was she kidding? Then I thought about it for a few seconds and, from the kitchen drawer, I selected a wicked-looking chef's knife. Then I gathered fresh clothes from among the scattered.

In the communal bath, I checked all the showers and, finding them empty, selected the farthest one from the door. I left the plastic curtain open while I washed up with soap in one hand and the knife in the other. Absurd? After what I'd been through last night?

I was exiting the shower when a young woman entered in a rumpled prom dress, smeared mascara, and tangled hair. She froze at the sight of the knife, turned and ran.

Time to put glamping in the rearview mirror. I quickly got dressed.

By the time I'd returned to the Wee Wind, Mother was loading our suitcases into the van. I took one last swing through the trailer for anything left behind, then joined her in the vehicle.

"We should settle up with Ma," Mother said, "then hit the road."

When we entered her trailer, Ma was seated at the little round kitchen table. Dressed in floral cotton blouse, and shorts that showed off surprisingly attractive legs, she had replaced the bottle of Wild Turkey with a ceramic squirrel coffee mug, its tail a handle.

"There'll be no bill," Ma announced with a flip of her free hand, ceramic squirrel mug in the other. "Just heard it on the scanner—Mrs. Butter-Wouldn't-Melt Mary Jo Stetson has been charged with the murders of Patrick Tool and Anna Fowler. Nice work, ladies."

Before Mother or I could protest about a free stay (actually I don't think either of us was about to), our hostess held up a hand. "You findin' who killed Patrick, that's payment enough."

"That's very generous of you, dear," Mother said.

And would go a long way toward lessening the debt we'd incurred on this trip.

Ma stared into her coffee. "He were a devil, Patrick Tool, but once upon a time, a handsome one. Charm the bark off a tree, that 'un. Some things you can't just explain! And I wouldn't've had my son, or Lacy, without that reprobate."

There didn't seem much else to say on the subject. After a respectful pause, Mother asked, "Were there any strangers in the camp last night?"

Ma frowned. "We don't run a real tight ship around here—Saloon's a money-maker welcome to one and all. You have somebody in mind?"

"Anyone not registered," Mother asked, "or a car you hadn't seen before?"

Her shrug spoke volumes. "Sometimes a guest will pick someone up in a local bar and bring 'em back here . . . but I ain't one to judge. So, no. Why?"

"Our trailer had been broken into while we were otherwise

occupied—solving a murder? And while nothing seems to be missing, it was ransacked. It's a tad troubling."

Visualizing any damages wiping out our free bill, I added, "But there wasn't any harm to the trailer."

That I'd noticed.

Ma said, "There was plenty of whoopin' and hollerin' in the night, but mostly from gals checked in here for the weekend, fixin' to leave today, gettin' friendly with some fellers they rounded up in town. Nothin' not normal."

I asked, "Do you have a security video system?"

"We have some security cameras around camp. Maybe you noticed 'em."

"Good!" Mother said.

Ma shook her head. "None of 'em hooked up. Strictly for show. Couldn't afford *really* puttin' in anything of that nature."

"Understood," Mother said, withdrawing something from her tote. "Dear, might I impose on you to deliver this to the receptionist at the police station?"

Mother handed Ma an autographed photo of Morgan Wallen. Vivian Borne always tried to keep her promises, particularly those tied to a bribe—she didn't want to damage her reputation, particularly with future prospective snitches. (Couldn't wait to see how she would deliver Ma her promised genuine Davy Crockett squirrel-tail cap.)

Ma nodded. "I'll see the little gal gets it. Now, you folks have a safe trip back to civil-ay-zation."

Seated behind the wheel in the van, I said, "Isn't that receptionist sure to know Moran Who's-It didn't really sign that photo? 'Dear Jenny, thanks for a wonderful night'? Why didn't you just forge his signature and leave it at that?"

"Because, my dear naive Brandy-kins, what I inscribed is what *I* would have wanted. This way, the photo won't ever enter the collecting market, because she'll never part with it."

There was some logic to that.

She flipped a hand toward my grip on the steering wheel. "Now let's go, dear. We have a long drive ahead of us. Chop chop! . . . That isn't offensive, is it? To Asian Americans?"

"Roughly, it's the equivalent of going 'woo woo woo' to a Native American."

"Well, then," Mother said, settling back, "we'll leave it out of the book."

Even though the route home we planned would add an extra three hours onto the eleven-hour trip, I headed east to avoid any Indian reservations. We couldn't afford either accidentally invading another shrine or Mother saying something inappropriate.

Once over the Texas border into Arkansas, I swung north, stopping only for gas, bathroom breaks, coffee, and convenience store food to eat on the way.

I also kept in touch with Tony via text to report our progress. What I didn't tell him, however, was that Mother would occasionally drive, an admittedly questionable decision I made after falling asleep at the wheel in Missouri, barely avoiding a side-trip into a deep ravine. Mother was back on her meds, so—assuming they'd had time to kick in—we should be fine. After all, the time she went driving across a cornfield she had maintained the speed limit.

When awake, I kept an eye on cars behind us, in case we were being followed, driving just under the limit so others would have to pass us, making a tail more apparent. The Tool case was over, apparently, but *somebody* had ransacked our Wee Wind. I really didn't relax until we'd crossed into Iowa for the last leg of the journey home.

It was a little after midnight when I pulled into the driveway of our two-story white stucco home, having left Tranquility around ten that morning. Just twenty-four hours ago we were breaking into Tool's mansion. Times flies when you're having felonious fun.

Tony, knowing I would want to see Sushi ASAP, texted he would drop her off (he had a key), since we'd be coming into Serenity from the south of town and his cabin was north.

And there Sushi was, meeting me at the door, so excited I was home that she (of course) piddled on the floor, which made me feel good (her excitement not the piddling) because of the way I'd been ignored not so long ago in favor of Rocky.

I scooped her up and told Mother not to wake us until mid-morning. Upstairs, I got out of my clothes and into some pajamas and warm socks. Then, snuggled with Sushi in my Art Deco bed, I finally felt safe.

You know how they say, "Had I but known," is a silly cliche to use in a book? Maybe so.

But . . . had I only known what was yet to come . . .

Brandy's Trash 'n' Treasures Tip

Pop-up stores that sell antiques are another option for finding fresh merchandise. Also known as flash retailing, these temporary businesses appear for a limited time in high foot-traffic areas, usually in an empty store front. Online sites such as "Storefront" and "Pop Up Shops" can aid in your search, as well as local newsprint advertising, and social media postings. Mother just calls Mrs. Clarence Weisenheimer, who knows everything.

THIRTEEN
Home on the Range

I woke to the familiar, reassuring smell of coffee and fried bacon.

Sushi had abandoned me, her loyalty vanishing at the first sound of Mother moving around in the kitchen—first rule of doggie-dom: meal over master (or mistress). I considered throwing back the covers and getting out of bed. I thought about that a while, then finally did. Put on a robe and my moose slippers, then descended the stairs on somewhat uncertain legs.

Wandering into the kitchen, I found Mother also in her bathrobe and slippers (non-moose variety), tending the stove. Sushi was standing so close to her, waiting for a morsel to drop, the animal could have been a furry appendage.

"Ah, Brandy, glad to see you among the living," she said cheerfully. "I was just about to send Sushi up to check on you."

A shih tzu alarm clock might sound cute, but getting roused by a ravenous Sushi wasn't. It consisted of a bop on the nose with a paw, repeated as often as necessary.

"What are we having," I asked, rubbing my eyes, "besides coffee and bacon?"

My stomach was growling worse than Sushi's after surviving a day of just enough on-the-road gas station food to maintain a pulse, yearning all the way for good old-fashioned bland Midwestern cuisine—any fare that didn't contain Tabasco or barbeque sauce. Nothing makes home sweet home seem sweeter than vacation days away, even working ones—murder-solving among them.

"Scrambled eggs," she replied as to the menu, adding, "And your favorite."

"Not Danish puffs?"

"Yes, Danish puffs."

My stomach was ready to stop growling and start barking!

Mother only made that delicious breakfast treat when she was trying to get back in my good graces. She would make use of a recipe she'd "borrowed" decades ago from the bakery chef at the Admiral Hotel in Copenhagen, which she had ever since passed off as an old Borne family favorite.

And she succeeded: all was forgiven.

(*Note to Anne Kaufman*: This isn't too hard, requiring only 2 mixing bowls, 1 saucepan, and 1 cookie sheet.)

Danish Puffs
(in three parts, translated from original recipe)

Part one:

½ cup soft butter or margarine
1 cup flour
2 tbsp. water

In a medium mixing bowl, cut butter into flour, sprinkle water over mixture, mix and roll into a ball and divide in half. On an ungreased cookie sheet, pat each half into a 12x3 inch strip, 3 inches apart.

Part two:

½ cup butter or margarine
1 tsp. almond extract
1 cup water
1 cup flour
3 eggs

Heat butter and water to rolling boil in a medium saucepan. Remove from heat and stir in almond extract and flour. Stir vigorously over low heat until mixture forms a ball— one minute or sooner. Remove from heat, beat in eggs until smooth and glossy. Divide ball in half and spread evenly over the two strips on the cookie sheet. Bake at 350 degrees for 60 minutes or until top is brown. Cool to room temperature.

Part three:

1½ cup powdered sugar
2 tbsp. soft butter
1½ tsp. vanilla
1–2 tbsp. warm water
sliced almonds

In a small mixing bowl, blend all together until smooth. Add glaze to cooled pastry and sprinkle with sliced almonds, or other nuts. Cut into serving pieces.

We sat in our bathrobes at the Duncan Phyfe table, eating in blessed silence but for the sounds of coffee slurping, pastry munching, and doggie yapping, as Sushi demanded her share of bacon.

Then Mother said, "I realize we just got back, dear, but I'll be going to the shop this morning."

We usually open on Tuesdays and today was definitely a Tuesday.

I growled and it wasn't Sushi or my stomach. "I don't think I'm up to it."

"Oh, come now," she chided, "what are you going to do with yourself? Sit around here and mope all day? When you fall off a horse, you get right back up in the saddle."

"You're thinking about bikes," I said, ready to shed all Western platitudes, "and I'm not moping about anything, just recovering. That was a tough trip going and returning and particularly in-between."

"Be that as it may, dear, we have a van filled with items we brought back that won't price and tag themselves."

I was tired and feeling sorry for myself and overall grumpy, and I guessed I could just as easily do all those things at the shop. Besides, I wouldn't be going to see Tony until this evening, which instead of looking forward to, I was dreading, fearing I'd no longer have a fiancé after he heard the details of our most recent escapade—what little he didn't already know, thanks to a couple of Southwestern police chiefs he'd spoken with on the phone.

Again, too many chiefs and not enough innocence.

"You win," I said to Mother. Not the first time I'd said that to her. Probably the hundredth. Just wasn't fair to have to deal with her when she'd been up a while and I'd just crawled back into being alive. But the Danish puffs bribery had helped.

Leaving Mother to the breakfast cleanup, I went upstairs where I took a long hot bubble bath, scrubbing off any remnants of Texas dust. And that helped, too, a whole heck of a lot.

With my hair freshly washed, some mascara and tinted lip balm (Beekman) expertly applied, I put on leggings and a pink cashmere cardigan I'd bought during the after-Christmas sales.

And now, finally feeling almost normal, I went downstairs to join Mother, out of her bathrobe and into her favorite emerald velour pantsuit, lovely wavy silver hair styled in a bun.

"Aren't you a *vision*, dear!" she said, uttering a rare compliment.

"Thank you?" Because such words from her usually were connected to something she was after.

"But I do believe you're due for a hair touch-up, or at least some highlights."

She just didn't know when to quit.

"I'm going to the shop with you," I said. "Don't bother pushing the soft soap. Already had my bubble bath."

Since the weather had turned frigid during the night, Mother and I donned warmer coats. Yesterday was Texas heat, but today it was snowing. No cowboy boots—UGGs.

In the foyer, Sushi pawed at my leggings, wanting to go along, and then tagged after me as I got the door open. I scooped the furball up, not giving her a chance to turn tail and run back into the warm house, as she'd occasionally do.

While I was happy or anyway relieved to be back in Serenity, I found driving through the downtown only brought back the town's almost spooky similarity to Tranquility. Hopefully that would fade like a bad dream with only the better moments lingering, unspecific, just a feeling.

In the alley behind the shop, I parked in our usual spot, and while Mother went in through the rear door to turn off the alarm, I began unloading the van.

In the kitchen, I set the boxes on the laminated boomerang-print table, then got busy making coffee, preheating the oven and putting peanut-butter dough from the fridge on a cookie sheet. (Yes, I washed my hands first.)

Mother, returning to the kitchen from her job of hoisting our flags outside, was shivering and rubbing her arms. "I do believe we're in for a real blizzard."

Which wasn't unusual for the end of March, and even early April in the Midwest.

That was fine by me. The fewer customers coming in with questions about our trip, the better. I wasn't anti-social, just recovering. Although, frankly, I could have used a vacation after that vacation.

With my kitchen tasks complete, I moved the boxes into the entryway and set them on the floor, then started the computer to begin researching the items we'd scored to determine how they should be priced.

Meanwhile, Mother began unpacking the new merchandise and making a list of what we had. Her contributions were: a Hopalong Cassidy glass coffee mug; six reproductions of shot glasses from old Western saloons; a vintage McCoy chuck wagon cookie jar; and a brass mantle clock with attached horse. Not bad for a woman who had also been busy solving two murders. My haul included: a Golden West Coffee tin; a silver longhorn belt buckle; those glued-together dancing frogs; the Frankoma book vase; a pair of brass cowboy bookends; tin gold-mining pan; the turquoise and silver bracelet; Navajo horse blanket; and the Cowboy Checkers board game.

Holdbacks would be the Grant Wood art nouveau necklace, which Mother was keeping; the BB branding iron I was keeping; and the minor-league baseball card collection that would bring the best price on the net.

"I guess we didn't do so badly," I admitted. Especially since Ma gave us free lodging.

Mother gestured to the curio cabinet near the front door where we showcased seasonal items. "They'll make a nice display, and we'll put a sale tag on the frogs for someone ambitious enough to have them professionally repaired."

The oven dinged, indicating it was pre-heated and ready for the cookies. But I was otherwise occupied at the moment.

"What do you want to do first?" I asked, fingers on the keyboard.

"The horse clock. It was made by United. Oh! And this was in the box with it." She held out a palm. "It's some kind of key."

I nodded at the small object with the little plastic handle. "I found it in the back of the van. I think maybe it goes with the clock."

"Not hardly, dear. It's too large for a clock key, and besides, our purchase is battery-operated."

She came around the counter. "It looks like it might go to a locker at an airport or bus station. Or possibly a storage unit."

"Is there a number imprinted on it?" I asked. "Or some indication of its source?"

Mother held her glasses out from her eyes to make the lenses magnify more. "Just the numbers one-one-four. *Where* did you say you found it?"

"In the back of the van on the floor."

She mulled that for a few moments. "You don't suppose this belonged to our red-haired hitchhiker?"

"Ruby?" I shrugged. "Maybe. She rode back there, after all. And since I cleaned the van out just before our trip, I'm sure I would have noticed it."

Sushi barked, *Put the cookies in!*

Mother replaced her glasses on her nose. Her eyes narrowed behind the lenses. "There was something a little off about that girl."

"Like what?"

"The way she acted at checkpoint Charlie."

"Like how? I didn't notice anything. But then I was driving and pretending you were having trouble breathing."

"Thinking back on it, she got quite nervous, and ducked down on the floor. Perhaps so the officers wouldn't notice her."

"Well, it *is* illegal to ride in a van like that, no seats in the back, no seat belts either, of course."

"Yes," she said with a frown, "and that would explain hiding from the law."

I frowned back at her. "They *were* looking for the casino robbers, remember."

Mother nodded. "Or robb-*er*."

I scoffed. "Oh, but that couldn't have been Ruby! She was nice."

"So was the Pied Piper," Mother said. "And look where it got the rats."

"Your analogy is all wrong. *We'd* be the Pied Piper in it."

"Well, that makes Ruby the rat, doesn't it? What do we *really* know about her?"

"Not much," I admitted, trying to recall conversations we'd had with her. "She said she was from some small town in North Dakota, and was a drifter, doing this and that."

"Precisely. She didn't even give us her last name."

"But Ruby was in a holding cell, like we were, the night of that casino heist."

Mother smiled slyly. "Now you're talking like a mystery writer—*think* like one, too. What better place to hide from the law than right under its nose?"

Sushi barked again. *Stop blabbing and put those cookies in the oven!*

Mother gestured with an open hand. "Picture this: she holds up the armored truck outside the casino—either by herself or with help—then hides the cash in a locker somewhere, goes to a bar and picks a fight to get herself arrested."

At least half-convinced Mother might be onto something, I picked up the possible scenario. "Then we give her a ride, and because the highway patrol has been alerted about us by Chief Hunter of the Cherokee tribe, we get waved on."

"A real piece of luck for Ruby," Mother said.

I tapped the little key on the counter. "But why leave this in our van?"

"To keep from being caught with it! And to be rid of it before any more highway stops by law enforcement. And, since we mentioned heading to Tranquility for a few days, Ruby thought she could retrieve the key there. We even told her where we were staying!"

I shook a fist at the air. "Which would explain the van's alarm going off! Plus, I thought I saw her once in the Saloon at the campground."

Mother was nodding. "It all fits, dear."

I frowned. "Only . . . she called from Austin, remember?"

"An old ploy. On a cell, anyone can say they're anywhere."

I played devil's advocate. "OK, but why didn't Ruby just tell the owner or manager, of wherever the locker was, that she'd lost her key, and get another one?"

"Because then she'd have to say what was *in* the locker to prove she was the one who'd rented it. And the owner of the lockers, or his manager or whatever, would likely be right there when she opened it. Particularly at an airport or bus station."

That made sense. "We can also rule out any storage unit that would require paperwork and/or renters who had to provide their own lock and key."

Mother was nodding. "Our best bet would be a bus station, where the lockers are automated to rent by the hour, and even days. But if this *was* Ruby, she'd have to stow the money away *before* she got a ride from us."

My fingers were dancing over the keyboard.

A disgruntled Sushi trotted in from the kitchen to find out what the holdup was with the cookies, the only holdup she was interested in.

"Tahlequah does have a Greyhound bus station downtown," I said.

"Go to its website."

I did.

"See if it has any photos," Mother instructed.

Yes, there were! I clicked on an inside-the-station image showing an area with customer seating to the left, a ticket counter to the right, and at the back, a row of lockers.

Mother asked excitedly, "Can you come in closer on the lockers?"

I could and did.

They were automated, numbering from 101 to 125, and the keys that remained in the lockers looked similar to the one we had.

"What do we do now?" I asked, indicating the little key she held between the thumb and middle finger of her right hand. "You know she could show up here or at the house, any time, looking for it."

"Let's put the key back in the van," Mother said. "She can't know we found it. In the meantime, I'll call Chief Hunter."

"Or Tony," I suggested.

"Or both," Mother affirmed.

But there wasn't time for calling either, much less returning the key to the van.

The old-fashioned bell sounded over the front door as it opened and our old pal Ruby blew in with the snow. She wore a North Dakota t-shirt under a denim jacket with torn jeans, not nearly warm enough for the weather. Not surprising, if her last stop had been Texas.

I shivered, but not from the wind blowing our way. The ill wind.

Mother, closing her fingers over the key, acted surprised. "Why, look who's here! Ruby! What a pleasant surprise! We're so glad you took us up on the offer to come visit our fair city." She jabbed me with an elbow. "Aren't we, Brandy? Glad?"

"Ecstatic," I replied, forcing a smile.

The redhead closed the door, then locked it with an ominous click. Turning, she said, "I want that key, Mrs. Borne."

"If I spoke of you getting the key to the city," Mother said, "that was only figurative, dear."

Ruby walked toward the counter, slow, steady, menacing, like an Earp heading to the O.K. Corral. "I'll have the *real* key, Mrs. Borne—the one in your hand. Think I didn't see you palm it?"

"Give it to her," I whispered.

"But it's our bargaining chip," Mother whispered back.

Ruby said, "I'm standing right here, ladies."

I turned to Mother and no whispering followed. I said right out loud, "There's no bargaining and there's no chip. This is no poker game. Give her the key."

Ruby sneered. "You'd better listen to your daughter, you crazy old broad."

Mother raised her chin. "There's no need for rudeness! . . . Very well. But you should know that I've already called Chief Hunter in Tahlequah and told him he could find the casino cash at the bus station in locker number one-one-four."

"And the local chief of police," I said firmly, "is on the way. You really *should* leave."

Maybe this *was* a poker game!

But Ruby called our bluff. From a pocket of the denim jacket came a small revolver. "I'm not leaving without what I came for!"

A fuzzy blur flew through the air and Sushi's sharp little teeth latched on to Ruby's forearm, the gun discharging. Mother and I had no time to react, the bullet hitting a Margaret Keane painting hanging high on the wall of a big-eyed cowgirl in a cowboy hat, giving the little gal a third eye in her forehead. A print, not an original, thankfully.

I was also thankful that this wasn't Sushi's (near) first gunfight, and the little doggie did not cotton to any hombre holding her pardners under the gun.

As Ruby struggled like a bucking bronco to remove the snarling Sushi from her arm, I leapt over the counter—Mother hightailing around it—and together we took the woman down like a steer we wrangled, Mother wrestling the gun from Ruby's hand.

Sushi, seeing we were in control, let go of Ruby, who promptly kicked me in the stomach, herding me back into Mother, whose shooting iron went flying. Ruby scrambled after the six-shooter and snatched it up.

Momentarily stunned, I watched helplessly while Ruby got the drop on Mother.

Using the counter to pull myself up, I grabbed the heavy brass horse clock and brought it down on Ruby's head, putting an end to the dust-up. The redhead went down like a mule kicked her in the noggin.

Mother, regaining possession of the gun, said, "Well, I hope that's the end of all this gunplay."

So did I.

"Now that we lassoed her," Mother said, spitting imaginary chaw, pulling up her velour trousers, "let's use some of our packing string and hogtie her, darlin'."

I did so, but not until after I had picked Sushi up and hugged her, telling her she was a good girl and that cookies were in her near future.

(*Brandy to the reader:* Mother insisted on revising much of the above confrontation scene with Ruby. Apologies.)

* * *

Two ambulances and three police cars descended on our shop, effectively blocking off the street, bringing bystanders out of stores and houses to gape and point and wag their heads. Not the neighborhood's first time at the Borne rodeo. (That one was me.).

Mother had told the dispatcher three people were injured. She herself had twisted her ankle in the battle over the gun, and I could barely walk after the kick to my stomach, while Ruby was still unconscious, her head bleeding from where I clocked her with the clock.

Mother and I were put into one ambulance, Ruby in the other, Mother advising Officer Munson, who arrived first on the scene not terribly happy to see us, that this woman was dangerous and might try to escape. So, even if he wasn't the sharpest knife in the Serenity drawer, he'd be on high alert as he rode with her.

Another officer, Shawntea Monroe—with whom we also had a history (but friendlier)—took charge of Sushi. In hindsight, it's quite possible the little furball attacked Ruby thinking the woman was the cause of the delay of the cookies getting baked.

In the ER I was given a CT scan of my stomach to check for internal bleeding, and when the doctor pulled up my pink cashmere sweater, he uncovered a purple and black imprint on my tummy of the bottom of Ruby's cowboy boot, like a particularly ugly tattoo. Mother had a series of X-rays of her ankle, which was swollen and red. I don't know what treatment Ruby received, and frankly didn't care.

After the tests, Mother and I were put in separate ER rooms to await our results.

I was lying on the exam table when Tony came in.

He was always a tough man to read.

I braced for the worst. But I wouldn't blame him for breaking off our reinstated engagement. He'd left the pressures of big-city law enforcement for a small-town, quieter job, only to encounter Mother and me, who weren't exactly quiet. And a small town with the highest per capita murder rate in America. Look it up in the Guinness Book of World Records.

Tony, in his trademark navy jacket over a light-blue shirt and navy striped tie, gray slacks, and brown Florsheim shoes, wheeled a doctor's stool over to the side of the exam table.

"How are you feeling?" he asked gently.

"Better. I'll know more when the doctor comes in with my test results."

Tony nodded. "Officer Munson filled me in on what happened."

"Ruby?"

"Fairly severe concussion. But she'll live."

I was relieved I hadn't killed her. Sort of.

He continued, "She'll face charges both here and in Oklahoma."

"Tony, the casino money—"

"Vivian's already told me."

"You . . . you talked to Mother before me?" I tried not to sound hurt.

"You were still having your scan when I arrived."

"Oh."

"Anyway," he went on, "Chief Hunter knows right where to look for the stolen money. We've already FedExed the evidence, that little locker key, to him."

"I bet Mother hated that she couldn't be the one to tell Hunter."

"Oh, she told him, all right. I wouldn't cheat her out of that. I put her on my cell before informing Hunter of Ruby's status."

Maybe I still had a fiancé.

"I'm taking you out of here," he said. "I've cleared it with the docs."

"Into a private room?"

"Home. Then we'll discuss a trip I'm going to, uh, propose."

I sat up, ignoring the pain. "Getting out of *this* town before sundown would be wonderful!" Then, "Are you sure you can take time off?"

"I've already arranged it. And I have vacation time I haven't used."

"How long will we be away?"

"Two weeks."

Two weeks without Mother!

I was so excited I almost forgot my boot-shaped bruise. "What? Are we going to Canada?"

Tony had always taken his solo summer vacations there, catching trout, and while this wasn't summer, he could always ice fish. I would stay nice and toasty in the lodge in front of a roaring fire, reading, resting, and resting some more, drinking hot chocolate—or maybe a hot toddy, with extra toddy.

He nodded. "I thought maybe we could go to Niagara Falls first. And while we're there, might as well get married." He took both my hands in his. "It's time, Brandy."

I can't describe the mixed feelings I had.

"I want to," I said, "but marriage is not going to change anything between me and Mother, and maybe make things worse."

"It's not about changing anything between you and her," Tony said earnestly, "it's about us starting a life together, supporting each other in a way we couldn't before. Two are stronger than one." He paused. "We'll figure it out as we go."

Those were more words strung together than I'd heard Tony say. Ever.

Why was I hesitating?

I'd married Roger because I thought I loved him, but mostly had wanted to get away from Mother, and I didn't want to make that mistake again.

But I knew in my heart, in my soul, this was different.

I put my arms around Tony's thick neck and whispered, "Let's do it, you big lug."

"Let's."

Five days later, Tony and I were standing in front of a male magistrate in the Niagara Falls clerk's office on the New York side, one of a dozen or so couples waiting their turn to tie the knot.

I was wearing a blue velvet dress with a sweetheart neckline and holding a bouquet of pink roses. Tony had on a charcoal-grey wool suit with a white shirt and silver tie, a pink rose from my bouquet in his lapel.

We had flown into the city and rented a car for our trip into Canada. Mother was home taking care of Sushi and Rocky, and Jake was still on spring vacation with his father and stepmother.

Prior to the ceremony, Tony and I had to present a photo ID and a birth certificate to the clerk's office in a grand old limestone building in the center of the city, then wait the required twenty-four hours, which we used to visit the Falls. They were spectacular in late winter, partially frozen, cascading water creating stunning ice formations, steam rising from below.

The ceremony itself was over in a minute, my engagement ring doubling as a wedding ring. Other than the magistrate and a female witness on staff, the only other person in the room was an elderly bearded man seated in a chair dressed in clothing decades out of fashion.

That night we had an elegant dinner at an Italian restaurant with a view of the Niagara River, and then later returned to our suite and ordered a bottle of champagne.

The rest of the evening, as Mother loves to say, is on a need-to-know basis.

And you don't need to know.

Brandy's Trash 'n' Treasures Tip

Mother and I have found some great furniture put out on the curb for trash pick-up. Granted, most need some restoration or a little clean-up and repair, but the expense can be well worth something gotten for free, unless the person restoring it lacks expertise, uses too harsh of a paint stripper, over-sands the wood, applies the stain unevenly, and improperly glues the joints. Me, me, me, me, and me!

FOURTEEN
Sweet Brandy From Serenity

Oh rapturous joy! Oh heavenly days! This is Vivian, by the way, not Brandy recounting her wedding night with Tony.

Well, not *her* wedding night—poor choice of words. Let's call it the wedding evening, and give those kids some dignity.

I rarely have the honor of writing the final chapter of one of our tomes; in fact it's only happened once before (*Antiques Frame*) in our twenty-book saga, and even then it was merely a *half* chapter.

After Brandy and Tony departed for Niagara Falls, I had much to do. But before we get into that, dear reader, allow me to tie up a few ends that may have you wondering.

Health news first. As you may have speculated, since she was well enough to travel, Brandy's injury was limited to a bad bruise, unsightly but not critical and thankfully temporary—mostly faded before the Niagara trip. My ankle (thank you for your interest) was merely sprained, and within a few days I was able to walk if not dance a jig, not that I'd ever known how. Also, you may find it of interest to learn that I've gone back on my bipolar medication, although I'm told it may take a few weeks to really kick in.

Ruby Johnson (I wish I had a more interesting last name to reveal for our antagonist) made a full recovery after Brandy lowered the boom on her with that equine clock; but of course, Ruby baby will be spending quite a few years in the pokey, between various charges filed in Iowa and Texas. I am planning to magnanimously send her a copy of this book, fresh off the presses, as her jailhouse spirits might be lifted on seeing her depiction in print—a more positive "charge" than those she faced in court(s).

The casino money was indeed found in locker 114 at the

Tahlequah bus station, not a wampum spent (can I say that?). Apparently (according to Big Chief Tony) Ruby had decided not to spend any of it until she got to Mexico, where it was less likely the bills might be traced. She had apparently acted alone in the robbery, having culled a "friendship" with one of the two armored-car guards, who was not found complicit in the heist, other than trusting Ruby too much with security information. Pillow talk, apparently. But we won't belabor that—not my business!

On a more pleasant note, Brandy and I were awarded ten percent of the cash from the casino's insurance company, which was a substantial amount, exactly what being none of your beeswax. A girl has to have some secrets, and I don't care to be prey to predators who might approach me with questionable investment opportunities.

I will say this much on the reward topic. In the days before Brandy left for Niagara Falls, we decided to give some of the reward money (again, an undisclosed amount) to the Diligwa replica village—where we'd caused so much trouble—for repairs and expansion; and also a portion to a new program implemented by the Cherokee Nation to preserve and promote their native language through film and media, as so many indigenous languages are being lost. *Osiyo!*

And what we did keep for ourselves covered the expenses from the trip, including jail fines, and the purchase of a new roof for the shop, which was starting to leak.

Regarding Sebastian the skilled forger, he copped a plea (as they say) with the Tranquility D.A., ratting out the late Wade and, in so doing, the much-alive Mary Jo as well, receiving a free pass on the larger crime when I offered my opinion that while he had indeed forged a document, he had not been otherwise involved in Wade and Mary Jo's criminal activities.

Perhaps you're wondering why I would back Sebastian up and keep him out of the hoosegow. I will answer that in a round-about fashion (approved by our attorney, Wayne Ekhardt).

Not long after returning from our Tranquility trip, I heard from Ma thanking me for sending her the squirrel-tailed cap (acquired from a squirrel enthusiast). On my advice, Ma banded together with Dixie and Zeke and began making an effort to break Tool's will, which left his fortune to the library fund in return for naming The Patrick C. Tool Memorial Library and a statue of himself out front (the egos some people have!).

In the aftermath of the Stetson crime(s) being exposed, however, Dixie and Zeke made a thorough search of the near-mansion they'd grown up in. Miraculously, they turned up a long-lost will written by their late mother in the same distinctive flowing hand as letters they'd saved from her and cherished in a lovely sentimental way. That will left everything to them, of course.

When she learned of this, Brandy said, "Rather convenient, wasn't it? Finding that will after all this time? Does it have anything to do with you helping keep Sebastian out of stir?"

"I'm afraid I don't follow you, dear."

"You did this, didn't you? You orchestrated this fraud!"

"Absolutely not, Brandy. But I do think it's punishment enough for Sebastian that his forgery of the Houston document was exposed and cost him his business and reputation. And Patrick Tool's stepchildren have announced a third of what they inherit will go to the new library, on the condition that it simply be named after the town and *not* include a statue of their late stepfather."

Brandy got very quiet before finally saying, "You're going to land *us* in stir one of these days. Again! Well, I don't approve of what you did. Exactly."

What else do I need to bring you up to date on? Oh. It occurred to me in the middle of last night that Tool is spelled *loot* backwards. While not an example of a true aptonym, the man certainly did love money.

I can't think of any more loose threads or ends or what-have-you; but if you do, please contact Severn House (marked ATTENTION: OLIVIA). I'm sure it can be addressed later, in the trade paperback edition.

Now, on a more personal note.

When Brandy told me she and Tony were going to Canada by way of Niagara Falls, New York, well, I wasn't born yesterday (never mind when I was born) (is Borne a true instance of an aptonym?). I wasn't about to miss my darling girl's second wedding after suffering through her first, when Roger was wrong for her (but their union did produce my wonderful grandson).

Internet research informed me that there was a twenty-four-hour waiting period after in-person filing for a marriage certificate in the Niagara Falls clerk's office. I booked the next flight after they'd left, knowing I'd be there in plenty of time for the ceremony.

Of course, I didn't want them to know I was in attendance, so—bundled up against the cold—I hopped on my Vespa and zipped to the Playhouse to retrieve a disguise. Sherlock Holmes has nothing on me!

Some years ago, before Brandy had come back to live with me after her divorce, I had played the lead role of Sheridan Whiteside in *The Man Who Came to Dinner*, a part made famous on Broadway in 1939 by Monty Woolley, who also starred in the 1942 movie co-starring Bette Davis. (Briefly, it's a story about an irascible literary critic invited to dine in someone's home who then slips on ice at the door, breaks his hip, and is confined to wheelchair as a houseguest where he makes intolerable demands of the homeowners.) Unfortunately, or fortunately depending on how you look at it, I had to step into the role after the local actor assigned to the part actually did slip on ice and break his hip on opening night. Irony isn't so funny in real life!

Over the years in my theatrical capacity, I had kept every costume ever used at the Playhouse in a storage room, and—lo and behold—I found the same costume I'd worn in that play, my wardrobe none-the-worse-for-wear save for a few minor moth holes. Gathering the tweed three-piece suit, cap and cane, I proceeded to the make-up room for the necessary white wig, matching beard, and handlebar mustache.

Leaving Sushi and Rocky in the care of Officer Shawntea—sworn to secrecy—I headed to the airport in Moline (not on my Vespa, rather taking a taxi). My plan was to arrive in Niagara Falls, stay at a hotel overnight, see the wedding the next day in the guise of an elderly male bystander, then return home that same night—with the newlyweds none the wiser.

Everything went splendidly. Dressed in my *Man Who Came to Dinner* duds, my make-up perfect, I got to the county clerk's office early in the morning and talked the clerk into letting me sit quietly in the special room for the ceremony, saying my wife of fifty years had recently died, and we had been married in this same grand old courthouse—which by the way looked disconcertingly like ours in Serenity. The Tranquility Effect again!

I'd had to suffer through quite a few knot-tyings before it was Brandy and Tony's turn. They made a lovely couple, and looked so happy, but the proceedings were over much too quickly, although the magistrate did do a nice job of acting as though he hadn't done this hundreds of times.

I even managed surreptitiously to take a few pictures on my new phone (the old one being in the Tranquility PD's evidence locker).

Going unrecognized as I did, I relished the thought of surprising them, once they'd returned to Serenity, not only with wedding photos but a big reception in the ballroom of the Merrill Hotel, opening the festivities to the whole town, which I'm sure the couple would appreciate. It only seemed an appropriate event for the police chief and half of Serenity's famous writing team.

Back in my hotel room, I exchanged my disguise for a comfortable outfit for travel, then packed my bag. But before leaving for the small airport to take a puddle-jumper to Newark, New Jersey—where I had a connecting flight on to Chicago, and then to Moline—I first gave Brandy a jingle on my cell.

"Hello, dear, this is your mother speaking."

"Yes, I know—I have caller ID."

"I hope I'm not phoning at an inopportune time." You never knew with a honeymoon couple!

"You're not."

"How did the wedding go?"

The phone seemed to go dead for a moment.

Then came Brandy's voice: "You should know. You were there."

And here I thought my disguise was Brandy-proof!

"How *could* you know? I was wearing something from a production you never saw me in!"

"You told me a hundred times about playing the lead in *The Man Who Came to Dinner*. Also, you forgot to take off your big glasses."

"Well, I needed them to see the ceremony. Did Tony spot me?"

"If he did, he didn't say."

I sighed into the phone. "You made such a lovely couple—the best one of the whole bunch I suffered through."

"Glad you approve. Mother?"

"Yes, dear?"

"You're not planning to follow us into Canada, are you?"

"No, I'm flying home. I really didn't mean to intrude, you know. That's why I kept such a low profile."

Another long pause.

Then Brandy's voice: "I'm glad you were there."

"I am too, dear. I am, too."

Arriving in Newark, I was greeted by a notice posted on the departure board of a three-hour delay with my flight to the Windy City, due to a snowstorm. Since I wasn't about to sit around an airport lounge for that long twiddling my thumbs, I came up with something else to do.

Some time ago, I had made an unlikely friend when Brandy and I attended a comic-book convention in New York (*Antiques Con*). So as not to spoil the details for those who have not read that book (and you really should), all I will say is that I had done this unlikely friend a great favor, and in return he did me one—a favor, I mean—without which my daughter's new husband might not have been alive to just have taken the plunge.

Anyhoo, I got a cab for a twenty-minute ride north of the airport to Teaneck, where my friend, an elderly gentleman, was staying at Royal Care, an exclusive assisted-living complex.

I had the taxi driver stop at an Italian restaurant on the way, where in no time flat they boxed up my friend's favorite meal. Now, it's always a good idea when dropping in on the former head of the New Jersey Mob (we'll call him Don Corleone, with thanks and appreciation to the late Mario Puzo) to show respect by bringing a gift. To sweeten this one, I also purchased the Don's favorite dessert, cannoli (ganool in Mafia parlance), from the bakery counter.

At the entrance of Royal Care, I pushed an intercom with a security camera (with my finger, not with a camera—I really am having trouble here until my meds kick in) to announce my presence. A female voice asked who I wanted to see and I gave her the Don's real name, then my own.

Several minutes ticked by while I held the boxed food, concerned that it might be getting cold. But I knew there was a kitchen in the Don's apartment, where it could be warmed, having been there before. So I wasn't too worried.

A buzzer sounded and I went on through the glass doors into a large modern reception area, where a middle-aged woman in a classy dress sat behind a mahogany desk—she might have been a CEO's secretary.

I thought I'd have to give her a photo ID, which is my passport these days, since my driver's license has REVOKED stamped across it; but she just waved me on to the elevators. The Don's digs were on the top floor—nice to have friends in high places. High places—ha!

Deftly switching the boxes to balance in one hand, I knocked at his suite with the other, recalling how the fireplug of a man in his eighties with a lumpy liver-spotted face and thinning silver hair had gruffly greeted me, clad in a navy nylon tracksuit and sneakers (him not me, as I was wearing—well, never mind, although I do remember that Brandy had claimed my top was inside-out when she saw me afterward).

But instead, a very threatening-looking gorilla (is that denigrating? To gorillas, I mean?) opened the door. It didn't take a detective (though I was one) to know by those bulging biceps that this was a bodyguard (another clue was the bulge of an apparent gun under the left arm of his rather loud sports jacket).

Without a word, he gestured for me to enter.

The once-opulent living area had been turned into a virtual hospital room, a bed placed where not that long ago the Don and I had sat playing Scrabble well into the night (he had insomnia), with a spectacular view of the lights of Manhattan across the Hudson River, from a window now covered in blackout drapes.

From the bed, surrounded by beeping equipment and poles with hanging bags, a voice asked weakly, "Is she here? Is she really here?"

The bodyguard grunted. Gorillas aren't known for being loquacious.

Don Corleone waved me over with a bony hand, the attached cord of an IV flapping. In the place of his tracksuit was a hospital gown.

I approached the bed, which had been raised slightly.

He was barely recognizable, cheeks sunken, skin gray.

"I brought you some linguine and clams," I said cheerfully, "and a cannolo."

"Ah, you remembered."

"Of course."

He looked past me, and suddenly the weakened voice took on its old gruffness. "Well, get the lady a damn seat, man!"

The bodyguard shuffled off and returned with a chair from the dining room and placed it next to the bed.

"Now beat it," the Don told him.

I sat, then waited until the guard disappeared before I asked, "Why the muscle?"

"Everybody's gettin' nervous now that, you know, the end is near." He poked his chest with a finger. "Lung cancer. Too far advanced to do a damn thing but wait."

"I'm so sorry." Then, "But what is there to be nervous about now? You've been retired for such a long time."

He gave a guttural grunt. "Nobody *really* retires, not until . . ."

. . . they go out in a body bag.

He changed the subject, as casually as if this were a normal conversation. "What brings you around, Vivian? I suppose I can manage giving you one more favor."

"No favor needed."

I told him about Brandy and Tony getting hitched, and a little about our recent trip to Texas. But his mind seemed to be elsewhere.

When his eyes began to close, I took his hand.

"I'll never forget you," I said, adding his first name, his real name, to my heartfelt expression.

"And I never forgot the time we spent together, brief as it was." He gestured for me to come closer.

"Phoenix," he whispered, through lips that had probably given countless orders for killings. But that was between him and his maker.

I whispered back, "Phoenix? Is that where you want to be . . . laid to rest?"

"It's everywhere."

I didn't understand. "You want . . . your ashes scattered everywhere?"

"Phoenix," he whispered again, squeezing my hand with sudden strength.

A hand the size of a catcher's mitt landed on my shoulder, and the Don's eyes took on a quality I'd never seen in him before—fright!

"It's time you leave, lady," the bodyguard said bluntly.

I stood and gazed down at the Don, who'd been a great man in his way. In his day. "Goodnight, sweet prince."

"Goodbye, Vivian." The finality unmistakable.

I stooped and gave his forehead a kiss.

At the desk in the lobby, I asked the receptionist to call a local taxi for me, then went outside to wait, eager to escape the building.

In the cab going back to Newark Airport, I went over and over the last few minutes the Don and I had spent together.

What was he trying to tell me?

Was Phoenix something more than just a city?

And if I did discover what he'd meant, what kind of danger would I be in? And Brandy? And Tony? And my grandson, Jake?

To be continued . . .

Vivian's Trash 'n' Treasures Tip

Rather than spending time tracking down merchandise, I let it come to our shop by encouraging customers to bring in their unwanted antiques and collectibles. Usually, they will settle for very little rather than lug the items back home. Horace Dusenberry is an exception, however, always coming round with interesting man-tiques and driving a hard bargain. But I can usually get him to throw in dinner.

BARBARA ALLAN

Is a joint pseudonym of husband-and-wife mystery writers, Barbara and Max Allan Collins.

BARBARA COLLINS made her entrance into the mystery field as a highly respected short-story writer with appearances in over a dozen top anthologies, including *Murder Most Delicious*, *Women on the Edge*, *Deadly Housewives* and the best-selling *Cat Crimes* series. She was the co-editor of (and a contributor to) the bestselling anthology *Lethal Ladies*, and her stories were selected for inclusion in the first three volumes of *The Year's 25 Finest Crime and Mystery Stories*.

Three acclaimed collections of her work have been published— *Too Many Tomcats* and (with her husband) *Murder—His and Hers* and *Suspense—His and Hers*. The couple's first novel together, the Baby Boomer thriller *Regeneration*, was a paperback bestseller; their second collaborative novel, *Bombshell*—in which Marilyn Monroe saves the world from World War III—was published in hardcover to excellent reviews. Recently they collaborated on the short suspense novel, *Cutout*.

Barbara also has been the production manager and/or line producer of several independent film projects.

MAX ALLAN COLLINS was named a Grand Master by the Mystery Writers of America in 2017. He has earned an unprecedented twenty-three Private Eye Writers of America "Shamus" nominations, many for his Nathan Heller historical thrillers, winning for *True Detective* (1983), *Stolen Away* (1991), and the short story, "So Long, Chief."

His classic graphic novel *Road to Perdition* (illustrated by Richard Piers Rayner) is the basis of the Academy Award-winning film. Max's other comics credits include "Dick Tracy"; "Batman"; his own "Ms Tree"; and "Wild Dog," featured on the *Arrow* TV series.

Max's body of work includes film criticism, short fiction, songwriting, trading-card sets, and movie/TV tie-in novels, such as the *New York Times*-bestseller *Saving Private Ryan,* numerous *USA Today* bestselling CSI novels, and the Scribe Award-winning *American Gangster*. His non-fiction includes *Scarface and the Untouchable: Al Capone, Eliot Ness & the Mad Butcher* (both with A. Brad Schwartz), and *Spillane—King of Pulp Fiction* with James L. Traylor.

An award-winning filmmaker, he wrote and directed the Lifetime movie *Mommy* (1996) and three other features; his produced screenplays include the 1995 HBO World Premiere *The Expert* and *The Last Lullaby* (2008). His 1998 documentary *Mike Hammer's Mickey Spillane* appears on the Criterion Collection release of the acclaimed film noir *Kiss Me Deadly*. The Cinemax TV series *Quarry* is based on his innovative book series.

Max's recent novels include a dozen-plus works begun by his mentor, the late mystery-writing legend Mickey Spillane, among them *Baby, It's Murder* with Mike Hammer, and the Caleb York western novels.

Max directed and (with Barbara) co-wrote the feature film *Death by Fruitcake* (2025), bringing Vivian and Brandy Borne (and Sushi) to life.

"BARBARA ALLAN" live(s) in Muscatine, Iowa, their Serenity-esque hometown. Son Nathan works as a translator of Japanese to English, with credits including video games, manga, and novels.